Earth, Air, Fire, Water

Robin Skelton was born in Yorkshire and educated at the University of Leeds. Since 1963 he has been teaching at the University of Victoria in British Columbia where he founded the Department of Creative Writing and, together with the late John Peter, *The Malahat Review*. He is the author or editor of over seventy books in the various fields of poetry, fiction, biography, drama, translation and the occult. He has edited *Poetry of the Thirties* and *Poetry of the Forties* for Penguin Books.

Born in Victoria BC in 1959, Margaret Blackwood is of Scottish and Irish descent. She is a visual artist, a poet and writer. She majored in Creative Writing at the University of Victoria, where she received her BFA degree in June 1989. *Earth, Air, Fire, Water* is her first collaboration with Robin Skelton. Her book, *The Monstrous Regiment*, a compilation of famous and lesser-known quotations about women through the centuries, will shortly be published. Her poems have appeared in Canadian literary magazines and she is currently working on a book of poetry.

Earth,
Air,
Fire,
Water

Pre-Christian and Pagan Elements in British Songs, Rhymes and Ballads

Robin Skelton

and

Margaret Blackwood

ARKANA

ARKANA

Published by the Penguin Group
27 Wrights Lane, London W8 5TZ, England
Viking Penguin Inc., 40 West 23rd Street, New York, New York 10010, USA
Penguin Books Australia Ltd, Ringwood, Victoria, Australia
Penguin Books Canada Ltd, 2801 John Street, Markham, Ontario, Canada L3R 1B4
Penguin Books (NZ) Ltd, 182–190 Wairau Road, Auckland 10, New Zealand

Penguin Books Ltd, Registered Offices: Harmondsworth, Middlesex, England

First published 1990
10 9 8 7 6 5 4 3 2 1

The Acknowledgements on p. 316
constitute an extension of this copyright page

Made and printed in Great Britain by
Cox and Wyman Ltd, Reading, Berks

Filmset in Linotron Goudy Old Style by
Rowland Phototypesetting Ltd, Bury St Edmunds, Suffolk

Contents

Spells

Blessings

Invocations and Incantations

Summer and Harvest

V The World of Faery

Song and Dance

Faery Ways

The Shape Changers

Trickery

Introduction

When Christian missionaries first came to Britain they faced a powerfully entrenched religion that had many regional differences and made use of many different names. This religion has been referred to by some commentators under the general heading of the Old Religion, a term later adopted by Catholics for the rites of the pre-Reformation Church, and, still later, after the rise and dominance of Protestantism, for Catholicism itself. Unfortunately the term suggests a degree of uniformity which was almost certainly not the case. Nevertheless it is clear that there were beliefs and attitudes held in common by the Celts of Ireland, Wales, Scotland and Cornwall, and also by the various other races of Nordic and Teutonic origin that made up the population of the British Isles.

These beliefs had resulted in the creation of many holy places, where the population would gather for their rites and celebrations. Many of these were at natural gathering places, such as fords across rivers, natural harbours, and places where the configuration of the landscape had led to the creation of meeting-places of tracks and roads, as well as at springs and wells. The missionaries were, of course, most interested in bringing their new religion to the main centres of population, and as a consequence these were first converted to the new faith, and those people who lived in the countryside were referred to as pagans (the word being derived from the Latin, *paganus*, which means rustic and unlearned; the allied word *pagus* meaning village or country folk).

The Christian Church set about changing the names of all the holy places and making them centres for the new religion. Consequently churches were built upon ancient sites, and the holy wells and places were given the names of saints. Nevertheless, for hundreds of years, the Old Religion was countenanced. In many churches there was a pagan altar, or altar for the country people, by the north door. Thus the country folk, coming to the small towns to market, had a place of worship where they could feel comfortable. Many people appear to have hedged their bets by paying their dues at both altars, as did King Harold, who is reported as having worshipped at both pagan and Christian altars before leaving Normandy for England after his visit to Duke William in 1064.

Gradually, however, the pagan north altars were taken down, and the north door in the majority of churches was sealed up, though the churches themselves still bore evidence of pagan beliefs in their gargoyles and in the carvings of the wooden miserere seats in the church choirs. Indeed, as the great churches and minsters and cathedrals rose after the Emperor Constantine established religious tolerance in the Edict of Milan, AD 313, the imagery of the carvings continued to be that of pre-Christian beliefs.

Over these centuries the populace was largely illiterate; only those in the service of the Church could read and write. The clerics were the only teachers of literacy, if we mean by literacy the ability to make use of the Roman alphabet. Other forms of literacy did, however, exist, for the pre-Christian populace was not ignorant of the need for other than oral communication. We have, indeed, a whole language of marks and signs, on relics of the earlier period, ranging from the sophistication of the Irish Ogham alphabet to runes, and to symbols carved in stone. It is more than likely that there were other signs and marks made upon wood, but these have not survived.

Oral tradition was, of course, the main way in which early beliefs and early learning were transmitted. During the process of transmission the various texts suffered many transformations. Some became christianized, the names of Christian traditions replacing older names. Some legends were reshaped. A good deal of folk wisdom which had been cast in the form of rhymes to make it more easily remembered was passed down to children as part of their education, and much of this became regarded as children's entertainment and found its way into the body of work we now refer to generally as nursery rhymes or Mother Goose. Although it has been stated that most of our nursery rhymes must be regarded, because of their language, as having been made no later than the early fifteenth century, it is obvious that they derive from much earlier texts. It is equally clear, as many scholars have pointed out, that an equally large number of nursery rhymes and of children's games and skipping rhymes were created as comments upon social happenings of the time. Indeed, when I was a boy, I remember chanting rhymes about Charlie Chaplin and Wallis Simpson, and Little Jack Horner refers to a scandal of the sixteenth century.

What do we know about this Old Religion that appears so waywardly in our nursery rhymes and ancient ballads? As Robert Graves has pointed out most effectively, and as other scholars have emphasized with less brilliance but more hard documentation, the pre-Christian religion in Europe was centred largely upon the worship of a Great Goddess and her consort. The Goddess was seen in four aspects; these have been identified as virgin (meaning simply a young woman, not necessarily a woman without sexual experience), a mother or mature woman, an old woman or crone, and the bringer of death, called Hecate in one tradition. Three of these aspects were emphasized – the virgin, mother and crone, for Hecate was somehow set a little apart and above. Nevertheless she is present in many stories, especially in the Irish tales of the Morrigu. The triple or quadruple Goddess had many names, and in continental Europe over the centuries she was worshipped as Gaea, the earth mother, as Rhea, as Isis, as Pallas Athena/Minerva, as Demeter, Goddess of Forests, and as Artemis/Diana. Diana eventually became the most favoured name, and there were many attempts by the Church to suppress the Dianic cult. As late as the fourteenth century some monks in Germany were discovered worshipping Diana in the forest.

The male God appeared in almost as many guises – Dionysus, Apollo and Pan in the Graeco-Roman tradition, and, in other traditions, Bran, the Sun God, whose main place of worship was what is now London, Lugh of Ireland and Herne the Hunter in the forests of England. In Scandinavia he had the three faces of Odin, Loki and Balder. This is indeed a fine and confused mixture.

It is better to abandon consideration of the nomenclature of the Goddess and the God and to look at their worship. This religion was based upon the seasons of the year and the great feasts were held at the solstices and equinoxes. These feasts were taken over by the Christian Church, and usually (except for the moving feast of Easter named after Eostre, the Goddess of Dawn) given specific dates which did not necessarily coincide with a calendar based firmly upon the movements of the sun and moon. Thus the mid-winter festival of Yule, now usually given as 21 December, became Christmas, the feast of the birth of Christ, though scholars tell us it is likely that the historical Jesus was born in April. The autumn feast, the Irish Samhain, the feast of the dead, became the Christian All Saints' Day or All Hallows, and Hallowe'en retains traces of ancient rites in North America today, though in Britain the festival was moved to 5 November in remembrance of Guy Fawkes' attempt to blow up Parliament on that day in 1605. Guy Fawkes' Day, also called Bonfire Night, remains a fire festival.

Other days were given saints' names. The day of Brigid, the Great Goddess of Ireland, was turned into the feast of Saint Brigid and into Candlemas. May Day, the ancient Beltaine, collected no less than six Irish saints' names, including that of Saint Oissin, or Oisin, whose name is that of the great poet of pagan Ireland, and therefore of an aspect of the God. It is also the feast day of Saints Asaph, Corentin, Joseph, Marcoul, Philip and James. May Day, however, with its attendant Maypole, retained its pagan rites more obviously than most other days in the year. Indeed, owing to May Day's pagan origins, it was felt that only 'bad' women married in May, and it was generally considered an unlucky month for marriages. The Scottish peasantry have a saying: 'Of the marriages in May,/ The bairns die o' decay.' Ironically, in his *Letters on Demonology and Witchcraft*, Sir Walter Scott says that originally the objection to marriages in May came from the Roman pagans. He goes on to mention that in 1684 a group of Scottish Dissenters called the Gibbites attempted to renounce May Day and other festivals and observances; they went so far as to term the names of months and days as profane.

All these feast days were celebrated in the rhymes and songs of oral tradition, and in terms which clearly suggest their origins.

The worshippers of the Old Religion had much lore which had to be handed down. The women of the villages were most frequently the repositories of this lore and the teachers of it, for they were the ones who could most easily pass it on to the children. The women, too, were the village physicians, and had the knowledge of herbs and their uses, as well as much weather lore. This folk wisdom found its way into verse from time to time, as did instructions for the correct foods and drinks for particular occasions. The 'wise woman' of the village was regarded as something of a threat to the urban physicians, for some patients preferred country potions and poultices to the cruder methods of the city surgeon and apothecary. As many of the country remedies involved the saying of charms, rather than prayers to the Christian God, these women were regarded as heretical, and as 'witches', and suffered accordingly. Moreover if a wise woman's patient died, the woman would immediately be accused of being a poisoner; the malpractice suit took the form of a witch trial. The urban physicians were left unscathed. The wise women were also knowledgeable about hallucinogens which produced altered states of consciousness, and which orthodox medicine only discovered in the twentieth century.

This is not the place to discuss the witchcraft mania that seized Europe in the Middle Ages and persisted in a weakened form until the nineteenth century. It is sufficient to point out that the figure of the wicked witch was created by the Christian Church for many reasons, some political, some economic and some few theological.

One of the theological, or, at least, ritualistic, points at issue was the difference between the Church and the Old Religion as regards prayer. The Church, faced with indubitable healings by wise women, felt that any 'miracles' not produced in the name of the Christian God must have been produced, for devious ends, by the Devil. This was not the whole of it, however. The Church perceived that members of the Old Religion cast spells, and that some spells differed from prayers in not being addressed to any supernatural power, pleading for assistance or intercession, but operated by way of the powers possessed by the spell-caster. Thus the widespread 'cures' for warts, some of which appear in this anthology, were made without any spiritual authority, divine or diabolic, but by the authority of the spell-caster, herself or himself. This cut at the root of theology itself. Mankind did not, could not, have the power to heal, curse or cure without supernatural aid. Members of the Old Religion were aware of psychosomatic illness and psychosomatic healings as the Church was not, and they combined their herbal remedies with spoken charms or with rituals, having discovered that these reinforced the power of their remedies. This was suspect to the Church, and had the effect of making the orthodox think that herbal remedies owed their effectiveness rather to the diabolic power of the charms than to the herbs themselves. Thus it was not until centuries had passed that the medical knowledge of practitioners of the Old Religion was translated into modern terms and provided the Pharmacopoeia with many important weapons. Nevertheless spells and charms remained in use for many years, and it is interesting to hear of Thomas Flatman writing of a spell used to cure a knife-wound as late as 1661.

There are many verses, poems and songs, and even hymns, which could be labelled spells because they command a change in the physical world, rather than intercede for it, or because they assert, or imply, the magical authority of either the speaker, or the spiritual powers of the natural world.

The magical practices of the individual 'witches' alarmed the Church. Their gatherings also were condemned. These often took place by moonlight, the moon being one aspect of the Goddess, or in the dark of night, not only to avoid discovery but also because the moon calendar of the Old Religion viewed the day as beginning and ending at noon; thus midnight, the 'witching hour', was the very centre of the 'day'. This theme of the importance of darkness appears in many poems addressed to the Spirit of Night.

One figure at the gatherings of members of the Old Religion was usually labelled by the Church as the Devil or Satan. This was a male member of the group, or coven, who would wear a horned head-dress – deer, goat or ram, according to the region and the local supply – as part of his costume. The Church had changed the image of Satan in the Bible, and modelled him upon Pan, giving him horns and cloven hoofs. It was not until the sixth century that he had begun to take centre stage in the theatre of Hell, but once there he was so attractive a figure that he remained. In oral tradition, however, the Goddess's consort lacked pitchfork and tail, and was usually presented as a divinity of the woodland and as a folk hero. He emerged into legend as Robin Hood, the opponent of tyranny, the protector of the poor, with near-magical powers as an archer, and devoted to the Goddess in the form of Maid Marian. The God also appeared in the form of a number of 'green men' and, indeed, The Green Man is still a popular pub sign in Britain, as also is Robin Hood, and in the depths of smoky, rainy Manchester I recall drinking in The Sherwood Arms.

With Robin Hood we are approaching legend, if not myth, and there are many stories which embody elements of the Old Religion. It does not take much perspicacity to see magical and pre-Christian elements in the many Arthurian romances in Britain and elsewhere. These romances also include many incursions into the world of faerie.

There are many theories about faerie and faerie lore. One view is that the faerie folk who live inside the hills in a timeless and paradisal world derive from the belief that the burial mounds still contain the spirits of those ancient people buried there. Another is that they represent the Old Religion which was driven literally underground by Christianity. A further view, supported by Shakespeare calling his faeries in *A Midsummer Night's Dream* by such names as Cobweb and Peaseblossom, is that faeries reveal the belief that every living thing has a spirit and a spiritual power and, that, in Blake's words, 'Everything that lives is holy.' Be that as it may, the faerie world clearly owes much to ancient beliefs and practices. The faeries dance in a ring, as 'witches' and followers of the Old Religion used to dance. The circle is an important image in old religions, as is evidenced by the many stone circles in Britain, and by the many references to circles in magical folk lore. The circle itself was, of course, very much a part of rural life. One does not form a square or rectangle round a fire in the open; one forms a circle. Early dwellings of the Celts in Ireland were circular; those still standing in Kerry are called beehive huts because of their conical shape. In a circle there is no dominant person, and all the people gathered there can see the rest of the group, whereas in rectangular gatherings, as in churches, those in authority face an audience or congregation who cannot see each other, but only the leaders and the backs of the heads in front of them. The circle also symbolizes the circular movement of the heavens and of the sun and the moon. 'Wave a circle round him thrice,' cried Coleridge in 'Kubla Khan', 'for he on honey dew hath fed, and drunk the milk of Paradise.' His 'damsel with a dulcimer' in that poem also seems to relate directly to the Goddess.

The poets, rhymesters and ballad-makers of the British Isles made considerable use of all this material over the centuries. Indeed, it seems that the poets were continually harking back to ancient beliefs, either by intent or intuitively. There were however a number of changes in the way this material was handled.

I have already referred to nursery rhymes and to folk ballads and songs, and many of these probably had their original texts in periods when the Old Religion was actively worshipped. One cannot however say this of the poetry written by specific authors for a reading public. Nevertheless, once one realizes that the writers consciously or intuitively made use of this material one begins to notice certain facts. The Goddess herself is celebrated frequently in different guises. In pre-Renaissance poetry she may appear as a Queen of the faerie, or be translated into the figure of the

Virgin Mary as either Mother of us all, the Mother Goddess, or as Inspirer, as Stella Maris – the star of the sea, the Goddess of tides – or as Muse. The figure of the Muse is often used, and it is clear that the Muse is regarded as a Goddess, even though she may be embodied in a particular woman whom the poet loves.

In the Renaissance the fashion for classical allusion made it possible for the poets to present pagan enthusiasms without danger of being called heretical, and so in the late sixteenth and the first half of the seventeenth century we find a good many poems about the Goddess as Venus and especially as Diana. We also find the God Pan emerging, and the pastoral poetry of the time, based somewhat upon Theocritus and Bion, celebrates the nature-worship that was part of the Old Religion. It also celebrates physical love in a manner that would not seem proper within a Christian tradition that, by then, had turned the erotic poetry of the Song of Solomon into a metaphysical allegory, though even Quarles, that most moral of poets, could not wholly avoid taking pleasure in eroticism in his verse paraphrase of the Song of Solomon which he called 'Sions Sonnets'.

While these Elizabethans and Jacobeans were playing pagan airs from their song-books, other poets, notably Robert Herrick, were recording rural feasts and customs in their poetry. Herrick frequently cast a classical disguise over his happy paganism, but not invariably.

The old themes remained in British poetry throughout the seventeenth century, but lost a little way during the Restoration and the Augustan age. They re-emerged with the Romantics, but by this time the original simple beliefs had become complicated by other influences. The Great Tradition of neo-platonism, of which Kathleen Raine has written so eloquently and convincingly, and which had been part of British poetry ever since the Renaissance, came into its own, and while we may point to the Old Religion in Shelley's 'The Witch of Atlas' and 'Queen Mab', and perceive a good deal of Goddess worship and of magical material in most of the Romantics of both generations, we cannot reasonably see much of this work as being primarily affected by the old rural beliefs, though it certainly derives from pre-Christian ones.

Nevertheless during the Romantic period some writers became fascinated by the Old Religion, most notably Sir Walter Scott, who wrote *Letters on Demonology and Witchcraft*, and who, in *The Border Minstrelsy*, collected and also somewhat reshaped and rewrote many old ballads. Joseph Ritson also collected a number of old songs and ballads, inspired perhaps by the earlier Percy's *Reliques of Ancient English Poetry*. In the nineteenth century the collecting of folk songs became fashionable and many pieces were discovered by Cecil Sharp, Baring Gould and others.

This interest in folk material led to the creation, in the late nineteenth and early twentieth century, of original poems and songs which are firmly based upon ancient material and beliefs. Many of the writers took the view that fairy tales were for children only, and therefore presented whimsy, as did Christina Rossetti in her *Goblin Market*. Others, however, took a different view and there are faery poems by W. B. Yeats, which derive directly from the faery traditions of Ireland which fascinated him. He collected and edited a number of these poems. Walter de la Mare also created many faery poems, and though some of these were included in books supposedly for children, a good many are far from childlike. Certain themes, images, beliefs persist as the landscape persists. As John Ceiriog Hughes (1832–1887) wrote in his epilogue to *Alun a Mabon*,

Still the mighty mountains stand,
  Round them still the tempests roar;
Still with dawn through all the land
  Sing the shepherds as of yore.
Round the foot of hill and scar
  Daisies still their buds unfold;
Changed the shepherds only are
  On those mighty mountains old.

Passing with the passing years
  Ancient customs change and flow;
Fraught with doom of joy or tears,
  Generations come and go.
Out of tears' and tempests' reach
  Alun Mabon sleeps secure; –
Still lives on the ancient speech,
  Still the ancient songs endure.

In making our selection, we have chosen to concentrate upon work which is either in the oral tradition or clearly derives from it, and upon work which appears to us to be dealing so directly with matters central to the Old Religion that it could not reasonably be excluded. We have avoided, for the most part, philosophical and metaphysical poetry, and where there are different versions of a particular ballad we have chosen the version that embodies our theme most clearly, whether or not it is in an early or a later and more reliable text.

Because many of these poems, rhymes, songs and ballads allude to ancient beliefs and customs without explanation we have provided a series of notes in commentary. We have also, for entirely practical reasons, provided titles for the many Mother Goose rhymes and Elizabethan songs which have come to us without them. These editorial inventions are presented in square brackets.

This book was made possible by a research grant from the University of Victoria, British Columbia, for which we are grateful.

ROBIN SKELTON, 1989

I
The Goddess and the God

The Goddess Worshipped
The Goddess and Muse
The Goddess and Nature
Love and the Goddess
Forms of the God

The Goddess Worshipped

Queen and Huntress

Queen and huntress, chaste and fair,
Now the sun is laid to sleep,
Seated in thy silver chair,
State in wonted manner keep:
  Hesperus entreats thy light,
  Goddess excellently bright.

Earth, let not thy envious shade
Dare itself to interpose;
Cynthia's shining orb was made
Heaven to clear when day did close:
  Bless us then, with wishèd sight,
  Goddess excellently bright.

Lay thy bow of pearl apart,
And thy crystal-shining quiver;
Give unto the flying hart
Space to breathe, how short soever;
  Thou that mak'st a day of night,
  Goddess excellently bright.

Ben Jonson

A Vow to Minerva

Goddesse, I begin an Art;
Come thou in, with thy best part,
For to make the Texture lye
Each way smooth and civilly:
And a broad-fac't Owle shall be
Offer'd up with Vows to Thee.

Robert Herrick

Ode to Psyche

O Goddess! hear these tuneless numbers, wrung
   By sweet enforcement and remembrance dear,
And pardon that thy secrets should be sung
   Even into thine own soft-conchèd ear;
Surely I dreamt today, or did I see
   The wingèd Psyche with awakened eyes?
I wandered in a forest thoughtlessly,
   And, on the sudden, fainting with surprise,
Saw two fair creatures, couchèd side by side
   In deepest grass, beneath the whisp'ring roof
   Of leaves and trembled blossoms, where there ran
      A brooklet, scarce espied:

'Mid hushed, cool-rooted flowers, fragrant-eyed,
   Blue, silver-white, and budded Tyrian,
They lay calm-breathing on the bedded grass;
   Their arms embracèd, and their pinions too;
   Their lips touched not, but had not bade adieu,
As if disjoinèd by soft-handed slumber,
And ready still past kisses to outnumber

At tender eye-dawn of aurorean love:
The wingèd boy I knew;
But who wast thou, O happy, happy dove?
His Psyche true!

O latest born and loveliest vision far
Of all Olympus' faded hierarchy!
Fairer than Phoebe's sapphire-regioned star,
Or Vesper; amorous glowworm of the sky;
Fairer than these, though temple thou hast none,
Nor altar heaped with flowers;
Nor virgin choir to make delicious moan
Upon the midnight hours;
No voice, no lute, no pipe, no incense sweet
From chain-swung censer teeming;
No shrine, no grove, no oracle, no heat
Of pale-mouthed prophet dreaming.

O brightest! though too late for antique vows,
Too, too late for the fond believing lyre,
When holy were the haunted forest boughs,
Holy the air, the water, and the fire;
Yet even in these days so far retired
From happy pieties, thy lucent fans,
Fluttering among the faint Olympians,
I see, and sing, by my own eyes inspired.
So let me be thy choir, and make a moan
Upon the midnight hours;
Thy voice, thy lute, thy pipe, thy incense sweet
From swingèd censer teeming;
Thy shrine, thy grove, thy oracle, thy heat
Of pale-mouthed prophet dreaming.

Yes, I will be thy priest, and build a fane
In some untrodden region of my mind,
Where branchèd thoughts, new grown with pleasant pain,
Instead of pines shall murmur in the wind:

Far, far around shall those dark-clustered trees
  Fledge the wind-ridgèd mountains steep by steep;
And there by zephyrs, streams, and birds, and bees,
  The moss-lain Dryads shall be lulled to sleep;
And in the midst of this wide quietness
A rosy sanctuary will I dress
With the wreathed trellis of a working brain,
  With buds, and bells, and stars without a name,
With all the gardener Fancy e'er could feign,
  Who breeding flowers, will never breed the same:
And there shall be for thee all soft delight
  That shadowy thought can win,
A bright torch, and a casement ope at night,
  To let the warm Love in!

John Keats

Dawn

Come into my dark oratory,
  be welcome the bright morn,
and blessed He who sent you,
  victorious, self-renewing dawn.

Maiden of good family.
  Sun's sister, daughter of Proud Night,
ever-welcome the fair morn
  that brings my mass-book light.

Anon.

Anima

Lady who came in dreams to aid John Clare,
beautiful, with disordered dress and hair,

so that he knew you well, and knew your care
for him, until at last you led him where
(seeing your calm compassion) he could hear
(not in ill terror but in modest fear)
judgment on him delivered, yet not hear
what said, but, seeing your glad smile, know there
all well, and from the body and the keeper's care
go unperturbed into the timeless outer air,

help each of us who sees your face to share
in his part understanding who you are.

John Knight

A Song to the Maskers

1. Come down, and dance ye in the toyle
   Of pleasures, to a Heate;
   But if to moisture, Let the oyle
   Of Roses be your sweat.

2. Not only to your selves assume
   These sweets, but let them fly;
   From this, to that, and so Perfume
   E'en all the standers by.

3. As Goddesse Isis (when she went,
   Or glided through the street)
   Made all that touch't her with her scent,
   And whom she touch't, turne sweet.

Robert Herrick

The Goddess and Muse

On Lucy, Countesse of Bedford

This morning, timely rapt with holy fire,
  I thought to forme unto my zealous Muse,
What kinde of creature I could most desire,
  To honour, serve, and love; as Poets use.
I meant to make her faire, and free, and wise,
  Of greatest bloud, and yet more good then great;
I meant the day-starre should not brighter rise,
  Nor lend like influence from his lucent seat.
I meant shee should be curteous, facile, sweet,
  Hating that solemne vise of greatnesse, pride;
I meant each softest vertue, there should meet,
  Fit in that softer bosome to reside.
Onely a learned, and a manly soule
  I purpos'd her; that should, with even powers,
The rock, the spindle, and the sheeres controule
  Of destinie, and spin her owne free houres.
Such when I meant to faine, and wish'd to see,
  My Muse bad, Bedford write, and that was shee.

Ben Jonson

A Hymn to the Muses

O! you the Virgins nine!
That doe our soules encline
To noble Discipline!
Nod to this vow of mine:
Come then, and now enspire
My violl and my lyre
With your eternall fire:
And make me one entire
Composer in your Quire.
Then I'le your Altars strew
With Roses sweet and new;
And ever live a true
Acknowledger of you.

Robert Herrick

The Crystal Cabinet

The maiden caught me in the wild,
  Where I was dancing merrily;
She put me into her cabinet,
  And locked me up with a gold key.

This cabinet is formed of gold,
  And pearl and crystal shining bright,
And within it opens into a world
  And a lovely moony night.

Another England there I saw,
  Another London with its Tower,
Another Thames and other hills,
  And another pleasant Surrey bower.

Another maiden like herself,
Translucent, lovely, shining clear,
Threefold, each in the other closed –
O, what a pleasant trembling fear!

O, what a smile! A threefold smile
Filled me that like a flame I burned;
I bent to kiss the lovely maid,
And found a threefold kiss returned.

I strove to seize the inmost form
With ardour fierce and hands of flame,
But burst the crystal cabinet,
And like a weeping babe became:

A weeping babe upon the wild,
And weeping woman pale reclined,
And in the outward air again,
I filled with woes the passing wind.

William Blake

The Goddess and Nature

Chloridia
Rites to Chloris and her Nymphs

The First Song

Zephyrus Come forth, come forth, the gentle Spring,
And carry the glad news I bring
  To earth, our common mother:
It is decreed by all the gods
The heav'n of earth shall have no odds,
  But one shall love another.

Their glories they shall mutual make,
Earth look on heaven for heaven's sake;
  Their honours shall be even;
All emulation cease, and jars;
Jove will have earth to have her stars
  And lights, no less than heaven.

Spring It is already done, in flowers
As fresh and new as are the hours,
  By warmth of yonder sun;
But will be multiplied on us
If from the breath of Zephyrus
  Like favour we have won.

Zephyrus Give all to him: his is the dew,
The heat, the humour –

Spring All the true –
Belovèd of the Spring!
Zephyrus The sun, the wind, the verdure –
Spring All
That wisest nature cause can call
Of quickening anything.

Ben Jonson

The Succession of the Foure Sweet Months

First, *April*, she with mellow showrs
Opens the way for early flowers;
Then after her comes smiling *May*,
In a more rich and sweet aray:
Next enters *June*, and brings us more
Jems, then those two, that went before:
Then (lastly) *July* comes, and she
More wealth brings in, then all those three.

Robert Herrick

To Spring

O thou with dewy locks, who lookest down
Through the clear windows of the morning, turn
Thine angel eyes upon our western isle,
Which in full choir hails thy approach, O Spring!

The hills tell each other, and the listening
Valleys hear; all our longing eyes are turned
Up to thy bright pavillions: issue forth,
And let thy holy feet visit our clime.

Come o'er the eastern hills, and let our winds
Kiss thy perfumèd garments; let us taste
Thy morn and evening breath; scatter thy pearls
Upon our love-sick land that mourns for thee.

O deck her forth with thy fair fingers; pour
Thy soft kisses on her bosom; and put
Thy golden crown upon her languished head,
Whose modest tresses were bound up for thee!

William Blake

[When Flora Fair]

When Flora fair the pleasant tidings bringeth
Of summer sweet with herbs and flowers adorned,
The nightingale upon the hawthorn singeth
And Boreas' blasts the birds and beasts have scorned;
When fresh Aurora with her colours painted,
Mingled with spears of gold, the sun appearing,
Delights the hearts that are with love acquainted,
And maying maids have then their time of cheering;
All creatures then with summer are delighted,
The beasts, the birds, the fish with scale of silver;
Then stately dames by lovers are invited
To walk in meads or row upon the river.
I all alone am from these joys exiled
No summer grows where love yet never smiled.

Richard Carlton

Be Still as You are Beautiful

Be still as you are beautiful,
  Be silent as the rose;
Through miles of starlit countryside
  Unspoken worship flows
To find you in your loveless room
  From lonely men whom daylight gave
The blessing of your passing face
  Impenetrably grave.

A white owl in the lichened wood
  Is circling silently,
More secret and more silent yet
  Must be your love to me.
Thus, while about my dreaming head
  Your soul in ceaseless vigil goes,
Be still as you are beautiful,
  Be silent as the rose.

Patrick MacDonogh

To Mistress Margery Wentworth

With marjoram gentle,
  The flower of goodlihead,
Embroidered the mantle
  Is of your maidenhead.
Plainly I cannot glose;
  Ye be, as I devine,
The pretty primrose,
  The goodly columbine.
With marjoram gentle,

The flower of goodlihead,
Embroidered the mantle
Is of your maidenhead.
Benign, courteous, and meek,
With wordes well devised;
In you, who list to seek,
Be virtues well comprised.
With marjoram gentle,
The flower of goodlihead,
Embroidered the mantle
Is of your maidenhead.

John Skelton

To Mistress Margaret Hussey

Merry Margaret,
As midsummer flower,
Gentle as falcon
Or hawk of the tower:
With solace and gladness,
Much mirth and no madness,
All good and no badness;
So joyously,
So maidenly,
So womanly
Her demeaning
In every thing,
Far, far passing
That I can indite,
Or suffice to write
Of Merry Margaret
As midsummer flower,

Gentle as falcon
Or hawk of the tower.
   As patient and still
And as full of good will
As fair Isaphill,
Coriander,
Sweet pomander,
Good Cassander,
Steadfast of thought,
Well made, well wrought,
Far may be sought
Ere that ye can find
So courteous, so kind
As Merry Margaret,
   This midsummer flower,
Gentle as falcon
Or hawk of the tower.

John Skelton

A Song of Yarrow

September, and the sun was low,
   The tender greens were flecked with yellow,
And autumn's ardent after-glow,
   Made Yarrow's uplands rich and mellow.

Between me and the sunken sun,
   Where gloaming gathered in the meadows,
Contented cattle, red and dun,
   Were slowly browsing in the shadows.

And out beyond them, Newark reared
   Its quiet tower against the sky,

As if its walls had never heard
  Of wassail-rout or battle-cry.

O'er moss-grown roofs that once had rung
  To reivers' riot, border brawl,
The slumberous shadows mutely hung,
  And silence deepened over all.

Above the high horizon bar
  A cloud of golden mist was lying,
And over it a single star
  Soared heavenward, as the day was dying.

No sound, no word, from field or ford,
  Nor breath of wind to float a feather,
While Yarrow's murmuring waters poured
  A lonely music through the heather.

In silent fascination bound,
  As if some mighty spell obeying,
The hills seemed listening to the sound
  And wondering what the stream was saying.

What secret to the inner ear,
  What happier message was it bringing,
What more of hope and less of fear,
  Than man dare mix with earthly singing?

Earth's song it was, yet heavenly growth –
  It was not joy, it was not sorrow,
A strange heart-fulness of them both
  The wandering singer seemed to borrow.

Like one that sings and does not know,
  But in a dream hears voices calling,
Of those that died long years ago,
  And sings although the tears be falling.

Oh Yarrow! garlanded with rhyme!
  That clothes thee in a mournful glory,
Though sunsets of an elder time
  Had never crowned thee with a story,

Still would I wander by thy stream,
  Still listen to the lonely singing,
That gives me back the golden dream
  Through which old echoes yet are ringing.

Love's sunshine! sorrow's bitter blast!
  Dear Yarrow, we have seen together,
For years have come and years have past,
  Since first we met among the heather.

Ah! those indeed were happy hours,
  When first I knew thee, gentle river;
But now thy bonny birken bowers
  To me, alas! are changed for ever.

The best, the dearest, all have gone,
  Gone like the bloom upon the heather,
And left us singing here alone
  Beside life's cold and winter weather.

I, too, pass on, but when I'm dead,
  Thou still shalt sing by night and morrow,
And help the aching heart and head
  To bear the burden of its sorrow.

And summer flowers shall linger yet,
  Where all thy mossy margins guide thee;
And minstrels, met as we have met,
  Shall sit and sing their songs beside thee.

J. B. Selkirk

All That's Past

Very old are the woods;
  And the buds that break
Out of the briar's boughs,
  When March winds wake,
So old with their beauty are –
  Oh, no man knows
Through what wild centuries
  Roves back the rose.

Very old are the brooks;
  And the rills that rise
Where snow sleeps cold beneath
  The azure skies
Sing such a history
  Of come and gone,
Their every drop is as wise
  As Solomon.

Very old are we men;
  Our dreams are tales
Told in dim Eden
  By Eve's nightingales;
We wake and whisper awhile,
  But, by the day gone by,
Silence and sleep like fields
  Of amaranth lie.

Walter de la Mare

Love and the Goddess

You Meaner Beauties

You meaner beauties of the night,
That poorly satisfie our eies
More by your number, than your light;
You common people of the skies,
What are you when the Moon shall rise?

Ye violets that first appeare,
By your pure purple mantles known
Like the proud virgins of the yeare,
As if the Spring were all your own;
What are you when the Rose is blown?

Ye curious chaunters of the wood,
That warble forth dame Nature's lays,
Thinking your passions understood
By your weak accents: what's your praise,
When Philomell her voyce shall raise?

So when my mistris shal be seene
In sweetnesse of her looks and minde;
By virtue first then choyce a queen;
Tell me, if she was not design'd
Th' eclypse and glory of her kind?

Sir Henry Wotton

[My Beauty Named]

Be thou then my Beauty named,
  Since thy will is to be mine;
For by that I am enflamed
  Which on all alike doth shine;
Others may the light admire,
I only truly feel the fire.

But if lofty titles move thee,
  Challenge then a Sovereign's place;
Say I honour when I love thee,
  Let me call thy kindness Grace:
State and Love things diverse be,
Yet will we teach them to agree.

Or if this be not sufficing,
  Be thou styled my Goddess then:
I will love thee, sacrificing;
  In thine honour hymns I'll pen:
To be thine, what canst thou more?
I'll love thee, serve thee, and adore.

Thomas Campion

[The Chain]

Have I found her? O rich finding!
  Goddess-like for to behold,
Her fair tresses seemly binding
  In a chain of pearl and gold.
Chain me, chain me, O most fair.
Chain me to thee with that hair!

Francis Pilinton

To Julia, The Flaminica Dialis, or Queen-Priest

Thou know'st, my Julia, that it is thy turne
This Mornings Incense to prepare, and burne.
The Chaplet, and Inarculum here be,
With the white Vestures, all attending Thee.
This day, the Queen-Priest, thou art made t'appease
Love for our very-many Trespasses.
One chiefe transgression is among the rest,
Because with Flowers her Temple was not drest:
The next, because her Altars did not shine
With daily Fyres: The last, neglect of Wine:
For which, her wrath is gone forth to consume
Us all, unlesse preserv'd by thy Perfume.
Take then thy Censer; Put in Fire, and thus,
O Pious-Priestesse! make a Peace for us.
For our neglect, Love did our Death decree,
That we escape. Redemption comes by thee.

Robert Herrick

Like the Idalian Queen

Like the Idalian queen,
Her hair about her eyne,
With neck and breast's ripe apples to be seen,
At first glance of the morn,
In Cyprus' gardens gathering those fair flow'rs
Which of her blood were born,
I saw, but fainting saw, my paramours.
The graces naked danc'd about the place,
The winds and trees amaz'd
With silence on her gaz'd;

The flow'rs did smile, like those upon her face,
And as their aspen stalks those fingers band,
That she might read my case,
A hyacinth I wish'd me in her hand.

William Drummond

To Venus

Oh, fair sweet goddess, queen of loves,
Soft and gentle as thy doves,
Humble-eyed, and ever ruing
Those poor hearts, their loves pursuing!
O, thou mother of delights,
Crowner of all happy nights,
Star of dear content and pleasure,
Of mutual loves the endless treasure!
Accept this sacrifice we bring,
Thou continual youth and spring;
Grant this lady her desires,
And every hour we'll crown thy fires.

John Fletcher

Forms of the God

Tom's Angel

No one was in the fields
But me and Polly Flint,
When, like a giant across the grass,
The flaming angel went.

It was budding time in May,
And green as green could be,
And all in his height he went along
Past Polly Flint and me.

We'd been playing in the woods,
And Polly up, and ran,
And hid her face, and said,
'Tom! Tom! The Man! The Man!'

And I up-turned; and there,
Like flames across the sky,
With wings all bristling, came
The Angel striding by.

And a chaffinch overhead
Kept whistling in the tree
While the Angel, blue as fire, came on
Past Polly Flint and me.

And I saw his hair, and all
The ruffling of his hem,
As over the clovers his bare feet
Trod without stirring them.

Polly she cried; and, oh!
We ran, until the lane
Turned by the miller's roaring wheel,
And we were safe again.

Walter de la Mare

Great God Pan

Sing his praises that doth keep
  Our flocks from harm,
Pan, the father of our sheep;
  And arm in arm
Tread we softly in a round,
Whilst the hollow neighbouring ground
Fills the music with her sound.

Pan, oh, great god Pan, to thee
  Thus do we sing!
Thou that keep'st us chaste and free
  As the young spring;
Ever be thy honour spoke,
From that place the morn is broke,
To that place day doth unyoke!

John Fletcher

Hymn of Pan

From the forests and highlands
  We come, we come;
From the river-girt islands,
  Where loud waves are dumb
    Listening to my sweet pipings.
The wind in the reeds and the rushes,
  The bees on the bells of thyme,
The birds on the myrtle bushes,
  The cicale above in the lime,
And the lizards below in the grass,
Were as silent as ever old Tmolus was,
    Listening to my sweet pipings.

Liquid Peneus was flowing,
  And all dark Tempe lay
In Pelion's shadow, outgrowing
  The light of the dying day,
    Speeded by my sweet pipings.
The Sileni, and Sylvans, and Fauns,
  And the Nymphs of the woods and the waves,
To the edge of the moist river-lawns,
  And the brink of the dewy caves,
And all that did then attend and follow,
Were silent with love, as you now, Apollo,
    With envy of my sweet pipings.

I sang of the dancing stars,
  I sang of the daedal Earth,
And of Heaven – and the giant wars,
  And Love, and Death, and Birth, –
    And then I changed my pipings, –
Singing how down the vale of Maenalus
  I pursued a maiden and clasped a reed.
Gods and men, we are all deluded thus!

It breaks in our bosom and then we bleed:
All wept, as I think both ye now would,
If envy or age had not frozen your blood,
At sorrow of my sweet pipings.

P. B. Shelley

The Satyrs' Dance

Round-a, round-a, keep your ring:
To the glorious sun we sing, –
Ho, ho!
He that wears the flaming rays,
And th' imperial crown of bays,
Him with shouts and songs we praise –
Ho, ho!
That in his bounty he'd vouchsafe to grace
The humble sylvans and their shaggy race.

Thomas Ravenscroft

Pan's Anniversary or The Shepherds' Holiday

Hymn 1

1st Arcadian Of Pan we sing, the best of singers, Pan,
That taught us swains how first to tune our lays,
And on the pipe more airs than Phoebus can.
Chorus Hear, O you groves, and hills resound his praise.

2nd Arcadian Of Pan we sing, the best of leaders, Pan,
That leads the Naiads and the Dryads forth,
And to their dances more than Hermes can.
Chorus Hear, O you groves, and hills resound his worth.
3rd Arcadian Of Pan we sing, the best of hunters, Pan,
That drives the hart to seek unusèd ways,
And in the chase more than Sylvanus can.
Chorus Hear, O you groves, and hills resound his praise.
4th Arcadian Of Pan we sing, the best of shepherds, Pan,
That keeps our flocks and us, and both leads forth
To better pastures than great Pales can.
Chorus Hear, O you groves, and hills resound his worth.
And while his powers and praises thus we sing,
The valleys let rebound, and all the rivers ring.

Hymn 2

Pan is our all, by him we breathe, we live,
We move, we are; 'tis he our lambs doth rear,
Our flocks doth bless, and from the store doth give
The warm and finer fleeces that we wear.
He keeps away all heats and colds,
Drives all diseases from our folds,
Makes everywhere the spring to dwell,
The ewes to feed, their udders swell;
But if he frown, the sheep (alas),
The shepherds wither, and the grass.
Strive, strive to please him then by still increasing thus
The rites are due to him, who doth all right for us.

Ben Jonson

Pan's Anniversary or The Shepherds' Holiday
[The Nymphs' Songs]

1st Nymph — Thus, thus, begin the yearly rites
Are due to Pan on these bright nights;
His morn now riseth and invites
To sports, to dances and delights:
All envious and profane, away;
This is the shepherds' holiday.

2nd Nymph — Strew, strew the glad and smiling ground
With every flower, yet not confound
The primrose drop, the spring's own spouse;
Bright day's-eyes and the lips of cows;
The garden star, the queen of May,
The rose to crown the holiday.

Ben Jonson

A Hymn in Praise of Neptune

Of Neptune's empire let us sing,
At whose command the waves obey;
To whom the rivers tribute pay,
Down the high mountain sliding:
To whom the scaly nation yields
Homage for the crystal fields
Wherein they dwell:
And every sea-god pays a gem
Yearly out of his wat'ry call
To deck great Neptune's diadem.

The Tritons dancing in a ring,
Before his palace-gates do make
The water with their echoes quake,

Like the great thunder sounding:
The sea-nymphs chant their accents shrill,
And the sirens, taught to kill
　　With their sweet voice,
Make ev'ry echoing rock reply,
Unto their gentle murmuring noise,
The praise of Neptune's empery.

Thomas Campion

The Smell of the Sacrifice

The Gods require the thighes
Of Beeves for sacrifice;
Which rosted, we the steam
Must sacrifice to them:
Who though they do not eat,
Yet love the smell of the meat.

Robert Herrick

II

Witches and Witchcraft

Flying and Bewitching

Witches, For and Against

Witches at Work

Flying and Bewitching

The Hagg

The staffe is now greas'd,
And very well pleas'd,
She cockes out her Arse at the parting,
To an old Ram Goat,
That rattles i'th'throat,
Halfe choakt with the stink of her farting.

In a dirtie Haire-lace
She leads on a brace
Of black-bore-cats to attend her;
Who scratch at the Moone,
And threaten at noone
Of night from Heaven for to rend her.

A hunting she goes;
A crackt horne she blowes;
At which the hounds fall a bounding;
While th'Moone in her sphere
Peepes trembling for feare,
And night's afraid of the sounding.

Robert Herrick

The Witch o' Fife

Hurray, hurray, the jade's away,
  Like a rocket of air with her bandalet!
I'm up in the air on my bonnie grey mare,
  But I see her yet, I see her yet.
I'll ring the skirts o' the gowden wain
  Wi' curb an' bit, wi' curb an' bit:
An' catch the Bear by the frozen mane –
  An' I see her yet, I see her yet.

Away, away, o'er mountain an' main,
  To sing at the morning's rosy yett;
An' water my mare at its fountain clear –
  But I see her yet, I see her yet.
Away, thou bonny witch o' Fife,
  On foam of the air to heave an' flit,
An' little reck thou of a poet's life,
  For he sees thee yet, he sees thee yet!

James Hogg

The Hag

  The Hag is astride,
  This night for to ride;
The Devill and shee together:
  Through thick, and through thin,
  Now out, and then in,
Though ne'r so foule be the weather.

  A Thorn or a Burr
  She takes for a Spurre:

With a lash of a Bramble she rides now,
  Through Brakes and through Bryars,
  O're Ditches, and Mires,
She followes the Spirit that guides now.

  No Beast, for his food,
  Dares now range the wood;
But husht in his laire he lies lurking:
  While mischeifs, by these,
  On Land and on Seas,
At noone of Night are a working.

  The storme will arise,
  And trouble the skies;
This night, and more for the wonder,
  The ghost from the Tomb
  Affrighted shall come,
Cal'd out by the clap of the Thunder.

Robert Herrick

The Ride-By-Nights

Up on their brooms the Witches stream,
Crooked and black in the crescent's gleam;
One foot high, and one foot low,
Bearded, cloaked, and cowled, they go.
'Neath Charlie's Wain they twitter and tweet,
And away they swarm 'neath the Dragon's feet,
With a whoop and a flutter they swing and sway,
And surge pell-mell down the Milky Way.
Between the legs of the glittering Chair
They hover and squeak in the empty air.

Then round they swoop past the glimmering Lion
To where Sirius barks behind huge Orion;
Up, then, and over to wheel amain
Under the silver, and home again.

Walter de la Mare

Witch's Broomstick Spell

Horse and hattock,
Horse and go,
Horse and pelatis, Ho, ho!

Isobel Gowdie

[Witch Song]

The silly bit chicken, gar cast her a pickle,
And she'll grow meikle, and she'll grow meikle;
And she'll grow meikle, and she'll do guid,
And lay an egg to my little brude.

Anon.

Witch's Milking Charm

Meares' milk, and deers' milk,
And every beast that bears milk
Between St Johnston and Dundee,
Come a' to me, come a' to me.

Anon.

The Witches' Cauldron

1 Witch Thrice the brinded cat hath mewed.
2 Witch Thrice and once the hedge-pig whined.
3 Witch Harpier cries 'Tis time, 'tis time.
1 Witch Round about the cauldron go:
In the poisoned entrails throw.
Toad, that under cold stone
Days and nights has thirty-one,
Sweltered venom sleeping got,
Boil thou first i' the charmed pot!
All Double, double toil and trouble;
Fire burn, and cauldron bubble.

2 Witch Fillet of a fenny snake,
In the cauldron boil and bake;
Eye of newt and toe of frog,
Wool of bat and tongue of dog,
Adder's fork and blind-worm's sting,
Lizard's leg and owlet's wing,
For a charm of powerful trouble,
Like a hell-broth boil and bubble.
All Double, double toil and trouble;
Fire burn, and cauldron bubble.

3 Witch Scale of dragon, tooth of wolf,
Witches' mummy, maw, and gulf
Of the ravined salt-sea shark,
Root of hemlock digged i' the dark,
Liver of blaspheming Jew,
Gall of goat, and slips of yew,
Slivered in the moon's eclipse,
Nose of Turk and Tartar's lips,
Finger of birth-strangled babe
Ditch-delivered by a drab,
Make the gruel thick and slab:

Add thereto a tiger's chaudron.
For the ingredients of our cauldron.
All Double, double toil and trouble;
Fire burn, and cauldron bubble.

2 Witch Cool it with a baboon's blood,
Then the charm is firm and good.

William Shakespeare

A Charm Song

Black spirits and white, red spirits and gray,
Mingle, mingle, mingle, you that mingle may!
Titty, Tiffin,
Keep it stiff in;
Firedrake, Puckey,
Make it lucky;
Laird, Robin,
You must bob in.
Round, around, around, about, about!
All ill come running in, all good keep out!
1 Witch Here's the blood of a bat.
Hecate Put in that, O put in that!
2 Witch Here's libbard's bane.
Hecate Put in again!
1 Witch The juice of toad, the oil of adder;
2 Witch Those will make the younker madder.
Hecate Put in – there's all – and rid the stench.
Firestone Nay, here's three ounces of the red-haired wench.
All Round, around, around, about, about!

Thomas Middleton

The Masque of Queens

9th Hag And I ha' been plucking, plants among,
Hemlock, henbane, adder's tongue,
Nightshade, moonwort, libbard's bane,
And twice by the dogs was like to be ta'en.
10th Hag I from the jaws of a gardener's bitch
Did snatch these bones, and then leaped the ditch;
Yet went I back to the house again,
Killed the black cat, and here's the brain.
11th Hag I went to the toad breeds under the wall,
I charmed him out and he came at my call;
I scratched out the eyes of the owl before,
I tore the bat's wing: what would you have more?

Ben Jonson

The Masque of Queens

Charm 4

Deep, O deep, we lay thee to sleep;
We leave thee drink by, if thou chance to be dry,
Both milk and blood, the dew and the flood.
We breathe in thy bed, at the foot and the head;
We cover thee warm, that thou take no harm;
And when thou dost wake,
  Dame earth shall quake,
  And the houses shake,
  And her belly shall ache
  As her back were brake
  Such a birth to make

As is the blue drake,
Whose form thou shalt take.
Dame Never a star yet shot?
Where be the ashes?
Hag Here i' the pot.
Dame Cast them up, and the flintstone
Over the left shoulder bone
Into the west.
Hag It will be best.

Charm 5

The sticks are a-cross, there can be no loss,
The sage is rotten, the sulfur is gotten
Up to the sky that was i' the ground.
Follow it then with our rattles, round,
Under the bramble, over the briar;
A little more heat will set it on fire;
Put it in mind to do it kind,
Flow water, and blow wind.
Rouncy is over, Robble is under,
A flash of light and a clap of thunder,
A storm of rain, another of hail.
We all must home i' the egg shell sail;
The mast is made of a great pin,
The tackle of cobweb, the sail as thin,
And if we go through and not fall in –
Dame Stay! All our charms do nothing win
Upon the night; our labor dies!
Our magic feature will not rise,
Nor yet the storm! We must repeat
More direful voices far, and beat
The ground with vipers till it sweat.

Ben Jonson

The Masque of Queens

Charm 7

Black go in, and blacker come out;
At thy going down we give thee a shout.
    Hoo!
At thy rising again thou shalt have two,
And if thou dost what we would have thee do,
Thou shalt have three, thou shalt have four,
Thou shalt have ten, thou shalt have a score
    Hoo! Har! Har! Hoo!

Charm 8

A cloud of pitch, a spur and a switch
To haste him away, and a whirlwind play
Before and after, with thunder for laughter
And storms for joy of the roaring boy,
His head of a drake, his tail of a snake.

Charm 9

About, about and about,
Till the mist arise and the lights fly out;
The images neither be seen nor felt;
The woolen burn and the waxen melt;
Sprinkle your liquors upon the ground
And into the air, around, around.
  Around, around,
  Around, around,
  Till a music sound
  And the pace be found
  To which we may dance
  And our charms advance.

Ben Jonson

Witches, For and Against

[The Night of Hallowe'en]

This is the night of Hallowe'en
When all the witches might be seen;
Some of them black, some of them green,
Some of them like a turkey bean.

Anon.

[Witches Gathering]

In the hinder end of harvest, on All-hallowe'en,
When our good neighbours does ride, if I read right,
Some buckled on a bunwand, and some on a bean,
Aye trottand in troups from the twilight.

Anon.

[Ride a Cock-Horse]

Ride a cock-horse to Banbury Cross,
To see a fine lady upon a white horse;
Rings on her fingers and bells on her toes,
And she shall have music wherever she goes.

Mother Goose

A Witch

There's thik wold hag, Moll Brown, look zee, just past!
I wish the ugly sly wold witch
Would tumble over into ditch;
I woulden pull her out not very vast.
No, no. I don't think she's a bit belied,
No, she's a witch, aye, Molly's evil-eyed.
Vor I do know o' many a-withrèn blight
A-cast on vo'k by Molly's mutter'd spite;
She did, woone time, a dreadvul deäl o' harm
To Farmer Gruff's vo'k, down at Lower Farm.
Vor there, woone day, they happened to offend her,
An' not a little to their sorrow,
Because they woulden gi'e or lend her
Zome'hat she come to bag or borrow;
An' zoo, they soon began to vind
That she'd agone an' left behind
Her evil wish that had such pow'r,
That she did meäke their milk an' eäle turn zour,
An' addle all the eggs their vowls did lay;
They coulden vetch the butter in the churn,
An' all the cheese begun to turn
All back ageän to curds an' whey;
The little pigs, a-runnèn wi' the zow,
Did zicken, zomehow, noobody know'd how,
An' vall, an' turn their snouts towárd the sky.
An' only gi'e woone little grunt, and die;
An' all the little ducks an' chickèn
Wer death-struck out in yard a-pickèn
Their bits o' food, an' vell upon their head,
An' flapp'd their little wings an' drapp'd down dead.
They coulden fat the calves, they woulden thrive;
They coulden seäve their lambs alive;
Their sheep wer all a-coath'd, or gi'ed noo wool;
The hosses vell away to skin an' bwones,

An' got so weak they coulden pull
A half a peck o' stwones:
The dog got dead-alive an' drowsy,
The cat vell zick an' woulden mousy;
An' every time the vo'k went up to bed,
They wer a-hag-rod till they wer half dead.
They us'd to keep her out o' house, 'tis true,
A-naïlèn up at door a hosses shoe;
An' I've a-heärd the farmer's wife did try
To dawk a needle or a pin
In drough her wold hard wither'd skin,
An' draw her blood, a-comèn by:
But she could never vetch a drap,
For pins would ply an' needles snap
Ageän her skin; an' that, in coo'se,
Did meäke the hag bewitch em woo'se.

William Barnes

Another [Charme] to Bring in the Witch

To house the Hag, you must doe this;
Commix with Meale a little Pisse
Of him bewitcht: then forthwith make
A little Wafer or a Cake;
And this rawly bak't will bring
The old Hag in. No surer thing.

Robert Herrick

Another Charme for Stables

Hang up Hooks, and Sheers to scare
Hence the Hag, that rides the Mare,
Till they be all over wet,
With the mire, and the sweat:
This observ'd, the Manes shall be
Of your horses, all knot-free.

Robert Herrick

Against Witches

Black luggie, lammer bead,
Rowan-tree, and Scarlet thread,
Put the witches to their speed.

Mother Goose

[The Protection]

Rowan-tree and red thread
Gar the witches tyne their speed.

Mother Goose

Charmes

Bring the holy crust of Bread,
Lay it underneath the head;
'Tis a certain Charm to keep
Hags away, while Children sleep.

Robert Herrick

Witches at Work

Alison Gross

O Alison Gross, that lives in yon tower,
  The ugliest witch in the north countrie,
She trysted me ae day up till her bower,
  And mony fair speeches she made to me.

She straiked my head and she kaimed my hair,
  And she set me doun saftly on her knee;
Says, 'Gin ye will be my lemman sae true,
  Sae mony braw things as I would you gie.'

She shaw'd me a mantle o' red scarlett,
  Wi' gouden flowers and fringes fine;
Says, 'Gin ye will be my lemman sae true,
  This gudely gift it sall be thine.'

'Awa', awa', ye ugly witch,
  Haud far awa', and lat me be!
I never will be your lemman sae true,
  And I wish I were out o' your company.'

She neist brought a sark o' the saftest silk,
  Well wrought wi' pearls about the band;
Says, 'Gin ye will be my ain true love,
  This gudely gift ye sall command.'

She shaw'd me a cup o' the gude red goud,
  Weel set in jewels sae fair to see;

Says, 'Gin ye will be my lemman sae true,
  This gudely gift I will ye gie.'

'Awa', awa', ye ugly witch,
  Haud far awa', and lat me be!
For I wadna ance kiss your ugly mouth
  For a' the gifts that you could gie.'

She's turned her richt and round about,
  And thrice she blew on a grass-green horn;
And she sware by the moon and the stars aboon
  That she'd gar me rue the day I was born.

Then out has she ta'en a silver wand,
  And she's turned her three times round and round;
She's mutter'd sic words that my strength it fail'd,
  And I fell doun senseless on the ground.

She turned me into an ugly worm,
  And gar'd me twine about the tree;
And aye on ilka Saturday's night
  Alison Gross she cam' to me;

Wi' silver basin and silver kaim,
  To kaim my headie upon her knee;
But ere that I'd kiss her ugly mouth,
  I'd sooner gae twining around the tree.

But as it fell out, on last Hallowe'en,
  When the Seely Court cam' ridin' by,
The Queen lighted down on a gowan bank,
  Close by the tree where I wont to lie.

She took me up in her milkwhite hand,
  She straiked me three times o'er her knee;
She changed me back to my proper shape,
  And nae mair do I twine about the tree.

Anon.

The Witch of Wokey

In aunciente days tradition showes
A base and wicked elfe arose,
  The Witch of Wokey hight:
Oft have I heard the fearful tale
From Sue, and Roger of the vale,
  On some long winter's night.

Deep in the dreary dismall cell,
Which seem'd and was ycleped hell,
  This blear-eyed hag did hide:
Nine wicked elves, as legends sayne,
She chose to form her guardian trayne,
  And kennel near her side.

Here screeching owls oft made their nest,
While wolves its craggy sides possest,
  Night-howling thro' the rock:
No wholesome herb could here be found;
She blasted every plant around,
  And blister'd every flock.

Her haggard face was foul to see;
Her mouth unmeet a mouth to bee;
  Her eyne of deadly leer,
She nought devis'd, but neighbour's ill;
She wreak'd on all her wayward will,
  And marr'd all goodly chear.

All in her prime, have poets sung,
No gaudy youth, gallant and young,
  E'er blest her longing armes;
And hence arose her spight to vex,
And blast the youth of either sex,
  By dint of hellish charms.

From Glaston came a lerned wight,
Full bent to marr her fell dispight,
  And well he did, I weene:
Sich mischief never had been known,
And, since his mickle lerninge shown,
  Sich mischief ne'er has been.

He chauntede out his godlie booke,
He crost the water, blest the brooke,
  Then – pater noster done, –
The ghastly hag he sprinkled o'er;
When lo! where stood a hag before,
  Now stood a ghastly stone.

Full well 'tis known adown the dale:
Tho' passing strange indeed the tale,
  And doubtfull may appear,
I'm bold to say, there's never a one,
That has not seen the witch in stone,
  With all her household gear.

But tho' this lernede clerke did well;
With grieved heart, alas! I tell,
  She left this curse behind:
That Wokey-nymphs forsaken quite,
Tho' sense and beauty both unite,
  Should find no leman kind.

For lo! even as the fiend did say,
The sex have found it to this day,
  That men are wonderous scant:
Here's beauty, wit, and sense combin'd,
With all that's good and virtuous join'd,
  Yet hardly one gallant.

Shall then such maids unpitied moane?
They might as well, like her, be stone,

As thus forsaken dwell.
Since Glaston now can boast no clerks;
Come down from Oxenford, ye sparks,
And, oh! revoke the spell.

Yet stay – nor thus despond ye fair;
Virtue's the god's peculiar care;
I hear the gracious voice:
Your sex shall soon be blest agen,
We only wait to find such men,
As best deserve your choice.

Dr Harrington

The Lunatic Lover

Grim king of the ghosts, make haste,
And bring hither all your train;
See how the pale moon does waste,
And just now is in the wane.
Come, you night-hags, with all your charms,
And revelling witches away,
And hug me close in your arms;
To you my respects I'll pay.

I'll court you, and think you fair,
Since love does distract my brain:
I'll go, I'll wed the night-mare,
And kiss her, and kiss her again:
But if she prove peevish and proud,
Then, a pise on her love! Let her go;
I'll seek me a winding shroud,
And down to the shades below.

A lunacy sad I endure,
  Since reason departs away;
I call to those hags for a cure,
  As knowing not what I say.
The beauty, whom I do adore,
  Now slights me with scorn and disdain;
I never shall see her more:
  Ah! how shall I bear my pain!

I ramble, and range about
  To find out my charming saint;
While she at my grief does flout.
  And smiles at my loud complaint.
Distraction I see is my doom,
  Of this I am now too sure;
A rival is got in my room,
  While torments I do endure.

Strange fancies do fill my head,
  While wandering in despair,
I am to the desarts lead,
  Expecting to find her there.
Methinks in a spangled cloud
  I see her enthroned on high;
Then to her I crie aloud,
  And labour to reach the sky.

Anon.

III

The Craft of Magic

Auguries and Foretellings
Spells
Herb Magic
Curses
Blessings
Invocations and Incantations

Auguries and Foretellings

[A Prayer to the Moon Goddess]

Luna, every woman's friend,
To me thy goodness condescend,
Let this night in visions see
Emblems of my destiny.

Mother Goose

[Spell for Babies]

Rock a cradle empty,
Babies will be plenty.

Mother Goose

To Know Whom One Shall Marry

This knot I knit,
To know the thing, I know not yet,
That I may see,
The man that shall my husband be,
How he goes, and what he wears,
And what he does, all days, and years.

Mother Goose

[For Everlasting Beauty]

The fair maid who, the first of May,
Goes to the fields at break of day,
And walks in dew from the hawthorn tree
Will ever handsome be.

Mother Goose

[Divination with Yarrow]

Good night, fair yarrow,
Thrice goodnight to thee;
I hope before tomorrow's dawn
My true love I shall see.

Mother Goose

[To Dream of a Future Husband]

Two make it,
Two bake it,
Two break it.

Mother Goose

[Beseeching the Mirror]

Mirror, mirror, tell me,
Am I pretty or plain?
Or am I downright ugly
And ugly to remain?

Shall I marry a gentleman?
Shall I marry a clown?
Or shall I marry old Knives-and-Scissors
Shouting through the town?

Mother Goose

[Sign of Rain]

Crow on the fence,
Rain will come hence.
Crow on the ground,
Rain will come down.

Mother Goose

[To See Your Beau]

Make a rhyme, make a rhyme,
See your beau before bedtime.

Mother Goose

[To Get a Wish]

Touch blue,
Your wish will come true.

Mother Goose

[Good Omens]

If you see the cuckoo sitting,
The swallow a-flitting,
And a filly-foal lying still,
You all the year shall have your will.

Mother Goose

[Magpie Omens]

Yen's sorry,
Twee's morry,
Three's a wedding,
Fower's death,
Five's hivin,
Six is hell,
And sivin's the deel's aan sel.

Anon.

[Crow Omens]

One's lucky,
Two's unlucky,
Three is health,
Four is wealth,
Five is sickness
And six death.

Mother Goose

[Black Cat]

Wherever the cat of the house is black,
Its lasses of lovers will have no lack.

Mother Goose

[Charms for Luck]

Yellow stones on Sunday,
Pearls on Monday,
Rubies on Tuesday,
Sapphires on Wednesday,
Garnets or red stones on Thursday,
Emeralds or green stones on Friday,
Diamonds on Saturday.

Mother Goose

[Winning a Pin]

I'll sing you a song,
Nine verses long,
  For a pin;
Three and three are six,
And three are nine;
You are a fool,
  And the pin is mine.

Mother Goose

[Four-Leaf Clover]

One leaf for fame, one leaf for wealth,
One for a faithful lover,
And one leaf to bring glorious health,
Are all in a four-leaf clover.

Mother Goose

[Even Ash]

If you find even ash, or four-leaved clover,
You will see your love afore the day's over.

Mother Goose

[Bad Luck]

The robin and the redbreast,
The robin and the wren –
If you take out their nest,
You'll never thrive again.

The robin and the redbreast,
The martin and the swallow –
If you touch one of their eggs,
Bad luck will sure to follow.

Mother Goose

Spells

[Windmill Spell]

Blow, wind, blow! and go, mill, go!
That the miller may grind his corn;
  That the baker may take it,
  And into bread make it,
And send us some hot in the morn.

Mother Goose

[Spell of Power]

One-ery, two-ery,
  Ziccary zan;
Hollow bone, crack a bone,
Ninery ten:
Spittery spot,
  It must be done;
Twiddleum twaddleum
  Twenty ONE.

Mother Goose

[Spell against Warts at the New Moon]

What I see is growing,
What I rub is going.

Mother Goose

[Ash Tree as a Cure for Warts]

Ash tree, ashen tree,
Pray buy this wart of me.

Mother Goose

[Bathe in Dew for Beauty]

Beauty come,
Freckles go,
Dewdrops make me
White as snow.

Mother Goose

[Spell for Marriage]

Hemp-seed I set,
    Hemp-seed I sow,
The young man that I love,
    Come after me and mow.

I sow, I sow,
    Then, my own dear,
Come hoe, come hoe,
    And mow and mow.

Mother Goose

[Spell for a Good Harvest]

Stand fast, root; bear well top;
God send us a yowling sop!
Every twig, apple big,
Every bough, apple enow,
Hats full, caps full,
Fill quarter sacks full.

Mother Goose

[Snail Spell]

Snail, Snail,
Come out of your hole,
Or else I'll beat you,
As black as a coal.

Snail, snail,
Put out your horns,
I'll give you bread
And barley corns.

Mother Goose

[Five Spells to Banish Rain]

Rain, rain, go away,
Come again another day.

Rain on the green grass,
  And rain on the tree,
Rain on the house-top,
  But not on me.

Rain, rain, go to Spain,
And never you come back again.

Rain, rain, go to Germany,
And remain there permanently.

Rain, rain, go away,
Don't come back till Christmas day,
Little Johnnie wants to play.

Mother Goose

[Spell for a Shower]

Rain, rain, come down and pour,
Then you'll only last an hour.

Mother Goose

[Self-Blessing Spell]

Magpie, magpie, chatter and flee,
Turn up thy tail, and good luck to me.

Mother Goose

[Horse's Spell]

Going up hill whip me not,
Coming down hill hurry me not,
On level ground spare me not,
Loose in the stable forget me not,
Of hay and corn rob me not,
Of clean water stint me not,
With sponge and water neglect me not,
Of soft bed deprive me not,
Tired and hot wash me not,
If sick or cold chill me not,
With bit or rein oh, jerk me not,
And when you are angry strike me not.

Mother Goose

[Milking Spell]

Cushy cow, bonny, let down thy milk,
And I will give thee a gown of silk;
A gown of silk and a silver tee,
If thou will let down thy milk to me.

Mother Goose

[Spell to Make Butter]

Come, butter, come,
Come, butter, come,
Peter stands at the gate
Waiting for a butter cake.
Come, butter, come.

Mother Goose

Charm of the Churn

Come will the free, come;
Come will the bond, come;
Come will the bells, come;
Come will the maers, come;
Come will the blade, come;
Come will the sharp, come;
Come will the hounds, come;
Come will the wild, come;
Come will the mild, come;
Come will the kind, come;
Come will the loving, come;
Come will the squint, come;
Come will he of the yellow cap,
That will set the churn a-running.

The free will come,
The bond will come,
The bells will come,
The maers will come,
The blades will come,
The sharp will come,

The hounds will come,
The wild will come,
The mild will come,
The kind will come,
The loving will come,
The devious will come,
The brim-full of the glove will come,
To set the churn a-running;
The kindly Columba will come in his array,
And the golden-haired Bride of the kine.

A splash is here,
A plash is here,
A plash is here,
A splash is here,
A crash is here,
A squash is here,
A squash is here,
A crash is here,
A big soft snail is here,
The sap of each of the cows is here,
A thing better than honey and spruce,
A bogle yellow and fresh is here.

A thing better than right is here,
The fist of the big priest is here,
A thing better than the carcase is here,
The head of the dead man is here,
A thing better than wine is here,
The full of the cog of Caristine
Of live things soft and fair are here,
  Of live things soft and fair are here.

Come, thou churn, come;
Come, thou churn, come;
Come, thou life; [?] come, thou breath; [?]
Come, thou churn, come;

Come, thou churn, come;
Come, thou cuckoo; come, thou jackdaw;
Come, thou churn, come;
Come, thou churn, come;
Come will the little lark from the sky,
Come will the little carlin of the black-cap.

Come, thou churn, come;
Come, thou churn, come;
Come will the merle, come will the mavis,
Come will the music from the bower;
Come, thou churn, come;
Come, thou churn, come;
Come, thou wild cat,
To ease thy throat;
Come, thou churn, come;
Come, thou churn, come.

Come, thou hound, and quench thy thirst;
Come, thou churn, come;
Come, thou churn, come;
Come, thou poor; come, thou naked;
Come, thou churn, come;
Come, thou churn, come;
Come, ye alms-deserver
Of most distressful moan;
Come, thou churn, come;
Come, thou churn, come;
Come, each hungry creature,
And satisfy the thirst of thy body.

Come, thou churn, come;
Come, thou churn, come;
It is the God of the elements who bestowed on us,
And not the charm of a carlin with plant.
Come, thou churn, come;
Come, thou churn, come;

Come, thou fair-white Mary,
And endow to me my means;
Come, thou churn, come;
Come, thou churn, come;
Come, thou beauteous Bride,
And bless the substance of my kine.
Come, thou churn, come;
Come, thou churn, come;
The churning made of Mary,
In the fastness of the glen,
To decrease her milk,
To increase her butter;
Butter-milk to wrist,
Butter to elbow;
  Come, thou churn, come;
  Come, thou churn, come.

Anon.

Charm for Rose

Thou rose deathly, deadly, swollen,
Leave the udder of the white-footed cow,
Leave the udder of the spotted cow,
Leave, leave that swelling,
  And betake thyself to other swelling.

Thou rose thrawn, obstinate,
Surly in the udder of the cow,
Leave thou the swelling and the udder,
Flee to the bottom of the stone.

I place the rose to the stone,
I place the stone to the earth,
I place milk in the udder,
I place substance in the kidney.

Anon.

Summoning Spell for a Fish

By the white sun's chill
By the dancing of the reeds
By the ripple's pull
  Come to my hook

    By the tang of your flesh
    By the gleam of your skin
    By your web of bone

By the shriek of my line
By the drone of my reel
By the blind maggot's spasm
  Come to my hook

    By the shiver of weed
    By the bubble's hiss
    By the river's drift

By the beat of your gill
By the flick of your fin
By the shadow's shift
  Come to my hook

    By the twitch of your lip
    By your rasping scale
    By the dark of your eye

By the menace of the pike
By the mayfly's wing
By the water's light
Come.

Jeni Couzyn

Spell to Bring Lost Creatures Home

Home, home,
Wild birds home!
Lark to the grass,
Wren to the hedge,
Rooks to the tree-tops,
Swallow to the eaves,
Eagle to its crag
And raven to its stone,
All birds home!

Home, home,
Strayed ones home,
Rabbit to burrow,
Fox to earth,
Mouse to the wainscot,
Rat to the barn,
Cattle to the byre,
Dog to the hearth,
All beasts home!

Home, home,
Wanderers home,
Cormorant to rock,
Gulls from the storm,
Boat to the harbour
Safe sail home!

Children home,
At evening home,
Boys and girls
From the roads come home,
Out of the rain
Sons come home,
From the gathering dusk,
Young ones home!

Home, home,
All souls home,
Dead to the graveyard,
Living to the lamplight,
Old to the fireside,
Girls from the twilight,
Babe to the breast
And heart to its haven,
Lost one home!

Kathleen Raine

Fath-Fith

Fath-fith
Will I make on thee,
By Mary of the augury,
By Bride of the corslet,
From sheep, from ram,
From goat, from buck,
From fox, from wolf,
From sow, from boar,
From dog, from cat,
From hipped-bear,
From wilderness-dog,

From watchful 'scan',
From cow, from horse,
From bull, from heifer,
From daughter, from son,
From the birds of the air,
From the creeping things of the earth,
From the fishes of the sea,
From the imps of the storm.

Anon.

A Charme, or an Allay for Love

If so be a Toad be laid
In a Sheeps-skin newly flaid,
And that ty'd to man 'twil sever
Him and his affections ever.

Robert Herrick

The Bondman

Bind me but to thee with thine haire,
And quickly I shall be
Made by that fetter or that snare
A bondman unto thee.

Or if thou tak'st that bond away,
Then bore me through the eare;
And by the Law I ought to stay
For ever with thee here.

Robert Herrick

The Bracelet to Julia

Why I tye about thy wrist,
Julia, this my silken twist;
For what other reason is't,
But to shew thee how in part,
Thou my pretty Captive art?
But thy Bondslave is my heart:
'Tis but silke that bindeth thee,
Knap the thread, and thou art free:
But 'tis otherwise with me;
I am bound, and fast bound so,
That from thee I cannot go;
If I co'd, I wo'd not so.

Robert Herrick

On Mistress S. W., who cured my hand by a plaster applied to the knife which hurt me

Wounded and weary of my life,
I to my fair one sent my knife;
The point had pierced my hand as far
As foe would foe in open war.
Cruel, but yet compassionate, she
Spread plasters for my enemy;
She hugg'd the wretch had done me harm,
And in her bosom kept it warm,
When suddenly I found the cure was done,
The pain and all the anguish gone,
Those nerves which stiff and tender were
Now very free and active are:
Not help'd by any power above,
But a true miracle of Love.

Henceforth, physicians, burn your bills,
Prescribe no more uncertain pills:
She can at distance vanquish pain,
She makes the grave to gape in vain:
'Mongst all the arts that saving be
None so sublime as sympathy.
Oh could it help a wounded breast,
I'd send my soul to have it dress'd.
Yet, rather, let herself apply
The sovereign med'cine to her eye:
There lurks the weapon wounds me deep,
There, that which stabs me in my sleep;
For still I feel, within, a mortall smart,
The salve that heal'd my hand can't cure my heart.

Thomas Flatman

The Holy Well

From thy forehead thus I take
These herbs, and charge thee not awake
Till in yonder holy well
Thrice, with powerful magic spell,
Filled with many a baleful word,
Thou hast been dipped. Thus, with my cord
Of blasted hemp, by moonlight twined,
I do thy sleepy body bind.
I turn thy head unto the east,
And thy feet unto the west,
Thy left arm to the south put forth,
And thy right unto the north.
I take thy body from the ground,
In this deep and deadly swound,
And into this holy spring

I let thee slide down by my string.
Take this maid, thou holy pit,
To thy bottom; nearer yet;
In thy water pure and sweet,
By thy leave I dip her feet;
Thus I let her lower yet,
That her ankles may be wet;
Yet down lower, let her knee
In thy waters washed be.
There stop. Fly away,
Everything that loves the day!
Truth, that hath but one face,
Thus do I charm thee from this place.
Snakes that cast your coats for new,
Chameleons that alter hue,
Hares that yearly sexes change,
Proteus altering oft and strange,
Hecate with shapes three,
Let this maiden changed be,
With this holy water wet,
To the shape of Amoret!
Cynthia, work thou with my charm!
Thus I draw thee free from harm,
Up out of this blessed lake:
Rise both like her and awake!

John Fletcher

A Conjuration to Electra

By those soft Tods of wooll
With which the aire is full:
By all those Tinctures there,
That paint the Hemisphere:

By Dewes and drisling Raine,
That swell the Golden Graine:
By all those sweets that be
I'th flowrie Nunnerie:
By silent Nights, and the
Three Formes of Heccate:
By all Aspects that blesse
The sober Sorceresse,
While juice she straines, and pith
To make her Philters with:
By Time, that hastens on
Things to perfection:
And by your self, the best
Conjurement of the rest:
O my Electra! be
In love with none, but me.

Robert Herrick

The Night-Piece, to Julia

Her Eyes the Glow-worme lend thee,
The Shooting Starres attend thee;
  And the Elves also,
  Whose little eyes glow,
Like the sparks of fire, befriend thee.

No Will-o'th'-Wispe mis-light thee;
Nor Snake, or Slow-worme bite thee:
  But on, on thy way
  Not making a stay,
Since Ghost ther's none to affright thee.

Let not the darke thee cumber;
What though the Moon do's slumber?
The Starres of the night
Will lend thee their light,
Like Tapers cleare without number.

Then 'Julia' let me wooe thee,
Thus, thus to come unto me:
And when I shall meet
Thy silv'ry feet,
My soule Ile poure into thee.

Robert Herrick

Love Charm

A love charm for thee,
Water drawn through a straw,
The warmth of him (her) thou lovest,
With love to draw on thee.

Arise betimes on Lord's day,
To the flat rock of the shore
Take with thee the pointed canopy,
And the cap of a priest.

A small quantity of embers
In the skirt of thy kirtle,
A special handful of sea-weed
In a wooden shovel.

Three bones of an old man,
Newly torn from the grave,
Nine stalks of royal fern,
Newly trimmed with an axe.

Burn them on a fire of faggots
And make them all into ashes;
Sprinkle in the fleshy breast of thy lover,
    Against the venom of the north wind.

Go round the 'rath' of procreation,
The circuit of the five turns,
And I will vow and warrant thee
    That man (woman) shall never leave thee.

Anon.

Love Spell

By the travelling wind
By the restless clouds
By the space of the sky,

By the foam of the surf
By the curve of the wave
By the flowing of the tide,

By the way of the sun,
By the dazzle of light
By the path across the sea,
    Bring my lover.

By the way of the air,
By the hoodie crow's flight
By the eagle on the wind,

By the cormorant's cliff
By the seal's rock
By the raven's crag,

By the shells on the strand
By the ripples on the sand
By the brown sea-wrack,
    Bring my lover.

By the mist and the rain
By the waterfall
By the running burn,

By the clear spring
By the holy well
And the fern by the pool
    Bring my lover.

By the sheepwalks on the hills
By the rabbit's tracks
By the stones of the ford,
    Bring my lover.

By the long shadow
By the evening light
By the midsummer sun
    Bring my lover.

By the scent of the white rose
Of the bog myrtle
And the scent of the thyme
    Bring my lover.

By the lark's song
By the blackbird's note
By the raven's croak
    Bring my lover.

By the voices of the air
By the water's song
By the song of a woman
    Bring my lover.

By the sticks burning on the hearth
By the candle's flame
By the fire in the blood
    Bring my lover.

By the touch of hands
By the meeting of lips
By love's unrest
    Bring my lover.

By the quiet of the night
By the whiteness of my breast
By the peace of sleep
    Bring my lover.

By the blessing of the dark
By the beating of the heart
By my unborn child,
    Bring my lover.

Kathleen Raine

Summoning Spell for a Husband

As your mind is a landscape, wide and changing
is growing and dying, knows the seasons
knows the flight of the bird and sleep of trees
  so let you come, so marry me.

As your body is straight and brown and smooth as stone
as your fingers are subtle as water
as your eyes are quick and sharp, as your nerves are
talking and listening

as your life is a wide river on its course
as I to you as bank and ocean and rain
as your love to me is sky and womb and storm
so let you come, so marry me.

As the child has been waiting for us now in the forest
a long long time, with growing and doing
and happiness to have before the world's ending
as my body now is the body of a woman

And I am strong to receive you now without bending
and strong to love without fearing
and strong to be in your harsh presence without forgetting
so let you come, so marry me.

Jeni Couzyn

Spell to Protect Our Love

By warm blood of bird
By wing of bird
By feather of bird
Let our love be safe.

By hot blood of mammal
By fur and by hair
By mammary gland
Let it come to no harm.

By chill blood of reptile
By scale of reptile
By lung of reptile
Let no ill damage it.

By four-legged amphibian
By gill and naked skin
By slow blood and lung
Adapt and be nourished.

By cool blood of fish
By gill and by fin
By scale and skeleton
Let no harm come to our love.

Jeni Couzyn

Spell for Jealousy

Be loved, my beloved.
Be sweetened, sour one.
Be filled, empty one.

Bring all the thief has given home to our house
Bring all the thief has given home to our bed
Bring all the thief has given home to our love
Bring all the thief has given home to me.

Light of her brighten me
Spite of her strengthen me
Joy of her gladden me.

Lady as candle is to the full sun of noon
As toad is to the great whale of the ocean
As leaf is to the mighty forest of the mountain
Are you now to me and my loved one.

Let the wind take you
Let the water take you
Let the rain take you.

You are burr in his sock
You are grain in his shoe
Now he will forget you.

Jeni Couzyn

Spell to Release the Furious Old Woman

This day I draw the spite from you
  Scorpion bear it,
This day I draw the anger from you
  Leopard bear it,
This day I draw the malice from you
  And bear it,
This day I draw the fear from you
  Bird release it.

  Old woman your face is softening
  Your words are the hail falling
  Your voice is the wind whining.

This day I draw the vengeance from you
  Snake use it,
This day I draw the loneliness from you
  Spirit enhance it.

  Heart fear not
Wisdom fault not
  Body hurt not
Death fail not.

Jeni Couzyn

Spell to Banish Fear

By the warmth of the sun
By the baby's cry
By the lambs on the hill
I banish thee.

By the sweetness of the song
By the warm rain falling
By the hum of grass
Begone.

Jeni Couzyn

Spell of Sleep

Let him be safe in sleep
As leaves folded together
As young birds under wings
As the unopened flower.

Let him be hidden in sleep
As islands under rain,
As mountains within their clouds,
As hills in the mantle of dusk.

Let him be free in sleep
As the flowing tides of the sea,
As the travelling wind on the moor,
As the journeying stars in space.

Let him be upheld in sleep
As a cloud at rest on the air,

As sea-wrack under the waves
When the flowing tide covers all
And the shells' delicate lives
Open on the sea-floor.

Let him be healed in sleep
In the quiet waters of night
In the mirroring pool of dreams
Where memory returns in peace,
Where the troubled spirit grows wise
And the heart is comforted.

Kathleen Raine

Charm of the Sprain

Bride went out
In the morning early,
With a pair of horses;
One broke his leg,
With much ado,
That was apart,
She put bone to bone,
She put flesh to flesh,
She put sinew to sinew,
She put vein to vein;
As she healed that
May I heal this.

Anon.

Charm for Chest Seizure

Power of moon have I over thee,
  Power of sun have I over thee,
Power of rain have I over thee,
  Power of dew have I over thee,
Power of sea have I over thee,
  Power of land have I over thee,
Power of stars have I over thee,
  Power of planets have I over thee,
Power of universe have I over thee,
  Power of skies have I over thee,
Power of saints have I over thee,
  Power of heaven have I over thee,
Power of heaven and power of God have I over thee,
  Power of heaven and God over thee.

A part of thee on the grey stones,
A part of thee on the steep mountains,
A part of thee on the swift cascades,
A part of thee on the gleaming clouds,
A part of thee on the ocean-whales,
A part of thee on the meadow-beasts,
A part of thee on the fenny swamps,
A part of thee on the cotton-grass moors,
  A part on the great surging sea –
    She herself has best means to carry,
      The great surging sea,
    She herself has best means to carry.

Anon.

The Counting of the Stye

Why came the two here
Without the three here?

After the incantation the Lord's Prayer is intoned, and the following is repeated:

Pater one,
Pater two,
Pater three,
Pater four,
Pater five,
Pater six,
Pater seven,
Pater eight,
Pater nine,
Pater one,
And eight,
Pater of Christ the kindly
Be upon thee to-night,
Pater of the Three of life
Upon thine eye without
harm.

Why came the one stye,
Without the two styes here?
Why came the two styes,
Without the three styes here?
Why came the three styes,
Without the four styes here?
Why came the four styes,
Without the five styes here?
Why came the five styes,
Without the six styes here?
Why came the six styes,

Without the seven styes
here?
Why came the seven styes,
Without the eight styes here?
Why came the eight styes,
Without the nine styes here?
Why came the nine,
Or one at all here?

Anon.

Charm for the Evil Eye

Whoso laid on thee the eye,
May it lie upon himself,
May it lie upon his house,
May it lie upon his flocks,
On the shuffling carlin,
On the sour-faced carlin,
On the bounding carlin,
On the sharp-shanked carlin,
Who arose in the morning,
With her eye on her flocks,
With her flocks in her 'seoin',
May she never own a fold,
May she never have half her desires,
The part of her which the ravens do not eat,
May the birds devour.

Four made to thee the eye,
Man and dame, youth and maid;
Three who will cast off thee the envy
The Father, the Son, and the Holy Spirit.

As Christ lifted the fruit,
From the branches of the bushes,
May He now lift off thee
Every ailment, every envy, every jealousy,
From this day forth till the last day of thy life.

Anon.

Herb Magic

The Charm of the Figwort

I will pluck the figwort,
With the fruitage of sea and land,
The plant of joy and gladness,
  The plant of rich milk.

As the King of kings ordained,
To put milk in pap and gland,
As the Being of life ordained,
To place substance in udder and kidney,
With milk, with milkiness, with butter milk,
With produce, with whisked whey, with milk-product,
With speckled female calves,
With progeny, with joy, with fruitage,
With love, with charity, with bounty,

Without man of evil wish,
Without woman of evil eye,
Without malice, without envy, without 'toirinn',
Without hipped bear,
Without wilderness dog,
Without 'scan foirinn',
Obtaining hold of the rich dainty
  Into which this shall go.
Figwort of bright lights,
Fruitage to place therein,
With fruit, with grace, with joyance.

Anon.

The Tree-Entwining Ivy

I will pluck the tree-entwining ivy,
As Mary plucked with her one hand,
As the King of life has ordained,
To put milk in udder and gland,
With speckled fair female calves,
As was spoken in the prophecy,
On this foundation for a year and a day,
Through the bosom of the God of life, and of all the powers.

Anon.

The Yarrow

I will pluck the yarrow fair,
That more benign shall be my face,
That more warm shall be my lips,
That more chaste shall be my speech,
Be my speech the beams of the sun,
Be my lips the sap of the strawberry.

May I be an isle in the sea,
May I be a hill on the shore,
May I be a star in waning of the moon,
May I be a staff to the weak,
Wound can I every man,
Wound can no man me.

Anon.

The Fairy Wort

Pluck will I the fairy wort,
With expectation from the fairy bower,
To overcome every oppression,
As long as it be fairy wort.

Fairy wort, fairy wort,
I envy the one who has thee,
There is nothing the sun encircles,
But is to her a sure victory.

Pluck will I mine honoured plant
Plucked by the great Mary, helpful Mother of the people,
To cast off me every tale of scandal and flippancy,
Ill-life, ill-love, ill-luck,
Hatred, falsity, fraud and vexation,
Till I go in the cold grave beneath the sod.

Anon.

The 'Mothan'

Pluck will I the 'mothan',
Plant of the nine joints,
Pluck will I and vow me,
To noble Bride and her Fosterling.

Pluck will I the 'mothan',
As ordained of the King of power,
Pluck will I and vow me,
To great Mary and her Son.

Pluck will I the 'mothan',
As ordained of the King of life,
To overcome all oppression,
And the spell of evil eye.

Anon.

St Columba's Plant

Plantlet of Columba,
Without seeking, without searching,
Plantlet of Columba,
Under my arm for ever!
For luck of men,
For luck of means,
For luck of wish [?],
For luck of sheep,
For luck of goats,
For luck of birds,
For luck of fields,
For luck of shell-fish,
For luck of fish,
For luck of produce and kine,
For luck of progeny and people,
For luck of battle and victory,
On land, on sea, on ocean,
Through the Three on high,
Through the Three a-nigh,
Through the Tree eternal,
Plantlet of Columba,
I cull thee now,
I cull thee now.

Anon.

[The Nine Good Herbs]

Remember, Mugwort, what you made known,
What you arranged at the Great Proclamation.
You were called Una, the oldest of herbs,
you have power against three and against thirty,
you have power against poison and against infection,
you have power against the loathsome foe roving through
the land.

And you, Plantain, mother of herbs,
open from the east, mighty inside.
Over you chariots creaked, over you queens rode,
over you brides cried out, over you bulls snorted.
You withstood all of them, you dashed against them.
May you likewise withstand poison and infection,
and the loathsome foe roving through the land.

'Stune' is the name of this herb, it grew on a stone,
it stands up against poison, it dashes against pain.
Unyielding it is called, it dashes against poison,
it drives out the hostile one, it casts out poison.
This is the herb that fought against the snake,
it has power against poison, it has power against infection,
it has power against the loathsome foe roving through the land.

Put to flight now, Venom-loather, the greater poisons,
though you are the lesser,
you the mightier, conquer the lesser poisons, until he
is cured of both.
Remember, Camomile, what you made known,
what you accomplished at Alorford,
that never a man should lose his life from infection,
after Camomile was prepared for his food.

This is the herb that is called 'Wergulu'.
A seal sent it across the sea-ridge,

a vexation to poison, a help to others.
It stands against pain, it dashes against poison,
it has power against three and against thirty,
against the hand of a fiend and against mighty devices,
against the spell of mean creatures.

There the Apple accomplished it against poison
that she (the loathsome serpent) would never dwell in the house.

Chervil and Fennel, two very mighty ones.
They were created by the wise Lord,
holy in heaven as He hung [on the cross];
He set and sent them to the seven worlds,
to the wretched and the fortunate, as a help to all.

These nine have power against nine poisons.
A worm came crawling, it killed nothing.
For Woden took nine glory-twigs,
he smote then the adder that it flew apart into nine parts.

Now these nine herbs have power against nine evil spirits,
against nine poisons and against nine infections;
Against the red poison, against the foul poison,
Against the white poison, against the purple poison,
against the yellow poison, against the green poison,
against the black poison, against the blue poison,
against the brown poison, against the crimson poison.
Against worm-blister, against water-blister,
against thorn-blister, against thistle-blister,
against ice-blister, against poison-blister.

> If any poison comes flying from the east,
> or any from the north, [or any from the south],
> or any from the west among the people.

Christ stood over diseases of every kind.

I alone know a running stream,
and the nine adders beware of it.
May all the weeds spring up from their roots,
the seas slip apart, all salt water,
when I blow this poison from you.

Anon.

Curses

[Curse on a Kitchen]

My mill grinds
Pepper, and Spice,
Your Mill grinds
Rats, and Mice.

Mother Goose

[Curse on a Drunk]

Piss a Bed,
Piss a Bed,
Barley Butt,
Your Bum is so heavy
You can't get up.

Mother Goose

Another

Who with thy leaves shall wipe (at need)
The place, where swelling Piles do breed:
May every ill, that bites, or smarts,
Perplex him in his hinder-parts.

Robert Herrick

Charm against Wens

Wen, wen, little wen,
here you shall not build, nor have any habitation,
but you shall go north, hence to the neighbouring hill,
where you wretch have a brother.
He shall lay a leaf on your head;
Under the wolf's paw, under the eagle's feather,
under the eagle's claw, ever may you wither.
May you be consumed as coal upon the hearth,
may you shrink as dung upon a wall,
and may you dry up as water in a pail.
May you become as small as a linseed grain,
and much smaller than the hipbone of an itchmite,
and may you become so small that you become nothing.

Anon.

The Curse

To a sister of an enemy of the author's who disapproved of 'the Playboy'

Lord, confound this surly sister,
Blight her brow with blotch and blister,
Cramp her larynx, lung, and liver,
In her guts a galling give her.
Let her live to eat her dinners
In Mountjoy with seedy sinners:
Lord, this judgement quickly bring,
And I'm your servant, J. M. Synge.

J. M. Synge

A Glass of Beer

The lanky hank of a she in the inn over there
Nearly killed me for asking the loan of a glass of beer;
May the devil grip the whey-faced slut by the hair,
And beat bad manners out of her skin for a year.

That parboiled ape, with the toughest jaw you will see
On virtue's path, and a voice that would rasp the dead,
Came roaring and raging the minute she looked at me,
And threw me out of the house on the back of my head!

If I asked her master he'd give me a cask a day;
But she, with the beer at hand, not a gill would arrange!
May she marry a ghost and bear him a kitten, and may
The High King of Glory permit her to get the mange.

James Stephens

Thief

To the galleys, thief, and sweat your soul out
With strong tugging under the curled whips,
That there your thievishness may find full play.
Whereas, before, you stole rings, flowers and watches,
Oaths, jests and proverbs,
Yet paid for bed and board like an honest man,
This shall be entire thiefdom: you shall steal
Sleep from chain-galling, diet from sour crusts,
Comradeship from the damned, the ten-year-chained –
And, more than this, the excuse for life itself
From a craft steered toward battles not your own.

Robert Graves

The Lament for O'Sullivan Beare (Made by His Nurse)

The sun of Ivera
No longer shines brightly,
The voice of her music
No longer is sprightly;
No more to her maidens
The light dance is dear,
Since the death of our darling
O'Sullivan Beare.

Scully! thou false one
You basely betrayed him;
In his strong hour of need
When thy right hand should aid him;

He fed thee – he clad thee –
You had all could delight thee:
You left him, you sold him
May heaven requite thee!

Scully! May all kinds
Of evil attend thee!
On thy dark road of life
May no kind one befriend thee!
May fevers long burn thee.
And agues long freeze thee!
May the strong hand of God
In his red anger seize thee!

Had he died calmly
I would not deplore him;
Or if the wild strife
Of the sea-war closed o'er him:
But with ropes round his white limbs
Through Ocean to trail him,
Like a fish after slaughter
'Tis therefore I wail him.

Long may the curse
Of his people pursue them;
Scully that sold him
And soldier that slew him!
One glimpse of Heaven's light
May they see never!
May the hearthstone of Hell
Be their best bed forever!

In the hole where the vile hands
Of soldiers had laid thee,
Unhonored, unshrouded,
And headless they laid thee,
No eye to rain o'er thee,

No dirge to lament thee,
No friend to deplore thee!

Dear head of my darling
How gory and pale
These aged eyes see thee,
High spiked on their jail!
That cheek in the summer sun
Ne'er shall grow warm;
Nor that eye e'er catch light
From the flash of the storm!

A curse, blessed ocean,
Is on thy green water
From the Haven of Cork
To Ivera of slaughter:
Since the billows were dyed
With the red wounds of fear
Of Muirtach Og
Our O'Sullivan Beare!

Anon.

A Curse on a Closed Gate

Be this the fate
Of the man who would shut his gate
On the stranger, gentle or simple, early or late.

When his mouth with a day's long hunger and thirst would wish
For the savour of salted fish,
Let him sit and eat his fill of an empty dish.

To the man of that ilk,
Let water stand in his churn, instead of milk
That turns a calf's coat silk.

And under the gloomy night
May never a thatch made tight
Shut out the clouds from his sight.

Above the ground or below it,
Good cheer, may he never know it,
Nor a tale by the fire, nor a dance on the road, nor a song by a
  wandering poet.

Till he open his gate
To the stranger, early or late,
And turn back the stone of his fate.

James H. Cousins

[Curse of Nine]

Ane's nane,
Twa's some,
Three's a pickle,
Four's a curn,
Five's a horse-lade,
Six'll gar his back bow,
Seven'll vex his breath,
Aught'll bear him to the ground,
And nine'll be his death.

Anon.

[The Kelpy]

Sair back and sair banes,
Drivin' the laird o' Morphie's stanes!
The laird o' Morphie'll never thrive
As lang's the kelpy is alive!

Anon.

Highland Execration on the Commonwealth

The Commonwealth that 'gramagh' thing,
Gar break him's word, gar die him's king,
Gar pay him's cess, or tak him's gears,
We'll no do that, de'il cow the leears;
We'll bide a while among the crows,
We'll scour the sword, and wisk the bows,
And when her nainsell see the 'Rie',
The deil may care for 'Gramaghee'!

Anon.

Blessings

[A Charm to Protect One's Home]

Saint Francis and Saint Benedight
Bless this house from wicked wight.
From the night-mare and the goblin,
That is hight Good-fellow Robin;
Keep it all from evil spirits,
Fairies, weezels, rats and ferrets,
From curfew time
To the next prime.

Mother Goose

[Sleep Blessing]

Good night,
Sleep tight,
Wake up bright
In the morning light,
To do what's right
With all your might.

Mother Goose

The Blessing of the Parching

Thou flame grey, slender, curved,
Coming from the top pore of the peat,
Thou flame of leaps, breadth, heat,
Come not nigh me with thy quips.

A burning steady, gentle, generous,
Coming round about my quicken roots,
A fire fragrant, fair, and peaceful,
Nor causes dust, nor grief, nor havoc.

Heat, parch my fat seed,
For food for my little child,
In name of Christ, King of the elements,
Who gave us corn and bread and blessing withal,
    In name of Christ, King of the elements,
    Who gave us corn and bread and blessing withal.

Anon.

The Beltane Blessing

Bless, O Threefold true and bountiful,
Myself, my spouse, and my children,
My tender children and their beloved mother at their head.
On the fragrant plain, on the gay mountain sheiling,
    On the fragrant plain, on the gay mountain sheiling.

Everything within my dwelling or in my possession,
All kine and crops, all flocks and corn,
From Hallow Eve to Beltane Eve,
With goodly progress and gentle blessing,
From sea to sea, and every river mouth,
    From wave to wave, and base of waterfall.

Be the Three Persons taking possession of all to me belonging,
Be the sure Trinity protecting me in truth;
Oh! satisfy my soul in the words of Paul,
And shield my loved ones beneath the wing of Thy glory,
    Shield my loved ones beneath the wing of Thy glory.

Bless everything and every one,
Of this little household by my side;
Place the cross of Christ on us with the power of love,
Till we see the land of joy,
    Till we see the land of joy.

What time the kine shall forsake the stalls,
What time the sheep shall forsake the folds,
What time the goats shall ascend to the mount of mist,
May the tending of the Triune follow them,
    May the tending of the Triune follow them.

Thou Being who didst create me at the beginning,
Listen and attend me as I bend the knee to Thee,
Morning and evening as is becoming in me,
In Thine own presence, O God of life,
    In Thine own presence, O God of life.

Anon.

The Clipping Blessing

Go shorn and come woolly,
Bear the Beltane female lamb,
Be the lovely Bride thee endowing,
And the fair Mary thee sustaining,
    The fair Mary thee sustaining.

Michael the chief be shielding thee
From the evil dog and from the fox,
From the wolf and from the sly bear,
And from the taloned birds of destructive bills,
From the taloned birds of hooked bills.

Anon.

[A Milking Prayer]

Bless, O God, my little cow,
Bless, O God, my desire;
Bless Thou my partnership
And the milking of my hand, O God.

Bless, O God, each teat,
Bless, O God each finger;
Bless Thou each drop
That goes into my pitcher, O God!

Anon.

Bless, O Chief of Generous Chiefs

Bless, O Chief of generous chiefs,
Myself and everything anear me,
Bless me in all my actions,
Make Thou me safe for ever,
Make Thou me safe for ever.

From every brownie and ban-shee,
From every evil wish and sorrow,
From every nymph and water-wraith,
From every fairy-mouse and grass-mouse,
From every fairy-mouse and grass-mouse.

From every troll among the hills,
From every siren hard pressing me,
From every ghoul within the glens,
Oh! save me till the end of my day.
Oh! save me till the end of my day.

Anon.

Good Wish

Wisdom of serpent be thine,
Wisdom of raven be thine,
Wisdom of valiant eagle.

Voice of swan be thine,
Voice of honey be thine,
Voice of the son of the stars.

Bounty of sea be thine,
Bounty of land be thine,
Bounty of the Father of heaven.

Anon.

Lob-Lie-by-the-Fire

Keep me a crust
Or starve I must;
Hoard me a bone
Or I am gone;
A handful of coals
Leave red for me;
Or the smouldering log
Of a wild-wood tree;
Even a kettle
To sing on the hob
Will comfort the heart
Of poor old Lob:
Then with his hairy
Hands he'll bless
Prosperous master,
And kind mistress.

Walter de la Mare

[The Crust]

If ye feare to be affrighted
When ye are (by chance) benighted:
In your Pocket for a trust,
Carrie nothing but a Crust:
For that holy piece of Bread,
Charmes the danger, and the dread.

Robert Herrick

The Wassaile

1 Give way, give way ye Gates, and win
An easie blessing to your Bin,
And Basket, by our entring in.

2 May both with manchet stand repleat;
Your Larders too so hung with meat,
That though a thousand, thousand eat;

3 Yet, ere twelve Moones shall whirl about
Their silv'rie Spheres, ther's none may doubt,
But more's sent in, then was serv'd out.

4 Next, may your Dairies Prosper so,
As that your plans no Ebbe may know;
But if they do, the more to flow.

5 Like to a solemne sober Stream
Bankt all with Lillies, and the Cream
Of sweetest Cow-slips filling Them.

6 Then, may your Plants be prest with Fruit,
Nor Bee, or Hive you have be mute;
But sweetly sounding like a Lute.

7 Next may your Duck and teeming Hen
Both to the Cocks-tread say Amen;
And for their two eggs render ten.

8 Last, may your Harrows, Shares and Ploughes,
Your Stacks, your Stocks, your sweetest Mowes,
All prosper by your Virgin-vowes.

9 Alas! we blesse, but see none here,
That brings us either Ale or Beere;
In a drie-house all things are neere.

10 Let's leave a longer time to wait,
Where Rust and Cobwebs bind the gate;
And all live here with needy Fate.

11 Where Chimneys do for ever weepe,
For want of warmth, and Stomachs keepe
With noise, the servants eyes from sleep.

12 It is in vain to sing, or stay
Our free-feet here; but we'l away:
Yet to the Lares this we'l say,

13 The time will come, when you'l be sad,
And reckon this for fortune bad,
T'ave lost the good ye might have had.

Robert Herrick

Invocations and Incantations

The Love-Charm

Rise from the shades below,
    All you that prove
The helps of looser love!
    Rise, and bestow
Upon this cup whatever may compel,
By powerful charm and unresisted spell,
A heart unwarmed to melt in love's desires!
Distil into this liquor all your fires;
    Heats, longings, tears;
  But keep back frozen fears;
That she may know, that has all power defied,
Art is a power that will not be denied.

John Fletcher

Pray and Prosper

First offer Incense, then thy field and meads
Shall smile and smell the better by thy beads.
The spangling Dew dreg'd o're the grasse shall be
Turn'd all to Mell, and Manna there for thee.
Butter of Amber, Cream, and Wine, and Oile

Shall run, as rivers, all throughout thy soyl.
Wod'st thou to sincere-silver turn thy mold?
Pray once, twice pray; and turn thy ground to gold.

Robert Herrick

To Larr

No more shall I, since I am driven hence,
Devote to thee my graines of Frankincense:
No more shall I from mantle-trees hang downe,
To honour thee, my little parsley crown:
No more shall I (I feare me) to thee bring
My chives of Garlick for an offering:
No more shall I, from henceforth, heare a quire
Of merry Crickets by my Country fire.
Go where I will, thou luckie Larr stay here,
Warme by a glit'ring chimnie all the yeare.

Robert Herrick

The Spell

Holy Water come and bring;
Cast in Salt, for seasoning:
Set the Brush for sprinkling:
Sacred Spittle bring ye hither;
Meale and it now mix together;
And a little Oyle to either:
Give the Tapers here their light,
Ring the Saints-Bell, to affright
Far from hence the evill Sp'rite.

Robert Herrick

[A Chant]

Dip, dip, allebadar,
Duck shee shantamar,
Shantamar allebadar,
Duck shee shantamar.

Anon.

You Spotted Snakes with Double Tongue

You spotted snakes with double tongue,
  Thorny hedge-hogs, be not seen;
Newts, and blind-worms, do no wrong;
  Come not near our fairy queen:
  Philomel, with melody,
  Sing in our sweet lullaby;
Lulla, lulla, lullaby, lulla, lullaby;
  Never harm,
  Nor spell, nor charm,
  Come our lovely lady nigh;
  So, good night, with lullaby.
Weaving spiders, come not here:
  Hence, you long-legged spinners, hence!
Beetles black, approach not near;
  Worm, nor snail, do no offence.
  Philomel, with melody, &c.

William Shakespeare

Lucy Ashton's Song

Look not thou on beauty's charming,
Sit thou still when kings are arming,
Taste not when the wine-cup glistens,
Speak not when the people listens,
Stop thine ear against the singer,
From the red gold keep thy finger;
Vacant heart and hand and eye,
Easy live and quiet die.

Sir Walter Scott

The Invocation of the Graces

I bathe thy palms
In showers of wine,
In the lustral fire,
In the seven elements,
In the juice of the rasps,
In the milk of honey,
And I place the nine pure choice graces
In thy fond face,
    The grace of form,
    The grace of voice,
    The grace of fortune,
    The grace of goodness,
    The grace of wisdom,
    The grace of charity,
    The grace of choice maidenliness,
    The grace of whole-souled loveliness,
    The grace of goodly speech.

Dark is yonder town,
Dark are those therein,
Thou art the brown swan,
Going in among them.
Their hearts are under thy control,
Their tongues are beneath thy sole,
Nor will they ever utter a word
  To give thee offence.

A shade art thou in the heat,
A shelter art thou in the cold,
Eyes art thou to the blind,
A staff art thou to the pilgrim,
An island art thou at sea,
A fortress art thou on land,
A well art thou in the desert,
  Health art thou to the ailing.

Thine is the skill of the Fairy Woman,
Thine is the virtue of Bride the calm,
Thine is the faith of Mary the mild,
Thine is the tact of the woman of Greece,
Thine is the beauty of Emir the lovely,
Thine is the tenderness of Darthula delightful,
Thine is the courage of Maebh the strong,
  Thine is the charm of Binne-bheul.

Thou art the joy of all joyous things,
Thou art the light of the beam of the sun,
Thou art the door of the chief of hospitality,
Thou art the surpassing star of guidance,
Thou art the step of the deer of the hill,
Thou art the step of the steed of the plain,
Thou art the grace of the swan of swimming,
  Thou art the loveliness of all lovely desires.

The lovely likeness of the Lord
Is in thy pure face,
The loveliest likeness that
Was upon the earth.

The best hour of the day be thine,
The best day of the week be thine,
The best week of the year be thine,
The best year in the Son of God's domain be thine.

Peter has come and Paul has come,
James has come and John has come,
Muriel and Mary Virgin have come,
Uriel the all-beneficent has come,
Ariel the beauteousness of the young has come,
Gabriel the seer of the Virgin has come,
Raphael the prince of the valiant has come,
And Michael the chief of the hosts has come,
   And Jesus Christ the mild has come,
   And the Spirit of true guidance has come,
   And the King of kings has come on the helm,
   To bestow on thee their affection and their love,
   To bestow on thee their affection and their love.

Anon.

God of the Moon, God of the Sun

God of the moon, God of the sun,
Who ordained to us the Son of mercy.
The fair Mary upon her knee,
Christ the King of life in her lap,
I am the cleric established,

Going round the founded stones,
I behold mansions, I behold shores,
I behold angels floating,
I behold the shapely rounded column
Coming landwards in friendship to us.

Anon.

Queen of the Night

Hail unto thee,
  Jewel of the night!

Beauty of the heavens,
  Jewel of the night!

Mother of the stars,
  Jewel of the night!

Fosterling of the sun,
  Jewel of the night!

Majesty of the stars,
  Jewel of the night!

Anon.

Benighted

'Frail crescent Moon, seven times I bow my head,
Since of the night you are the mystic queen:
May your sweet influence in her dews be shed!'

So ran by heart the rune in secret said:
Relic of heathen forebears centuries dead?
Or just a child's, in play with the Unseen?

Walter de la Mare

Deirín Dé

Deirín dé, deirín dé,
the brown goat calling in the heather,
deirín dé, deirín dé,
the ducks are squawking in the marsh.

Deirín dé, deirín dé,
cows go West at dawn of day,
deirín dé, deirín dé,
and my babe will mind them on the grass.

Deirín dé, deirín dé,
moon will rise and sun will set,
deirín dé, deirín dé,
and you are my babe and share of life.

Deirín dé, deirín dé,
a thrush's nest in my little press,
deirín dé, deirín dé,
yes, and gold for my little darling.

Deirín dé, deirín dé,
I'll let my babe out picking berries,
deirín dé, deirín dé,
if he'll just sleep sound till the round of day.

Anon.

Greeting

Over the wave-patterned sea-floor,
Over the long sunburnt ridge of the world,
I bid the winds seek you.
I bid them cry to you
Night and morning
A name you loved once;
I bid them bring to you
Dreams, and strange imaginings, and sleep.

Ella Young

[Invocation for Love]

Change me, O heavens into the ruby stone
  That on my love's fair locks doth hang in gold,
Yet leave me speech to her to make my moan,
  And give me eyes her beauties to behold;
Or if you will not make my flesh a stone,
Make her hard heart seem flesh that now seems none.

John Wilbye

Invocation for Justice

God, I am bathing my face
In the nine rays of the sun,
As Mary bathed her Son
    In generous milk fermented.

Sweetness be in my face,
Riches be in my countenance,
Comb-honey be in my tongue,
    My breath as the incense.

Black is yonder house,
Blacker men therein;
I am the white swan,
    Queen over them.

I will go in the name of God,
In the likeness of deer, in likeness of horse,
In likeness of serpent, in likeness of king,
    More victorious am I than all persons.

Anon.

Incantation

Vervain . . . basil . . . orison –
Whisper their syllablings till all meaning is gone,
And sound all vestige loses of mere word . . .
'Tis then as if, in some far childhood heard,
A wild heart languished at the call of a bird,
Crying through ruinous windows, high and fair,
A secret incantation on the air:
A language lost; which, when its accents cease,
Breathes, voiceless, of a pre-Edenic peace.

Walter de la Mare

Fragment

As it was,
As it is,
As it shall be
Evermore,
O Thou Triune
Of grace!
With the ebb,
With the flow,
O Thou Triune
Of grace!
With the ebb,
With the flow.

Anon.

IV

Country Folk and Feasts

In the Green Wood

Love and Marriage

The Blacksmith

Yule

Twelfth Night

Candlemas

May

Summer and Harvest

In the Green Wood

[Making the Fire]

Oak-logs will warm you well,
That are old and dry;
Logs of pine will sweetly smell
But the sparks will fly.
Birch-logs will burn too fast,
Chestnut scarce at all;
Hawthorn-logs are good to last –
Catch them in the fall.
Holly-logs will burn like wax,
You may burn them green;
Elm-logs like to smouldering flax,
No flame to be seen.
Beech-logs for winter time,
Yew-logs as well;
Green elder-logs it is a crime
For any man to sell.
Pear-logs and apple-logs,
They will scent your room,
Cherry-logs across the dogs
Smell like flower of the broom.
Ash-logs, smooth and grey,
Burn them green or old,
Buy up all that come your way –
Worth their weight in gold.

Mother Goose

[In Sherwood]

In Sherwood lived stout Robin Hood,
  An archer great, none greater,
His bow and shafts were sure and good,
  Yet Cupid's were much better;
Robin could shoot at many a hart and miss,
Cupid at first could hit a heart of his.
  Hey, jolly Robin Hood! ho, jolly Robin Hood!
    Love finds out me
    As well as thee,
  To follow me to the green-wood.

A noble thief was Robin Hood,
  Wise was he could deceive him;
Yet Marian in his bravest mood
  Could of his heart bereave him:
No greater thief lies hidden under skies,
Than beauty closely lodged in women's eyes.
  Hey, jolly Robin &c.

An outlaw was this Robin Hood,
  His life free and unruly,
Yet to fair Marian bound he stood
  And love's debt paid her duly:
Whom curb of strictest law could not hold in,
Love to obedience with a wink could win.
  Hey, jolly Robin &c.

Now wend we home, stout Robin Hood,
  Leave we the woods behind us,
Love-passions must not be withstood,
  Love everywhere will find us.
I lived in field and town, and so did he;
I got me to the woods, Love followed me.
  Hey, jolly Robin &c.

Robert Jones

[Green Brooms]

There was an old man, and he liv'd in a wood;
  And his lazy son Jack would snooze till noon:
Nor followed his trade although it was good
  With a bill and a stump for making brooms, green brooms;
  With a bill and a stump for making of brooms,

One morn in a passion, and sore with vexation,
  He swore he would fire the room,
If he did not get up and go to his work,
  And fall to the cutting of brooms, green brooms,
  And fall to the cutting of brooms.

Then Jack he arose and slip't on his clothes,
  And away to the woods very soon,
Where he made up his pack, and put it on his back,
  Crying, Maids, do you want any brooms? green brooms?
  Crying, Maids, do you want any brooms?

Mother Goose

[A Soul-Cake]

A soul-cake, a soul-cake,
Please good mistress a soul-cake;
    One for Peter and one for Paul
And one for the Lord who made us all;
An apple, a pear, a plum or a cherry,
Any good thing to make us merry.

Mother Goose

Green Besoms

I am a besom maker,
Come listen to my song.
With a bundle of green besoms
I trudge the land along.
Sweet pleasures that I do enjoy
Both morning, night and noon
As I walk o'er the hills so high
A gathering of green broom.
  O come and buy my besoms,
  Bonny green, green besoms,
    Besoms fine and new,
  Bonny green-broom besoms,
    Better never grew.

One day as I was trudging
Down by my native cot
I saw a jolly farmer,
O happy is his lot.
He ploughs his furrows deep,
The seed he layeth low,
And there it bides asleep
Until the green broom blow.

One day as I was walking
'Twas down in yonder vale
I met Jack Spratt the miller
That taketh toll and tale.
His mill, O how it rattles,
The grist it grindeth clean.
I ease him of his jingling
By selling besoms green.

One day as I was walking
Across the hills so high

I saw the wealthy squire
Who hath a rolling eye.
I sing my song, he tips a wink,
And glad the squire did seem.
I ease him of his jingling chink
By selling besoms green.

One day as I was walking
Along the King's high-way
I met the parson riding
And ventured him to stay.
The parish tythe that is your due
Collecting you have been,
But tythe I'll also take of you
By selling besoms green.

O when the yellow broom is ripe
Upon its native soil
It's like a pretty baby bright
With sweet and wavily smile.
My cuts that make the besom
I bundle tight and spare
All honest folks to please 'em
I'm the darling of the fair.

Mother Goose

Hollin, Green Hollin

Alone in greenwood must I roam,
  Hollin, green hollin,
A shade of green leaves is my home,
  Birk and green hollin.

Where nought is seen but boundless green,
  Hollin, green hollin,
And spots of far blue sky between,
  Birk and green hollin.

A weary head a pillow finds,
  Hollin, green hollin,
Where leaves fall green in summer winds,
  Birk and green hollin.

Enough for me, enough for me,
  Hollin, green hollin,
To live at large with liberty,
  Birk and green hollin.

Anon.

The Keeper

O the keeper he a shooting goes
And all amongst his bucks and does
And O for to shoot at the barren doe
She's amongst the leaves of the green O.
  Jacky boy, Martin
    Sing 'ee well. Very well
    Hey Down Ho down
    Derry derry down

She's amongst the leaves of the green O.
To my hey down down
To my ho down down
Hey down, ho down
Derry derry down
She's amongst the leaves of the green O.

The first doe that he shot at he missed
And the second doe he trimmed he kissed
And the third ran away in a young man's heart
She's amongst the leaves of the green O.

The fourth doe then she crossed the plain
The keeper fetched her back again
O and he tickled her in a merry vein
She's amongst the leaves of the green O.

The fifth doe then she crossed the brook
The keeper fetched her back with his long hook
And what he done at her you must go and look
For she's amongst the leaves of the green O.

Anon.

Under the Greenwood Tree

In summer time when leaves grow green
   And birds sit on the tree,
Let all the lords say what they can,
   There's none so merry as we.
There's Jeffrey and Tom, there's Ursula and Joan,
   With Roger and bonny Bettee,
O how they do firk it, caper and jerk it
   Under the greenwood tree.

Our music is the Choir Pipe,
   And he so well can play;
We hire him from Whitsuntide
   To latter Lammas Day:
On Sundays and on holidays
   After even song comes he,
And then they do firk it, caper and jerk it
   Under the greenwood tree.

Come play we Adam and Eve, said Dick.
  What's that? quoth Choir Pipe.
It is the beginning of the World,
  Thou most illiterate wight.
If that be it, then have at all,
  And he plays with a merry glee,
And then they did firk it, caper and jerk it
  Under the greenwood tree.

Then in comes Gaffer Underwood,
  And he sits him on the bench,
With his wife and his daughter Mary,
  That pretty round-fac'd wench;
There was Goodman Chuck and Habbacock,
  And all sit there to see
How they did firk it, caper and jerk it
  Under the greenwood tree.

We must not forget my Lord's son,
  For he's full of merry conceits,
And brake a jest among the maids
  And he capers, leaps and sweats,
And he gives them a flap with his fox-tail,
  And he thrust it in, to see
How they did firk it, caper and jerk it
  Under the greenwood tree.

And then we went to Sir Harry's house,
  A rich old cob was he,
And there we danc'd a round, a round,
  But the devil a penny we see.
From thence we went to Somerton,
  Where the boys be jolly and free,
And then we did firk it, caper and jerk it
  Under the greenwood tree.

Anon.

Love and Marriage

[Come, Lusty Ladies]

Come, lusty ladies, come, come, come!
With pensive thoughts you pine.
Come, learn the gilliard now of us,
For we be masquers [fine].
We sing, we dance, and we rejoice
With mirth in modesty:
Come, ladies, then and take a part,
And, as we sing, dance ye!
Tarranta ta-ta-ta-ta-tararantina, &c.

Anon.

Song of the Cauld Lad of Hilton

Wae's me, wae's me,
The acorn is not yet
Fallen from a tree
That's to grow the wood
That's to make the cradle
That's to rock the bairn
That's to grow to a man
That's to slay me.

Anon.

The Merry-ma-Tanzie

(Verses for a marrying game)

Here we go the jingo-ring,
The jingo-ring, the jingo-ring,
Here we go the jingo-ring,
About the merry-ma-tanzie.

Twice about, and then we fa,
Then we fa, then we fa,
Twice about and then we fa,
About the merry-ma-tanzie.

Guess ye wha's the young goodman,
The young goodman, the young goodman,
Guess ye wha's the young goodman,
About the merry-ma-tanzie?

Honey is sweet, and so is he,
So is he, so is he,
Honey is sweet and so is he,
About the merry-ma-tanzie.

He's married wi a gay gold ring,
A gay gold ring, a gay gold ring,
He's married wi a gay gold ring,
About the merry-ma-tanzie.

A gay gold ring's a cankerous thing,
A cankerous thing, a cankerous thing,
A gay gold ring's a cankerous thing,
About the merry-ma-tanzie.

Now they're married I wish them joy,
I wish them joy, I wish them joy,

Now they're married I wish them joy,
  About the merry-ma-tanzie.

Father and mother they must obey,
  Must obey, must obey,
Father and mother they must obey,
  About the merry-ma-tanzie.

Loving each other like sister and brother,
  Sister and brother, sister and brother,
Loving each other like sister and brother
  About the merry-ma-tanzie.

We pray this couple may kiss together,
  Kiss together, kiss together,
We pray this couple may kiss together,
About the merry-ma-tanzie.

Anon.

The Bride-Cake

This day my Julia thou must make
For Mistresse Bride, the wedding Cake:
Knead but the Dow and it will be
To paste of Almonds turn'd by thee:
Or kisse it thou, but once, or twice,
And for the Bride-Cake ther'l be Spice.

Robert Herrick

The Blacksmith

[Making Horseshoes]

A shoemaker makes shoes without leather,
With all the four elements together,
Fire, Water, Earth, Air,
And every customer takes two pair.

Mother Goose

The Blacksmith's Song

Here's a health to the blacksmith, the best of all fellows,
He works at the anvil while the boy blows the bellows,
Which makes my bright hammer to rise and to fall.
Here's to old Cole, and to young Cole, and the old Cole of all.
Twanky dillo, twanky dillo, twanky dillo, dillo, dillo, dillo,
A roaring pair of bagpipes made of the green willow,
Willow, willow, willow, willow. Willow, willow, willow, willow.
A roaring pair of bagpipes made of the green willow.

Anon.

The Deathless Blacksmith

'Tis the Tamer of Iron,
  The wrestler whose thews
Were made for subduing
  The Thing That Subdues.
In a splendour of darkness
  Encaverned he stands,
Amid Pow'rs, amid Terrors,
  The slaves of his hands.

Is he human and mortal,
  With frailties like mine,
Or a demigod rather,
  Of lineage divine?
For the fierce things and stubborn
  Grow meek in his gaze.
The Fire loves to serve him;
  The Iron obeys.

He is child of the daybreak, –
  His furnaces roared
Ere yet the first ploughshare
  Beheld the first sword;
And over far war-shout,
  And over far pain,
The voice of his hammer
  Comes pealing amain.

He labours where round him
  The demonlight flares;
He is patience that conquers
  When fury despairs.
'Whatsoever is mighty,'
  He sings in his glee,
'Twixt hammer and anvil
  Was fashioned by me.'

And he smites with the sureness,
  And moulds with the joy,
Of the gods that for pastime
  Create and destroy; –
The gods at whose bidding
  The fuel was hurled
On the fires of the forges
  Where shaped is the world.

Sir William Watson

Song of the Cyclops

Brave iron, brave hammer, from your sound
The art of music has her ground;
On the anvil thou keep'st time,
Thy knick-a-knock is a smith's best chime.
  Yet thwick-a-thwack, thwick, thwack-a-thwack, thwack,
  Make our brawny sinews crack:
  Then pit-a-pat, pat, pit-a-pat, pat
  Till thickest bars be beaten flat.

We shoe the horses of the sun,
Harness the dragons of the moon;
Forge Cupid's quiver, bow, and arrows,
And our dame's coach that's drawn with sparrows.
    Till thwick-a-thwack, &c.

Jove's roaring cannons and his rammers
We beat out with our Lemnian hammers;
Mars his gauntlet, helm, and spear,
And Gorgon shield are all made here.
    Till thwick-a-thwack, &c.

The grate which shut the day outbars,
Those golden studs which nail the stars,
The globe's case and the axle-tree,
Who can hammer these but we?
Till thwick-a-thwack, &c.

A warming-pan to heat earth's bed,
Lying i' th' frozen zone half-dead;
Hob-nails to serve the man i' th' moon,
And sparrowbills to clout Pan's shoon,
Whose work but ours?
Till thwick-a-thwack, &c.

Venus' kettles, pots, and pans
We make, or else she brawls and bans;
Tongs, shovels, andirons have their places,
Else she scratches all our faces.
Till thwick-a-thwack, &c.

Thomas Dekker

Yule

Ceremonies for Christmasse

Come, bring with a noise,
My merrie merrie boyes,
The Christmas Log to the firing;
While my good Dame, she
Bids ye all be free;
And drink to your hearts desiring.

With the last yeeres brand
Light the new block, and
For good successe in his spending,
On your Psaltries play,
That sweet luck may
Come while the Log is a tending.

Drink now the strong Beere,
Cut the white loafe here,
The while the meat is a shredding
For the rare Mince-Pie;
And the Plums stand by
To fill the Paste that's a kneading.

Robert Herrick

[New Year]

Wassail, wassail, to our town,
The cup is white, the ale is brown:
The cup is made of the ashen tree,
And so is the ale of the good barley.

Little maid, pretty maid, turn the pin,
Open the door and let us come in:
God be here, God be there,
I wish you all a Happy New Year.

Mother Goose

Saint Distaffs Day, or the Morrow after Twelfth Day

Partly worke and partly play
Ye must on S. *Distaffs* day:
From the Plough soone free your teame;
Then come home and fother them.
If the Maides a spinning goe,
Burne the flax, and fire the tow:
Scortch their plackets, but beware
That ye singe no maiden-haire.
Bring in pailes of water then,
Let the Maides bewash the men.
Give S. *Distaff* all the right,
Then bid Christmas sport *good-night*.
And next morrow, every one
To his owne vocation.

Robert Herrick

Twelfth Night

Twelfe Night, or King and Queene

Now, now the mirth comes
With the cake full of plums,
Where Beane's the King of the sport here;
Besides we must know,
The Pea also
Must revell, as Queene, in the Court here.

Begin then to chuse,
(This night as ye use)
Who shall for the present delight here,
Be a King by the lot,
And who shall not
Be Twelfe-day Queene for the night here.

Which knowne, let us make
Joy-sops with the cake;
And let not a man then be seen here,
Who unurg'd will not drinke
To the base from the brink
A health to the King and the Queene here.

Next crowne the bowle full
With gentle lambs-wooll;
Adde sugar, nutmeg and ginger,
With store of ale too;
And thus ye must doe
To make the wassaile a swinger.

Give then to the King
And Queene wassailing;
And though with ale ye be whet here;
Yet part ye from hence,
As free from offence,
As when ye innocent met here.

Robert Herrick

Candlemas

Ceremony upon Candlemas Eve

Down with the Rosemary, and so
Down with the Baies, & misletoe:
Down with the Holly, Ivie, all,
Wherewith ye drest the Christmas Hall:
That so the superstitious find
No one least Branch there left behind:
For look how many leaves there be
Neglected there (maids trust to me)
So many Goblins you shall see.

Robert Herrick

May

The May-Pole

The May-pole is up,
Now give me the cup;
I'le drink to the Garlands a-round it:
But first unto those
Whose hands did compose
The glory of flowers that crown'd it.

A health to my Girles,
Whose husbands may Earles
Or Lords be, (granting my wishes)
And when that ye wed
To the Bridall Bed,
Then multiply all, like to Fishes.

Robert Herrick

[Song for the First of May]

Trip and go, heave and hoe,
Up and down, to and fro,
From the town to the grove
Two and two, let us rove;
A-maying, a-playing;

Love hath no gainsaying;
So merrily trip and go,
So merrily trip and go.

Mother Goose

The Milk-Maid's Life

Upon the first of May,
With garlands, fresh and gay,
With mirth and music sweet, for such a season meet,
They pass the time away.
They dance away sorrow, and all the day thorough
Their legs do never fail,
For they nimbly their feet do ply,
And bravely try the victory,
In honour o' the milking-pail.

Anon.

The Rural Dance about the Maypole

Come lasses and lads,
Take leave of your dads,
And away to the Maypole hie;
For every he
Has got him a she
With a minstrel standing by;
For Willy has gotten his Jill,
And Jonny has got his Jone,
To jig it, jig it, jig it, jig it,
Jig it up and down.

Strike up, says Wat,
Agreed, says Kate,
And I prithee, Fiddler, play,
Content, says Hodge,
And so, says Madge,
For this is a holiday,
For every man did put
His hat off to his lass,
And every girl did curchy,
Curchy, curchy on the grass.

Begin, says Hall,
Aye, aye, says Mall,
We'll lead up Packington's Pound;
No, no, says Noll,
And so, says Doll,
We'll first have Sellinger's Round;
Then every man began to foot it round about,
And every girl did jet it, jet it, jet it in and out.

Y'are out, says Dick,
'Tis a lie, says Nick,
The Fiddler played it false;
'Tis true, says Hugh,
And so, says Sue,
And so, says nimble Alice;
The Fiddler then began to play the tune agen,
And every girl did trip it, trip it, trip it, to the men.

Let's kiss, says Jane,
Content, says Nan,
And so says every she;
How many, says Batt,
Why three, says Matt,
For that's a maiden's fee;
But they instead of three did give 'em half a score,
And they in kindness gave 'em, gave 'em, gave 'em as many more.

Then after an hour
They went to a bower
And played for ale and cakes,
And kisses too
Until they were due,
The lasses held the stakes.
The girls did then begin to quarrel with the men,
And bid 'em take their kisses back, and give 'em their own agen.

Yet there they sate,
Until it was late
And tired the Fiddler quite,
With singing and playing,
Without any paying
From morning until night.
They told the Fiddler then they'd pay him for his play,
And each a 2 pence, 2 pence, 2 pence gave him and went away.

Anon.

Corinna's Going a Maying

Get up, get up for shame, the Blooming Morne
Upon her wings presents the god unshorne.
See how Aurora throwes her faire
Fresh-quilted colours through the aire:
Get up, sweet-Slug-a-bed, and see
The Dew-bespangling Herbe and Tree.
Each Flower has wept, and bow'd toward the East,
Above an houre since; yet you not drest,
Nay! not so much as out of bed?
When all the Birds have Mattens seyd,
And sung their thankfull Hymnes: 'tis sin,

Nay, profanation to keep in,
When as a thousand Virgins on this day,
Spring, sooner then the Lark, to fetch in May.

Rise; and put on your Foliage, and be seene
To come forth, like the Spring-time, fresh and greene;
And sweet as Flora. Take no care
For Jewels for your Gowne, or Haire:
Feare not; the leaves will strew
Gemms in abundance upon you:
Besides, the childhood of the Day has kept,
Against you come, some Orient Pearls unwept:
Come, and receive them while the light
Hangs on the Dew-locks of the night:
And Titan on the Eastern hill
Retires himselfe, or else stands still
Till you come forth. Wash, dresse, be briefe in praying:
Few Beads are best, when once we goe a Maying.

Come, my Corinna, come; and comming, marke
How each field turns a street; each street a Parke
Made green, and trimm'd with trees: see how
Devotion gives each House a Bough,
Or Branch: Each Porch, each doore, ere this,
An Arke a Tabernacle is
Made up of white-thorn neatly enterwove;
As if here were those cooler shades of love.
Can such delights be in the street,
And open fields, and we not see't?
Come, we'll abroad; and let's obay
The Proclamation made for May:
And sin no more, as we have done, by staying;
But my Corinna, come. Let's goe a Maying.
There's not a budding Boy, or Girle, this day,
But is got up, and gone to bring in May.
A deale of Youth, ere this, is come
Back, and with White-thorn laden home.

Some have dispatcht their Cakes and Creame,
Before that we have left to dreame:
And some have wept, and woo'd, and plighted Troth,
And chose their Priest, ere we can cast off sloth:
Many a green-gown has been given;
Many a kisse, both odde and even:
Many a glance too has been sent
From out the eye, Loves Firmament:
Many a jest told of the Keyes betraying
This night, and Locks pickt, yet w'are not a Maying.

Come, let us goe, while we are in our prime;
And take the harmlesse follie of the time.
We shall grow old apace, and die
Before we know our liberty.
Our life is short; and our dayes run
As fast away as do's the Sunne:
And as a vapour, or a drop of raine
Once lost, can ne'r be found againe:
So when or you or I are made
A fable, song, or fleeting shade;
All love, all liking, all delight
Lies drown'd with us in endlesse night.
Then while time serves, and we are but decaying;
Come, my Corinna, come, let's goe a Maying.

Robert Herrick

It was a Lover and His Lass

It was a lover and his lass,
With a hey, and a ho, and a hey nonino,
That o'er the green corn-field did pass

In the spring time, the only pretty ring time,
When birds do sing, hey ding a ding, ding:
Sweet lovers love the spring.

Between the acres of the rye,
With a hey, and a ho, and a hey nonino,
These pretty country folk would lie,
In spring time, &c.

This carol they begun that hour,
With a hey, and a ho, and a hey nonino,
How that a life was but a flower
In spring time, &c.

And therefore take the present time,
With a hey, and a ho, and a hey nonino,
For love is crowned with the prime
In spring time, &c.

William Shakespeare

[The Month of May]

Now is the month of maying,
When merry lads are playing
Each with his bonny lass
Upon the greeny grass.
Fa la la!

The spring clad all in gladness
Doth laugh at winter's sadness,
And to the bagpipe's sound
The nymphs tread out their ground.
Fa la la!

Fie then, why sit we musing,
Youth's sweet delight refusing?
Say, dainty nymphs, and speak,
Shall we play barley-break.
Fa la la!

Thomas Morley

[Sing Care Away]

On a fair morning, as I came by the way,
Met I with a merry maid in the merry month of May,
When a sweet love sings his lovely lay
And every bird upon the bush bechirps it up so gay,
With a heave and ho! with a heave and ho!
Thy wife shall be thy master, I trow.
Sing, care away, care away, let the world go!
Hey, lustily all in a row, all in a row,
Sing, care away, care away, let the world go!

Thomas Morley

Padstow May Song

The Morning Song

Unite and unite, and it's all how white,
For summer is a-come in to-day
And whither we are going we all will unite
In the merry morning of May.

I warn you young men every one
To go to the greenwood and fetch your may home.

Arise, Master . . . and joy you betide,
And bright is your bride that lies by your side.

Arise, Mistress . . . and gold be your ring
And give us a cup of ale that merrier we may sing.

With the merry sing and now joyful spring,
How happy are the birds that merrily do sing.

Arise, Master . . . with your sword by your side,
Your steed is in stable awaiting you to ride.

Arise, Master . . . and reach me your hand
And you shall have a lovely lass with a thousand pounds in hand.

Arise, Master . . . for I know you well and fine,
You've a shilling in your purse, I wish it were in mine.

Arise, Miss . . . and strew all your flowers,
It is but a little while since we strewed ours.

With the merry sing and now joyful spring,
How happy are the birds that merrily do sing.

Arise, Miss . . . from out of your bed,
Your chamber shall be spread with the white rose and red.

Arise, Miss . . . all in your smock of silk,
And all your body under as white as any milk.

Where are the young men that now here should dance?
Some they are in England and some are in France.

Where are the maidens that now here should sing?
They are all in the meadows a flower gathering.

For the merry sing now the joyful spring,
How happy are the birds that merrily do sing.

The young men of Padstow they might if they wold,
They might ha' built a ship and gilded her with gold.

The maidens of Padstow they might if they wold,
They have made a garland and gilded it with gold.

Now fare you well and we wish you good cheer,
We will come no more unto your house until another year.

For the merry sing now the joyful spring,
How happy are the birds that merrily do sing.

Anon.

Padstow May Song

The Day Song

Awake St George, our English knight O,
For summer is a come, and winter is a go.
Where is St George and where is he O?
He's down in his long boat upon the salt sea O.
For to fetch summer home, summer and may O,
For summer is a come and winter is a go.

Where are the French dogs that make such boast O?
They shall eat the goose feathers and we'll eat the roast O.

Thou mightst ha' shown a knavish face, or tarried at home O,
But thou shall be a cuckold and wear the horns O.

Up flies the kite, down falls the lark O,
Aunt Ursula Birdwood, she had an old ewe.
Aunt Ursula Birdwood, she had an old ewe,
And she died in her own park long ago.

Anon.

The Padstow Night Song (For May Day)

Unite, unite, let us all unite,
For Summer is a-come unto day
And whither we are going we will all unite
  On the merry morning of May.

The young men of Padstow they might if they would,
For Summer is a-come unto day.
They might have built a ship and gilded her with gold
  On the merry morning of May.

The maidens of Padstow they might if they would,
For Summer is a-come unto day.
They might have made a garland of the white rose and the red
  On the merry morning of May.

Up Merry Spring, and up the merry ring,
For Summer is a-come unto day.
How happy are those little birds that merrily do sing
  On the merry morning of May.

Anon.

[Spring]

The peaceful western wind
  The winter storms hath tamed,
And Nature in each kind
  The kind heat hath inflamed:
The forward buds so sweetly breathe
  Out of their earthly bowers,
That heaven, which views their pomp beneath,
  Would fain be decked with flowers.

See how the morning smiles
  On her bright eastern hill,
And with soft steps beguiles
  Them that lie slumbering still!
The music-loving birds are come
  From cliffs and rocks unknown,
To see the trees and briars bloom
  That late were overthrown.

What Saturn did destroy,
  Love's Queen revives again;
And now her naked boy
  Doth in the fields remain,
Where he such pleasing change doth view
  In every living thing,
As if the world were born anew
  To gratify the spring.

Thomas Campion

[Chloris Fresh as May]

Now is my Chloris fresh as May,
Clad all in green and flowers gay.
Fa la la!

O might I think August were near
That harvest joy might soon appear.
Fa la la!

But she keeps May throughout the year,
And August never comes the near.
Fa la la!

Yet will I hope, though she be May,
August will come another day.
Fa la la!

Thomas Weelkes

The Masque of May

The chiffchaff and the celandine
The blackbird and the bee
The chestnut branches topped with green
Have met my love and me
And we have played the masque of May
So sweet and commonplace and gay

The sea's first miracle of blue
Bare trees that glitter near the sky
Grow with a love and longing new
Where went my love and I
And there we played the masque of May
So old and infinite and gay.

J. M. Synge

Summer and Harvest

The Haymaker's Song

In the merry month of June,
  In the prime time of the year;
Down in yonder meadows
  There runs a river clear:
And many a little fish
  Doth in that river play;
And many a lad, and many a lass,
  Go abroad a-making hay.

In come the jolly mowers,
  To mow the meadows down;
With budget and with bottle
  Of ale, both stout and brown,
All labouring men of courage bold
  Come here their strength to try;
They sweat and blow, and cut and mow,
  For the grass cuts very dry.

Here's nimble Ben and Tom,
  With pitchfork, and with rake;
Here's Molly, Liz, and Susan,
  Come here their hay to make.
While sweet, jug, jug, jug!
  The nightingale doth sing,
From morning unto even-song,
  As they are hay-making.

And when that bright day faded,
  And the sun was going down,
There was a merry piper
  Approachèd from the town:
He pulled out his pipe and tabor,
  So sweetly he did play,
Which made all lay down their rakes,
  And leave off making hay.

Then joining in a dance,
  They jig it o'er the green;
Though tired with their labour,
  No one less was seen.
But sporting like some fairies,
  Their dance they did pursue,
In leading up, and casting off,
  Till morning was in view.

And when that bright daylight,
  The morning it was come,
They lay down and rested
  Till the rising of the sun:
Till the rising of the sun,
  When the merry larks do sing,
And each lad did rise and take his lass,
  And away to hay-making.

Anon.

The Ripe and Bearded Barley

Come out, 'tis now September,
  The hunter's moon's begun,
And through the wheaten stubble
  We hear the frequent gun.

The leaves are turning yellow,
  And fading into red,
While the ripe and bearded barley
  Is hanging down its head.

      All among the barley
        Who would not be blithe,
      While the ripe and bearded barley
        Is smiling on the scythe.

The wheat is like a rich man,
  It's sleek and well-to-do.
The oats are like a pack of girls,
  They're thin and dancing, too.
The rye is like a miser,
  Both sulky, lean and small,
Whilst the ripe and bearded barley
  Is the monarch of them all.

      All among the barley
        Who would not be blithe,
      While the ripe and bearded barley
        Is smiling on the scythe.

The spring is like a young maid
  That does not know her mind,
The summer is a tyrant
  Of most ungracious kind.
The autumn is an old friend
  That pleases all he can,
And brings the bearded barley
  To glad the heart of man.

      All among the barley
        Who would not be blithe,
      While the ripe and bearded barley
        Is smiling on the scythe.

Anon.

[Harvest Time]

The boughs do shake and bells do ring,
So merrily comes our harvest in,
Our harvest in, our harvest in,
So merrily comes our harvest in.

We've ploughed, we've sowed,
We've reaped, we've mowed,
We've got our harvest in.

Mother Goose

Sir John Barleycorn

There came three men from out of the west
Their victory to try;
And they have ta'en a solemn oath,
Poor Barleycorn should die.

They took a plough and ploughed him in,
Clods harrowed on his head;
And then they took a solemn oath
John Barleycorn was dead.

There he lay sleeping in the ground
Till rain on him did fall;
Then Barleycorn sprung up his head,
And so amazed them all.

There he remained till Midsummer
And look'd both pale and wan;
Then Barleycorn he got a beard
And so became a man.

Then they sent men with scythes so sharp
To cut him off at knee;
And then poor Johny Barleycorn
They served most barbarouslie.

Then they sent men with pitchforks strong
To pierce him through the heart;
And like a doleful Tragedy
They bound him in a cart.

And then they brought him to a barn
A prisoner to endure;
And so they fetched him out again,
And laid him on the floor.

Then they set men with holly clubs,
To beat the flesh from th' bones;
But the miller served him worse than that,
He ground him 'twixt two stones.

O! Barleycorn is the choicest grain
That e'er was sown on land:
It will do more than any grain
By the turning of your hand.

It will make a boy into a man,
A man into an ass:
To silver it will change your gold,
Your silver into brass.

It will make the huntsman hunt the fox,
That never wound a horn;
It will bring the tinker to the stocks
That people may him scorn.

O! Barleycorn is the choicest grain
That e'er was sown on land.
And it will cause a man to drink
Till he neither can go nor stand.

Anon.

V

The World of Faery

Song and Dance

Faery Ways

Encounters

The Fairies Farewell

Song and Dance

The Fairies' Dance

Dare you haunt our hallow'd green?
None but fairies here are seen.
Down and sleep,
Wake and weep,
Pinch him black, and pinch him blue,
That seeks to steal a lover true!
When you come to hear us sing,
Or to tread our fairy ring,
Pinch him black, and pinch him blue!
O thus our nails shall handle you!

Thomas Ravenscroft

The Ruin

When the last colours of the day
Have from their burning ebbed away,
About that ruin, cold and lone,
The cricket shrills from stone to stone;
And scattering o'er its darkened green,
Bands of the fairies may be seen,
Chattering like grasshoppers, their feet
Dancing a thistledown dance round it:
While the great gold of the mild moon
Tinges their tiny acorn shoon.

Walter de la Mare

[The Fairy Ring]

Let us in a lover's round
Circle all this hallowed ground;
Softly, softly trip and go,
The light-foot Fairies jet it so.
Forward then, and back again,
Here and there and everywhere,
Winding to and fro,
Skipping high and louting low;
And, like lovers, hand in hand,
March around and make a stand.

George Mason and John Earsden

The Elves' Dance

Round about in a fair ring-a,
Thus we dance and thus we sing-a;
Trip and go, to and fro,
Over this green-a;
All about, in and out,
Over this green-a.

Thomas Ravenscroft

[Song to the Spirit of the Wind]

She who sits by haunted well,
Is subject to the Nixies' spell;
She who walks on lonely beach,
To the Mermaid's charmed speech;
She who walks round ring of green,
Offends the peevish Fairy Queen;
And she who takes rest in the dwarfie's cave,
A weary weird of woe shall have.

Sir Walter Scott

[Fairy Song]

The wind blows out of the gates of the day,
The wind blows over the lonely of heart,
And the lonely of heart is withered away,
While the fäeries dance in a place apart,
Shaking their milk-white feet in a ring,
Tossing their milk-white arms in the air:
For they hear the wind laugh and murmur and sing
Of a land where even the old are fair,
And even the wise are merry of tongue;
But I heard a reed of Coolaney say,
'When the wind has laughed and murmured and sung,
The lonely of heart is withered away!'

W. B. Yeats

[Invocation to Fairies]

Thrice toss these oaken ashes in the air,
Thrice sit thou mute in this enchanted chair,
Then thrice-three times tie up this true love's knot,
And murmur soft 'She will or she will not.'

Go, burn these poisonous weeds in yon blue fire,
These screech-owl's feathers and this prickling briar,
This cypress gathered at a dead man's grave,
That all my fears and cares an end may have.

Then come, you Fairies! dance with me a round!
Melt her hard heart with your melodious sound!
In vain are all the charms I can devise:
She hath an art to break them with her eyes.

Thomas Campion

Faery Ways

[The Barge]

There are men in the village of Erith
Whom nobody seeth or heareth,
  And there looms, on the marge
  Of the river, a barge
That nobody roweth or steereth.

Mother Goose

The Shepherd's Calendar

She from her memory oft repeats
Witches' dread powers and fairy feats:
How one has oft been known to prance
In cowribs, like a coach, to France,
And ride on sheep-trays from the fold
A race-horse speed to Burton-hold,
To join the midnight mystery's rout,
Where witches meet the yews about:
And how, when met with unawares,
They turn at once to cats or hares,
And race along with hellish flight,
Now here, now there, now out of sight!
And how the other tiny things
Will leave their moonlight meadow-rings,

And, unperceiv'd, through key-holes creep,
When all around have sunk to sleep,
And crowd in cupboards as they please,
As thick as mites in rotten cheese,
To feast on what the cotter leaves –
Mice are not reckon'd greater thieves.
They take away, as well as eat,
And still the housewife's eye they cheat,
In spite of all the folks that swarm
In cottage small and larger farm;
They through each key-hole pop and pop,
Like wasps into a grocer's shop,
With all the things that they can win
From chance to put their plunder in;
As shells of walnuts, split in two
By crows, who with the kernels flew;
Or acorn-cups, by stock-doves pluck'd,
Or egg-shells by a cuckoo suck'd;
With broad leaves of the sycamore
They clothe their stolen dainties o'er,
And when in cellar they regale,
Bring hazel-nuts to hold their ale,
With bung-holes bor'd by squirrels well,
To get the kernel from the shell,
Or maggots a way out to win,
When all is gone that grew within;
And be the key-holes e'er so high,
Rush poles a ladder's help supply,
Where soft the climbers fearless tread
On spindles made of spiders' thread.

John Clare

[Little Lad]

Little lad, little lad, where were you born?
Far off in Lancashire, under a thorn,
Where they sup butter-milk
With a ram's horn;
And a pumpkin scoop'd
With a yellow rim,
Is the bonny bowl they breakfast in.

Mother Goose

[In Myrtle Arbours]

Hark, all you ladies that do sleep!
The fairy-queen Proserpina
Bids you awake and pity them that weep:
You may do in the dark
What the day doth forbid;
Fear not the dogs that bark,
Night will have all hid.

But if you let your lovers moan,
The fairy-queen Proserpina
Will send abroad her fairies every one,
That shall pinch black and blue
Your white hands and fair arms
That did not kindly rue
Your paramours' harms.

In myrtle arbours on the downs
The fairy-queen Proserpina,
This night by moonshine leading merry rounds,

Holds a watch with sweet love,
  Down the dale, up the hill;
No plaints or groans may move
  Their holy vigil.

Thomas Campion

The Hosts of Faery

White shields they carry in their hands,
With emblems of pale silver;
With glittering blue swords,
With mighty stout horns.

In well-devised battle array,
Ahead of their fair chieftain
They march amid blue spears,
Pale-visaged, curly-headed bands.

They scatter the battalions of the foe,
They ravage every land they attack,
Splendidly they march to combat,
A swift, distinguished, avenging host!

No wonder though their strength be great:
Sons of queens and kings are one and all;
On their heads are
Beautiful golden-yellow manes.

With smooth comely bodies,
With bright blue-starred eyes,
With pure crystal teeth,
With thin red lips.

Good they are at man-slaying,
Melodious in the ale-house,
Masterly at making songs,
Skilled at playing fidchell.

Anon.

The Tale of the Wyf of Bathe

In th'olde dayes of the king Arthour,
Of which that Britons speken greet honour,
Al was this land fulfild of fayerye.
The elf-queen, with hir joly companye,
Daunced ful ofte in many a grene mede;
This was the olde opinion, as I rede.
I speke of manye hundred yeres ago;
But now can no man see none elves mo.
For now the grete charitee and prayeres
Of limitours and othere holy freres,
That serchen every lond and every streem,
As thikke as motes in the sonne-beem,
Blessinge halles, chambres, kichenes, boures,
Citees, burghes, castels, hye toures,
Thropes, bernes, shipnes, dayeryes,
This maketh that ther been no fayeryes.
For ther as wont to walken was an elf,
Ther walketh now the limitour him-self
In undermeles and in morweninges,
And seyth his matins and his holy thinges
As he goth in his limitacioun.
Wommen may go saufly up and doun,
In every bush, or under every tree;
Ther is noon other incubus but he,
And he ne wol doon hem but dishonour.

Geoffrey Chaucer

Oberon's Feast

'Shapcot! To thee the Fairy State
I with discretion, dedicate.
Because thou prizest things that are
Curious, and un-familiar.
Take first the feast; these dishes gone;
Wee'l see the Fairy-Court.' anon

A little mushroome table spred,
After short prayers, they set on bread;
A Moon-parcht grain of purest wheat,
With some small glit'ring gritt, to eate
His choyce bitts with; then in a trice
They make a feast lesse great then nice.
But all this while his eye is serv'd,
We must not thinke his eare was sterv'd:
But that there was in place to stir
His Spleen, the chirring Grashopper;
The Merry Cricket, puling Flie,
The piping Gnat for minstralcy.
And now, we must imagine first,
The Elves present to quench his thirst
A pure seed-Pearle of Infant dew,
Brought and besweetned in a blew
And pregnant violet; which done,
His kilting eyes begin to runne
Quite through the table, where he spies
The hornes of paperie Butterflies,
Of which he eates, and tastes a little
Of that we call the Cuckoes spittle.
A little Fuz-ball-pudding stands
By, yet not blessed by his hands,
That was too coorse; but then forthwith
He ventures boldly on the pith
Of sugred Rush, and eates the sagge

And well bestrutted Bees sweet bagge:
Gladding his pallat with some store
Of Emits eggs; what wo'd he more?
But Beards of Mice, a Newt's stew'd thigh,
A bloated Earewig, and a Flie;
With the Red-capt worme, that's shut
Within the concave of a Nut,
Browne as his Tooth. A little Moth,
Late fatned in a piece of cloth:
With withered cherries; Mandrakes eares;
Moles eyes; to these, the slain-Stags teares:
The unctuous dewlaps of a Snaile;
The broke-heart of a Nightingale
Ore-come in musicke; with a wine,
Ne're ravisht from the flattering Vine,
But gently prest from the soft side
Of the most sweet and dainty Bride,
Brought in a dainty daizie, which
He fully quaffs up to bewitch
His blood to height; this done, commended
Grace by his Priest; The feast is ended.

Robert Herrick

Queen Mab

I am the Fairy MAB: to me 'tis given
The wonders of the human world to keep:
The secrets of the immeasurable past,
In the unfailing consciences of men,
Those stern, unflattering chroniclers, I find:
The future, from the causes which arise
In each event, I gather: not the sting
Which retributive memory implants

In the hard bosom of the selfish man;
Nor that ecstatic and exulting throb
Which virtue's votary feels when he sums up
The thoughts and actions of a well-spent day,
Are unforeseen, unregistered by me:
And it is yet permitted me, to rend
The veil of mortal frailty, that the spirit
Clothed in its changeless purity, may know
How soonest to accomplish the great end
For which it hath its being, and may taste
That peace, which in the end all life will share.

P. B. Shelley

The Fairies

If ye will with Mab find grace,
Set each Platter in his place:
Rake the Fier up, and get
Water in, ere Sun be set.
Wash your Pailes, and clense your Dairies;
Sluts are loathsome to the Fairies:
Sweep your house: Who doth not so,
Mab will pinch her by the toe.

Robert Herrick

Now the Hungry Lion Roars

Now the hungry lion roars,
  And the wolf behowls the moon;
Whilst the heavy ploughman snores,
  All with weary task fordone.
Now the wasted brands do glow,
  Whilst the scritch-owl, scritching loud,
Puts the wretch that lies in woe
  In remembrance of a shroud.
Now it is the time of night
  That the graves, all gaping wide,
Everyone lets forth his sprite,
  In the churchway paths to glide:
And we fairies, that do run
  By the triple Hecate's team,
From the presence of the sun,
  Following darkness like a dream,
Now are frolic; not a mouse
Shall disturb this hallowed house:
I am sent with broom before,
To sweep the dust behind the door.

Through the house give glimmering light,
  By the dead and drowsy fire;
Every elf and fairy sprite
  Hop as light as bird from brier;
And this ditty, after me,
Sing, and dance it, trippingly.
First rehearse your song by rote,
To each word a warbling note:
Hand in hand, with fairy grace,
Will we sing, and bless this place.

Now, until the break of day,
Through this house each fairy stray.

To the best bride-bed will we,
Which by us shall blessed be;
And the issue there create
Ever shall be fortunate.
So shall all the couples three
Ever true in loving be;
And the blots of Nature's hand
Shall not in their issue stand;
Never mole, hare-lip, nor scar,
Nor mark prodigious, such as are
Despised in nativity,
Shall upon their children be.
With this field-dew consecrate,
Every fairy take his gait;
And each several chamber bless,
Through this palace with sweet peace:
And the owner of it blest,
Ever shall in safety rest.
  Trip away;
  Make no stay:
Meet me all by break of day.

William Shakespeare

Over Hill, Over Dale

Over hill, over dale,
  Thorough bush, thorough brier,
Over park, over pale,
  Thorough flood, thorough fire,
I do wander everywhere,
Swifter than the moon's sphere;
And I serve the fairy queen,

To dew her orbs upon the green.
The cowslips tall her pensioners be;
In their gold coats spots you see,
Those be rubies, fairy favours,
In those freckles live their savours:
I must go seek some dewdrops here,
And hang a pearl in every cowslip's ear.

William Shakespeare

The Fairy Queen

Come, follow, follow me,
You, fairy elves that be:
Which circle on the greene,
Come, follow Mab your queene.
Hand in hand let's dance around,
For this place is fairye ground.

When mortals are at rest,
And snoring in their nest:
Unheard, and unespy'd,
Through key-holes we do glide;
Over tables, stools, and shelves,
We trip it with our fairy elves.

And, if the house be foul
With platter, dish, or bowl,
Up stairs we nimbly creep,
And find the sluts asleep:
There we pinch their armes and thighes;
None escapes, nor none espies.

But if the house be swept,
And from uncleanness kept,
We praise the household maid,
And duely she is paid:
For we use before we goe
To drop a tester in her shoe.

Upon a mushroomes head
Our table-cloth we spread;
A grain of rye, or wheat,
Is manchet, which we eat;
Pearly drops of dew we drink
In acorn cups fill'd to the brink.

The brains of nightingales,
With unctuous fat of snailes,
Between two cockles stew'd,
Is meat that's easily chew'd;
Tailes of wormes, and marrow of mice,
Do make a dish, that's wonderous nice.

The grasshopper, gnat, and fly,
Serve for our minstrelsie;
Grace said, we dance a while,
And so the time beguile:
And if the moon doth hide her head,
The gloe-worm lights us home to bed.

On tops of dewie grasse
So nimbly do we passe,
The young and tender stalk
Ne'er bends when we do walk:
Yet in the morning may be seen
Where we the night before have been.

Anon.

Song by Fairies

Omnes Pinch him, pinch him, black and blue,
Saucy mortals must not view
What the queen of stars is doing,
Nor pry into our fairy wooing.
1 Fairy Pinch him black.
2 Fairy And pinch him black.
3 Fairy Let him not lack
Sharp nails to pinch him blue and red,
Till sleep has rocked his addlehead,
4 Fairy For the trespass he hath done,
Spots o'er all his flesh shall run.
Kiss Endymion, kiss his eyes,
Then to our midnight haydegyes.

John Lyly

Robin Good-Fellow

From Oberon, in fairye land,
The king of ghosts and shadowes there,
Mad Robin I, at his command,
Am sent to viewe the night-sports here.
What revell rout
Is kept about,
In every corner where I go,
I will o'ersee,
And merry bee,
And make good sport, with ho, ho, ho!

More swift than lightening can I flye
About this aery welkin soone,

And, in a minutes space, descrye
Each thing that's done belowe the moone,
There's not a hag
Or ghost shall wag,
Or cry, ware Goblin's! where I go,
But Robin I
Their feates will spy,
And send them home, with ho, ho, ho!

Whene'er such wanderers I meete,
As from their night-sports they trudge home;
With counterfeiting voice I greete
And call them on, with me to roame
Thro' woods, thro' lakes,
Thro' bogs, thro' brakes;
Or else, unseene, with them I go,
All in the nicke
To play some tricke
And frolicke it, with ho, ho, ho!

Sometimes I meete them like a man;
Sometimes, an ox, sometimes, a hound;
And to a horse I turn me can;
To trip and trot about them round.
But if, to ride,
My backe they stride,
More swift than wind away I go,
Ore hedge and lands,
Thro' pools and ponds
I whirry, laughing, ho, ho, ho!

Ben Jonson (attrib.)

Encounters

The Man Who Dreamed of Faeryland

He stood among a crowd at Drumahair;
His heart hung all upon a silken dress,
And he had known at last some tenderness,
Before earth took him to her stoney care;
But when a man poured fish into a pile,
It seemed they raised their little silver heads,
And sang what gold morning or evening sheds
Upon a woven world-forgotten isle
Where people love beside the raveled seas;
That Time can never mar a lover's vows
Under that woven changeless roof of boughs:
The singing shook him out of his new ease.

He wandered by the sands of Lissadell;
His mind ran all on money cares and fears,
And he had known at last some prudent years
Before they heaped his grave under the hill;
But while he passed before a plashy place,
A lug-worm with its gray and muddy mouth
Sang that somewhere to north or west or south
There dwelt a gay, exulting, gentle race
Under the golden or the silver skies;
That if a dancer stayed his hungry foot
It seemed the sun and moon were in the fruit:
And at that singing he was no more wise.

He mused beside the well of Scanavin,
He mused upon his mockers: without fail

His sudden vengeance were a country tale,
When earthly night had drunk his body in;
But one small knot-grass growing by the pool
Sang where – unnecessary cruel voice –
Old silence bids its chosen race rejoice,
Whatever raveled waters rise and fall
Or stormy silver fret the gold of day,
And midnight there enfold them like a fleece
And lover there by lover be at peace.
The tale drove his fine angry mood away.

He slept under the hill of Lugnagall;
And might have known at last unhaunted sleep
Under that cold and vapor-turbaned steep,
Now that the earth had taken man and all:
Did not the worms that spired about his bones
Proclaim with that unwearied, reedy cry
That God has laid His fingers on the sky,
That from those fingers glittering summer runs
Upon the dancer by the dreamless wave.
Why should those lovers that no lovers miss
Dream, until God burn Nature with a kiss?
The man has found no comfort in the grave.

W. B. Yeats

La Belle Dame Sans Merci

O what can ail thee Knight at arms
  Alone and palely loitering?
The sedge has withered from the Lake
  And no birds sing!

O what can ail thee Knight at arms
  So haggard and so woe begone?

The Squirrel's granary is full
  And the harvest's done.

I see a lilly on thy brow
  With anguish moist and fever dew
And on thy cheek a fading rose
  Fast withereth too.

I met a Lady in the Meads
  Full beautiful – a faery's child,
Her hair was long, her foot was light
  And her eyes were wild –

I made a garland for her head,
  And bracelets too, and fragrant zone;
She looked at me as she did love
  And made sweet moan –

I set her on my pacing steed –
  And nothing else saw all day long
For sidelong would she bend and sing
  A faery's song –

She found me roots of relish sweet
  And honey wild and manna dew
And sure in language strange she said
  I love thee true.

She took me to her elfin grot
  And there she wept and sighed full sore,
And there I shut her wild wild eyes
  With Kisses four.

And there she lullèd me asleep
  And there I dreamed. Ah Woe betide!
The latest dream I ever dreamt
  On the cold hill side.

I saw pale Kings, and Princes too,
  Pale warriors death pale were they all;
They cried – 'La belle dame sans merci
  Thee hath in thrall.'

I saw their starved lips in the gloam
  With horrid warning gapèd wide
And I awoke, and found me here
  On the cold hill's side.

And this is why I sojourn here
  Alone and palely loitering;
Though the sedge is withered from the Lake
  And no birds sing.

John Keats

The Stolen Child

Where dips the rocky highland
Of Sleuth Wood in the lake,
There lies a leafy island
Where flapping herons wake
The drowsy water-rats;
There we've hid our faery vats,
Full of berries
And of reddest stolen cherries.
  Come away, O human child!
To the waters and the wild
With a faery, hand in hand,
For the world's more full of weeping than you can understand.

Where the wave of moonlight glosses
The dim grey sands with light,
Far off by furthest Rosses
We foot it all the night,
Weaving olden dances,
Mingling hands and mingling glances
Till the moon has taken flight;
To and fro we leap
And chase the frothy bubbles,
While the world is full of troubles
And is anxious in its sleep.
Come away, O human child!
To the waters and the wild
With a faery, hand in hand,
For the world's more full of weeping than you can understand.

Where the wandering water gushes
From the hills above Glen-Car,
In pools among the rushes
That scarce could bathe a star,
We seek for slumbering trout
And whispering in their ears
Give them unquiet dreams;
Leaning softly out
From ferns that drop their tears
Over the young streams.
Come away, O human child!
To the waters and the wild
With a faery, hand in hand,
For the world's more full of weeping than you can understand.

Away with us he's going,
The solemn-eyed:
He'll hear no more the lowing
Of the calves on the warm hillside
Or the kettle on the hob
Sing peace into his breast,

Or see the brown mice bob
Round and round the oatmeal-chest.
For he comes, the human child!
To the waters and the wild
With a faery, hand in hand,
From a world more full of weeping than he can understand.

W. B. Yeats

The Wee Wee Man

As I was walking all alone
Between the water and the green,
There I spied a wee wee man,
The least wee man that ever was seen.

His legs were scarce an effet's length,
But thick his arms as any tree.
Between his brows there was a span,
Between his shoulders there were three.

He took up a boulder stone,
And flung it as far as I could see.
Though I had been a miller's man,
I could not lift it to my knee.

O wee wee man, but thou art strang!
O tell me where thy haunt may be.
My dwelling's down by yon bonny bower,
O will you mount and ride with me?

On we leapt, and off we rode,
Till we came to far away,
We lighted down to bait our horse,
And out there came a bonny may.

Four and twenty at her back,
  And they were all dressed out in green,
And though King Harry had been there,
  The worst o' them might be his queen.

On we leapt, and off we rode,
  Till we came to yon bonny hall.
The roof was o' the beaten gold,
  Of gleaming crystal was the wall.

When we came to the door of gold,
  The pipes within did whistle and play,
But ere the tune of it was told,
  My wee wee man was clean away.

Anon.

The Elfin Knight

My plaid awa, my plaid awa,
  And ore the hill and far awa,
And far awa to Norrowa,
  My plaid shall not be blown awa.

The elfin knight sits on yon hill,
  Ba, ba, lilli ba.
He blaws his horn both lowd and shril.
  The wind hath blown my plaid awa.

He blowes it east, he blowes it west,
He blowes it where he lyketh best.

I wish that horn were in my kist,
Yea, and the knight in my armes two.

She had no sooner these words said,
When that the knight came to her bed.

Thou art over young a maid, quoth he,
Married with me thou wouldst be.

I have a sister younger than I,
And she was married yesterday.

Married with me if thou wouldst be,
A courtesie thou must do to me.

For thou must shape a sark to me,
Without any cut or heme, quoth he.

Thou must shape it knife-and-sheerlesse,
And also sue it needle-threadlesse.

If that piece of courtesie I do thee,
Another thou must do to me.

I have an aiker of good ley-land,
Which lyeth low by yon sea-strand.

For thou must eare it with thy horn,
So thou must sow it with thy corn.

And bigg a cart of stone and lyme,
Robin Redbreast he must trail it hame.

Thou must barn it in a mouse-holl,
And thrash it into thy shoes' soll.

And thou must winnow it in thy looff,
And also seek it in thy glove.

For thou must bring it over the sea,
And thou must bring it dry home to me.

When thou hast gotten thy turns well done,
Then come to me and get thy sark then.

I'l not quit my plaid for my life,
It haps my seven bairns and my wife.
    The wind shall not blow my plaid awa.

My maidenhead I'l then keep still,
Let the elphin knight do what he will.
    The wind's not blown my plaid awa.

Anon.

Lady Isabel and the Elf-Knight

Fair lady Isabel sits in her bower sewing,
    Aye as the gowans grow gay
There she heard an elf-knight blawing his horn.
    The first morning in May.

'If I had yon horn that I hear blawing,
And yon elf-knight to sleep in my bosom.'

This maiden had scarcely these words spoken,
Till in at her window the elf-knight has luppen.

'It's a very strange matter, fair maiden,' said he,
'I canna blaw my horn but ye call on me.

'But will ye go to yon greenwood side?
If ye canna gang, I will cause you to ride.'

He leapt on a horse, and she on another,
And they rode to the greenwood together.

'Light down, light down, Lady Isabel,' said he,
'We are come to the place where you are to die.'

'Hae mercy, hae mercy, kind sir, on me,
Till ance my dear father and mother I see.'

'Seven king's-daughters here hae I slain,
And ye shall be the eight o' them.'

'O sit down a while, lay your head on my knee,
That we may hae some rest before that I die.'

She stroak'd him sae fast, the nearer he did creep,
Wi' a sma' charm she lull'd him fast asleep.

Wi' his ain sword-belt sae fast as she ban him,
Wi' his ain dag-durk sae sair as she dang him.

'If seven king's-daughters here ye hae slain,
Lye ye here, a husband to them a'.'

Anon.

Thomas the Rhymer

True Thomas lay on Huntlie bank;
  A ferlie he spied wi' his e'e;
And there he saw a lady bright,
  Come riding down by the Eildon Tree.

Her skirt was o' the grass-green silk,
  Her mantle o' the velvet fyne,
An ilka tett of her horse's mane
  Hang fifty siller bells and nine.

True Thomas he pull'd aff his cap,
  And louted low down to his knee:
'All hail, thou mighty Queen of Heaven!
  For thy peer on earth I never did see.'

'O no, O no, Thomas,' she said,
  'That name does not belang to me;
I am but the queen of fair Elfland,
  That am hither come to visit thee.

'Harp and carp, Thomas,' she said,
  'Harp and carp, along wi' me,
And if ye dare to kiss my lips,
  Sure of your bodie I will be!'

'Betide me weal, betide me woe,
  That weird sall never daunton me;'
Syne he has kissed her rosy lips,
  All underneath the Eildon Tree.

'Now, ye maun go wi' me,' she said,
  'True Thomas, ye maun go wi' me,
And ye maun serve me seven years,
  Thro' weal or woe as may chance to be.'

She mounted on her milk-white steed,
  She's taen True Thomas up behind,
And aye whene'er her bridle rung,
  The steed flew swifter than the wind.

O they rade on, and farther on –
  The steed gaed swifter than the wind –
Until they reached a desart wide,
  And living land was left behind.

'Light down, light down, now, True Thomas,
  And lean your head upon my knee;

Abide and rest a little space,
   And I will show you ferlies three.

'O see ye not yon narrow road,
   So thick beset with thorns and briers?
That is the path of righteousness,
   Tho' after it but few enquires.

'And see ye not that braid braid road,
   That lies across that lily leven?
That is the path of wickedness,
   Tho' some call it the road to heaven.

'And see not ye that bonny road,
   That winds about the fernie brae?
That is the road to fair Elfland,
   Where thou and I this night maun gae.

'But, Thomas, ye maun hold your tongue,
   Whatever ye may hear or see,
For, if you speak word in Elfyn land,
   Ye'll ne'er get back to your ain countrie.'

O they rade on, and farther on,
   And they waded thro' rivers aboon the knee,
And they saw neither sun nor moon,
   But they heard the roaring of the sea.

It was mirk mirk night, and there was nae stern light,
   And they waded thro' red blude to the knee;
For a' the blude that's shed on earth
   Rins thro' the springs o' that countrie.

Syne they came on to a garden green,
   And she pu'd an apple frae a tree:
'Take this for thy wages, True Thomas,
   It will give the tongue that can never lie.'

'My tongue is mine ain,' True Thomas said,
'A gudely gift ye wad gie to me!
I neither dought to buy nor sell,
At fair or tryst where I may be.

'I dought neither speak to prince or peer,
Nor ask of grace from fair ladye:'
'Now hold thy peace,' the lady said,
'For as I say, so must it be.'

He has gotten a coat of the even cloth,
And a pair of shoes of velvet green,
And till seven years were gane and past
True Thomas on earth was never seen.

Anon.

The Young Tamlane

'O I forbid ye, maidens a',
That wear gowd on your hair,
To come or gae by Carterhaugh,
For young Tamlane is there.

'There's nane that gaes by Carterhaugh,
But maun leave him a wad,
Either gowd rings or green mantles,
Or else their maidenheid.

'Now gowd rings ye may buy, maidens,
Green mantles ye may spin;
But, gin ye lose your maidenheid,
Ye'll ne'er get that agen.' –

But up then spake her, fair Janet,
The fairest o' her kin;
'I'll cum and gang to Carterhaugh,
And ask nae leave o' him.' –

Janet haw kilted her green kirtle,
A little abune her knee;
And she has braided her yellow hair,
A little abune her bree.

And when she came to Carterhaugh,
She gaed beside the well;
And there she fand his steed standing,
But away was himsell.

She hadna pu'd a red red rose,
A rose but barely three;
Till up and starts a wee wee man,
At lady Janet's knee.

Says – 'Why pu' ye the rose, Janet?
What gars ye break the tree?
Or why come ye to Carterhaugh,
Withouten leave o' me?' –

Says – 'Carterhaugh it is mine ain;
My daddie gave it me:
I'll come and gang to Carterhaugh,
And ask nae leave o' thee.'

He's ta'en her by the milk-white hand,
Among the leaves sae green;
And what they did, I cannot tell –
The green leaves were between.

He's ta'en her by the milk-white hand,
Among the roses red;

And what they did, I cannot say –
  She ne'er return'd a maid.

When she cam to her father's ha',
  She looked pale and wan;
They thought she'd dreed some sair sickness,
  Or been with some leman.

She didna comb her yellow hair,
  Nor make meikle o' her head;
And ilka thing that lady took,
  Was like to be her deid.

It's four and twenty ladies fair
  Were playing at the ba';
Janet, the wightest of them anes,
  Was faintest o' them a'.

Four and twenty ladies fair
  Were playing at the chess;
And out there came the fair Janet,
  As green as any grass.

Out and spak an auld grey-headed knight,
  Lay o'er the castle wa' –
'And ever, alas! for thee, Janet,
  But we'll be blamed a'!' –

'Now haud your tongue, ye auld grey knight!
  And an ill deid may ye die,
Father my bairn on whom I will,
  I'll father nane on thee.' –

Out then spak her father dear,
  And he spak meik and mild –
'And ever, alas! my sweet Janet,
  I fear ye gae with child.' –

'And if I be with child, father,
  Mysell maun bear the blame;
There's ne'er a knight about your ha'
  Shall hae the bairnie's name.

'And if I be with child, father,
  'Twill prove a wondrous birth;
For weel I swear I'm not with bairn
  To any man on earth.

'If my love were an earthly knight,
  As he's an elfin grey,
I wadna gie my ain true love
  For nae lor that ye hae.' –

She prink'd hersell and prinn'd hersell,
  By the ae light of the moon,
And she's away to Carterhaugh,
  To speak wi' young Tamlane.

And when she cam to Carterhaugh,
  She gaed beside the well;
And there she saw the steed standing,
  But away was himsell.

She hadna pu'd a double rose,
  A rose but only twae,
When up and started young Tamlane,
Says – 'Lady, thou pu's nae mae!

'Why pu' ye the rose, Janet,
  Within this garden grene,
And a' to kill the bonny babe,
  That we got us between?' –

'The truth ye'll tell to me, Tamlane:
  A word ye mauna lie;

Gin e'er ye was in haly chapel,
 Or sained in Christentie?' –

'The truth I'll tell to thee, Janet,
 A word I winna lie;
A knight me got, and a lady me bore,
 As well as they did thee.

'Randolph, Earl Murray, was my sire,
 Dunbar, Earl March, is thine;
We loved when we were children small,
 Which yet you well may mind.

'When I was a boy just turn'd of nine,
 My uncle sent for me,
To hunt, and hawk, and ride with him,
 And keep him companie.

'There came a wind out of the north,
 A sharp wind and a snell;
And a deep sleep came over me,
 And frae my horse I fell.

'The Queen of Fairies keppit me
 In yon green hill to dwell;
And I'm a fairy, lyth and limb;
 Fair ladye, view me well.

'But we, that live in Fairy-land,
 No sickness know, nor pain,
I quit my body when I will,
 And take to it again.

'I quit my body when I please,
 Or unto it repair;
We can inhabit, at our ease,
 In either earth or air.

'Our shapes and size we can convert
To either large or small;
An old nut-shell's the same to us
As is the lofty hall.

'We sleep in rose-buds soft and sweet,
We revel in the stream;
We wanton lightly on the wind,
Or glide on a sunbeam.

'And all our wants are well supplied
From every rich man's store,
Who thankless sins the gifts he gets,
And vainly grasps for more.

'Then would I never tire, Janet,
In Elfish land to dwell;
But aye, at every seven years,
They pay the teind to hell;
And I am sae fat and fair of flesh,
I fear 'twill be mysell.

'This night is Hallowe'en, Janet,
The morn is Hallowday;
And gin ye dare your true love win,
Ye hae nae time to stay.

'The night it is good Hallowe'en,
When fairy folk will ride;
And they that wad their true-love win,
At Miles Cross they maun bide.' –

'But how shall I thee ken, Tamlane?
Or how shall I thee knaw,
Amang so many unearthly knights,
The like I never saw?' –

'The first company that passes by,
  Say na, and let them gae;
The next company that passes by,
  Sae na, and do right sae;
The third company that passes by,
  Then I'll be ane o' thae.

'First let pass the black, Janet,
  And syne let pass the brown;
But grip ye to the milk-white steed,
  And pu' the rider down.

'For I ride on the milk-white steed,
  And aye nearest the town;
Because I was a christen'd knight,
  They gave me that renown.

'My right hand will be gloved, Janet,
  My left hand will be bare;
And these the tokens I gie thee,
  Nae doubt I will be there.

'They'll turn me in your arms, Janet,
  An adder and a snake;
But haud me fast, let me not pass,
  Gin ye wad buy me maik.

'They'll turn me in your arms, Janet,
  An adder and an ask;
They'll turn me in your arms, Janet,
  A bale that burns fast.

'They'll turn me in your arms, Janet,
  A red-hot gad o' airn;
But haud me fast, let me not pass,
  For I'll do you no harm.

'First dip me in a stand o' milk,
  And then in a stand o' water;
But haud me fast, let me not pass –
  I'll be your bairn's father.

'And, next, they'll shape me in your arms,
  A tod, but an eel;
But haud me fast, nor let me gang,
  As you do love me weel.

'They'll shape me in your arms, Janet,
  A dove, but and a swan;
And, last, they'll shape me in your arms
  A mother-naked man:
Cast your green mantle over me –
  I'll be myself again.' –

Gloomy, gloomy, was the night,
  And eiry was the way,
As fair Janet in her green mantle,
  To Miles Cross she did gae.

The heavens were black, the night was dark,
  And dreary was the place;
But Janet stood, with eager wish,
  Her lover to embrace.

Betwixt the hours of twelve and one,
  A north wind tore the bent;
And straight she heard strange elritch sounds,
  Upon that wind which went.

About the dead hour o' the night,
  She heard the bridles ring;
And Janet was as glad o' that
  As any earthly thing.

Their oaten pipes blew wondrous shrill,
  The hemlock small blew clear;
And louder notes from hemlock large,
  And bog-reed, struck the ear;
But solemn sounds, or sober thoughts,
  The Fairies cannot bear.

They sing, inspired with love and joy,
  Like skylarks in the air;
Of solid sense, or thought that's grave,
  You'll find no traces there.

Fair Janet stood, with mind unmoved,
  The dreary heath upon;
And louder, louder wax'd the sound,
  As they came riding on.

Will o' Wisp before them went,
  Sent forth a twinkling light;
And soon she saw the Fairy bands
  All riding in her sight.

And first gaed by the black black steed,
  And then gaed by the brown;
But fast she gript the milk-white steed,
  And pu'd the rider down.

She pu'd him frae the milk-white steed,
  And loot the bridle fa';
And up there raise an erlish cry –
  'He's won among us a'!' –

They shaped him in fair Janet's arms,
  An esk, but and an adder;
She held him fast in every shape –
  To be her bairn's father.

They shaped him in her arms at last,
  A mother-naked man;
She wrapt him in her green mantle,
  And sae her true love wan!

Up then spake the Queen o' Fairies,
  Out o' a bush o' rye –
'She's ta'en awa the bonniest knight
  In a' my cumpanie.

'But had I kenn'd, Tamlane,' she says,
  'A lady wad borrow'd thee –
I wad ta'en out thy twa grey een,
  Put in twa een o' tree.

'Had I but kenn'd, Tamlane,' she says,
  'Before ye came frae hame –
I wad ta'en out your heart o' flesh,
  Put in a heart o' stane.

'Had I but had the wit yestreen
  That I hae coft the day –
I'd paid my kane seven times to hell
  Ere you'd been won away!'

Sir Walter Scott

[The Piper's Son]

Tom, he was a piper's son,
He learnt to play when he was young,
And all the tune that he could play,
Was, 'Over the hills and far away';
Over the hills and a great way off,
The wind shall blow my top-knot off.

Tom with his pipe made such a noise,
That he pleased both the girls and boys,
And they stopped to hear him play,
'Over the hills and far away.'

Tom with his pipe did play with such skill
That those who heard him could never keep still;
As soon as he played they began to dance,
Even pigs on their hind legs would prance.

As Dolly was milking her cow one day,
Tom took his pipe and began for to play,
So Doll and the cow danced 'The Cheshire Round',
Till the pail was broken and the milk ran on the ground.

He met old Dame Trot with a basket of eggs,
He used his pipe and she used her legs;
She danced about till the eggs were all broke,
She began for to fret, but he laughed at the joke.

Tom saw a cross fellow was beating an ass,
Heavy laden with pots, pans, dishes, and glass;
He took out his pipe and he played them a tune,
And the poor donkey's load was lightened full soon.

Mother Goose

The Elphin Nourice

I heard a cow low, a bonnie cow low,
  An' a cow low doun in yon glen,
Lang, lang will my young son greet,
  Or his mither bid him come ben.

I heard a cow low, a bonnie cow low,
An' a cow low doun in yon fauld,
Lang, lang, will my young son greet
Or his mither take him frae cauld.

Waken, Queen of Elfan,
An' hear your Nourice moan.
O moan ye for your meat,
Or moan ye for your fee,
Or moan ye for the ither bounties
That ladies are wont to gie?

I moan na for my meat,
Nor yet for my fee,
But I mourn for Christened land –
It's there I fain would be.

O nurse my bairn, Nourice, she says,
Till he stan' at your knee,
An' ye win hame to Chrisen land,
Whar fain it's ye wad be.

O keep my bairn, Nourice,
Till he gang by the hauld,
An ye's win hame to your young son,
Ye left in four nights auld.

Anon.

The Deserted Home

Sadly talks the blackbird here.
Well I know the woe he found:
No matter who cut down his nest,
For its young it was destroyed.

I myself not long ago
Found the woe he now has found.
Well I read thy song, O bird,
For the ruin of thy home.

Thy heart, O blackbird, burnt within
At the deed of reckless man:
Thy nest bereft of young and egg
The cowherd deems a trifling tale.

At thy clear notes they used to come,
Thy new-fledged children, from afar;
No bird now comes from out thy house,
Across its edge the nettle grows.

They murdered them, the cowherd
  lads,
All thy children in one day:
One the fate to me and thee,
My own children live no more.

There was feeding by thy side
Thy mate, a bird from o'er the sea:
Then the snare entangled her,
At the cowherds' hands she died.

O Thou, the Shaper of the world!
Uneven hands Thou layst on us:
Our fellows at our side are spared,
Their wives and children are alive.

A fairy host came as a blast
To bring destruction to our house:
Though bloodless was their taking off,
Yet dire as slaughter by the sword.

Woe for our wife, woe for our young!
The sadness of our grief is great:
No trace of them within, without –
And therefore is my heart so sad.

Anon.

The Night Swans

'Tis silence on the enchanted lake,
And silence in the air serene,
Save for the beating of her heart,
The lovely-eyed Evangeline.

She sings across the waters clear
And dark with trees and stars between,
The notes her fairy godmother
Taught her, the child Evangeline.

As might the unrippled pool reply,
Faltering and answer far and sweet,
Three swans as white as mountain snow
Swim mantling to her feet.

And still upon the lake they stay,
Their eyes black stars in all their snow,
And softly, in the glassy pool,
Their feet beat darkly to and fro.

She rides upon her little boat,
Her swans swim through the starry sheen,
Rowing her into Fairyland –
The lovely-eyed Evangeline.

'Tis silence on the enchanted lake,
And silence in the air serene;
Voices shall call in vain again
On earth the child Evangeline.

'Evangeline! Evangeline!'
Upstairs, downstairs, all in vain.
Her room is dim; her flowers faded;
She answers not again.

Walter de la Mare

The Fairies Farewell

The Fairies Farewell

Farewell rewards and Fairies!
  Good housewives now you may say;
For now foule sluts in dairies,
  Doe fare as well as they:
And though they sweepe their hearths no less
  Than mayds were wont to doe,
Yet who of late for cleaneliness
  Finds sixe-pence in her shoe?

Lament, lament old Abbies,
  The fairies lost command;
They did but change priests babies,
  But some have chang'd your land:
And all your children stoln from thence
  And now growne Puritanes,
Who live as changelings ever since,
  For love of your demaines.

At morning and at evening both
  You merry were and glad,
So little care of sleepe and sloth,
  These prettie ladies had.
When Tom came home from labour,
  Or Ciss to milking rose,
Then merrily went their tabour,
  And nimbly went their toes.

Witness those rings and roundelayes
  Of theirs, which yet remaine;
Were footed in queene Maries dayes
  On many a grassy playne.
But since of late Elizabeth
  And later James came in;
They never danc'd on any heath,
  As when the time hath bin.

By which wee note the fairies
  Were of the old profession:
Their songs were 'Ave Maries',
  Their dances were procession.
But now, alas! they all are dead,
  Or gone beyond the seas,
Or farther for religion fled,
  Or else they take their ease.

A tell tale in their company
  They never could endure;
And whoso kept not secretly
  Their mirth, was punished sure:
It was a just and christian deed
  To pinch such blacke and blue:
O how the common-welth doth need
  Such justices as you!

Now they have left our quarters;
  A register they have,
Who can preserve their charters;
  A man both wise and grave.
An hundred of their merry pranks
  By one that I could name
Are kept in store; con twenty thanks
  To William for the same.

To William Churne of Staffordshire
  Give laud and praises due,
Who every meale can mend your cheare
  With tales both old and true:
To William all give audience,
  And pray yee for his noddle:
For all the fairies evidence
  Were lost, if it were addle.

Richard Corbet

VI
Visions and Transformations

Love and Death

The Shape Changers

Trickery

Love and Death

[The Tasks]

Can you make me a cambrick shirt,
  Parsley, sage, rosemary and thyme,
Without any seam or needle work?
  And you shall be a true lover of mine.

Can you wash it in yonder well,
  Parsley, sage, rosemary and thyme,
Where never spring water, nor rain ever fell?
  And you shall be a true lover of mine.

Can you dry it on yonder thorn,
  Parsley, sage, rosemary and thyme,
Which never bore blossom since Adam was born?
  And you shall be a true lover of mine.

Now you have ask'd me questions three,
  Parsley, sage, rosemary and thyme,
I hope you'll answer as many for me,
  And you shall be a true lover of mine.

Can you find me an acre of land,
  Parsley, sage, rosemary and thyme,
Between the salt water and the sea sand?
  And you shall be a true lover of mine.

Can you plow it with a ram's horn,
  Parsley, sage, rosemary and thyme,

And sow it all over with one pepper corn?
  And you shall be a true lover of mine.

Can you reap it with a sickle of leather,
  Parsley, sage, rosemary and thyme,
And bind it up with a peacock's feather?
  And you shall be a true lover of mine.

When you have done and finish'd your work,
  Parsley, sage, rosemary and thyme,
Then come to me for your cambrick shirt,
  And you shall be a true lover of mine.

Mother Goose

The Youthful Quest

His Lady queen of woods to meet,
    He wanders day and night:
The leaves have whisperings discreet,
    The mossy ways invite.

Across a lustrous ring of space,
    By covert woods and caves,
Is promise of her secret face
    In film that onward waves.

For darkness is the light astrain,
    Astrain for light the dark.
A grey moth down a larches' lane
    Unwinds a ghostly spark.

Her lamp he sees, and young desire
Is fed while cloaked she flies.
She quivers shot of violet fire
To ash at look of eyes.

George Meredith

The Unquiet Grave

'The wind doth blow today, my love,
And a few small drops of rain;
I never had but one true-love,
In cold grave she was lain.

'I'll do as much for my true-love
As any young man may;
I'll sit and mourn all at her grave
For a twelvemonth and a day.'

The twelvemonth and a day being up,
The dead began to speak:
'Oh who sits weeping on my grave,
And will not let me sleep?'

''Tis I, my love, sits on your grave,
And will not let you sleep;
For I crave one kiss of your clay-cold lips,
And that is all I seek.'

'You crave one kiss of my clay-cold lips,
But my breath smells earthly strong;
If you have one kiss of my clay-cold lips,
Your time will not be long.

‘’Tis down in yonder garden green,
 Love, where we used to walk,
The finest flower that e’er was seen
 Is withered to a stalk.

‘The stalk is withered dry, my love,
 So will our hearts decay;
So make yourself content, my love,
 Till God calls you away.’

Anon.

Fair Margaret and Sweet William

When day was gone, and night was come,
 And all men fast asleep,
Then came the spirit of Fair Margaret,
 And stood at William’s feet.

‘God give you joy, you two true lovers,
 In bride-bed fast asleep;
Loe I am going to my green grass grave,
 And I am in my winding-sheet.’

When day was come, and night was gone,
 And all men wak’d from sleep,
Sweet William to his lady said,
 ‘My dear, I have cause to weep.

‘I dream’d a dream, my dear lady;
 Such dreams are never good;
I dream’d my bower was full of red swine,
 And my bride-bed full of blood.’

'Such dreams, such dreams, my honoured lord,
They never do prove good,
To dream thy bower was full of swine,
And thy bride-bed full of blood.'

Anon.

Song of the Murdered Child whose Bones Grew into a Milk-White Dove

Pew, pew,
My minny me slew,
My daddy me chew,
My sister gathered my banes,
And put them between twa milk-white stanes,
And I grew and I grew
To a milk-white doo,
And I took to my wings
And away I flew.

Anon.

[Cock Robin]

Who did kill Cock Robin?
I, said the Sparrow,
With my bow and Arrow,
And I did kill Cock Robin.

Who did see him die?
I, said the Fly,
With my little Eye,
And I did see him die.

And who did catch his blood?
I, said the Fish,
With my little Dish,
And I did catch his blood.

And who did make his shroud?
I, said the Beetle,
With my little Needle,
And I did make his shroud.

Who'll dig his grave?
I, said the Owl,
With my pick and shovel,
I'll dig his grave.

Who'll be the parson?
I, said the Rook,
With my little book,
I'll be the parson.

Who'll be the clerk?
I, said the Lark,
If it's not in the dark,
I'll be the clerk.

Who'll carry the link?
I, said the Linnet,
I'll fetch it in a minute,
I'll carry the link.

Who'll be the chief mourner?
I, said the Dove,

I mourn for my love,
I'll be chief mourner.

Who'll carry the coffin?
I, said the Kite,
If it's not through the night,
I'll carry the coffin.

Who'll bear the pall?
We, said the Wren,
Both the cock and the hen,
We'll bear the pall.

Who'll sing a psalm?
I, said the Thrush,
As she sat on a bush,
I'll sing a psalm.

Who'll toll the bell,
I, said the Bull,
Because I can pull,
I'll toll the bell.

All the birds of the air
Fell a-sighing and a-sobbing,
When they heard the bell toll
For poor Cock Robin.

Mother Goose

The Raven's Tomb

'Build me my tomb,' the Raven said
'Within the dark yew-tree,
So in the Autumn yewberries,
Sad lamps, may burn for me,
Summon the haunted beetle,
From twilight bud and bloom,
To drone a gloomy dirge for me
At dusk above my tomb.
Beseech ye too the glowworm
To rear her cloudy flame,
Where the small, flickering bats resort,
Whistling in tears my name.
Let the round dew a whisper make,
Welling on twig and thorn;
And only the grey cock at night
Call through his silver horn.
And you, dear sisters, don your black
For ever and a day,
To show how true a raven
In his tomb is laid away.'

Walter de la Mare

The Shape Changers

The Hare

In the black furrow of a field
I saw an old witch-hare this night;
And she cocked a lissome ear,
And she eyed the moon so bright,
And she nibbled of the green;
And I whispered 'Shsst! witch-hare,'
Away like a ghostie o'er the field
She fled, and left the moonlight there.

Walter de la Mare

The Twa Magicians

The lady stands in her bower door,
   As straight as willow wand,
The blacksmith stood a little forebye,
   Wi hammer in his hand.

Weel may ye dress ye, lady fair,
   Into your robes o red,
Before the morn at this same time
   I'll gain your maidenhead.

Awa, awa, ye coal-black smith,
  Woud ye do me the wrang
To think to gain my maidenhead,
  That I hae kept sae lang

Then she has hauden up her hand,
  And she sware by the mold,
I wudna be a blacksmith's wife
  For the full o a chest o gold.

I'd rather I were dead and gone,
  And my body laid in grave,
Ere a rusty stock o coal-black smith
  My maidenhead should have.

But he has hauden up his hand,
  And he sware by the mass,
I'll cause ye be my light leman
  For the hauf o that and less.

'O *bide, lady, bide,*
  And aye he bade her bide
The rusty smith your leman shall be
  For a' your muckle pride.'

Then she became a turtle dow,
  To fly up in the air,
And he became another dow,
  And they flew pair and pair.
'O *bide, lady, bide,'* &c.

She turned hersell into an eel,
  To swim into yon burn,
And he became a speckled trout,
  To gie the eel a turn.
'O *bide, lady, bide,'* &c.

Then she became a duck, a duck,
  To puddle in a peel,
And he became a rose-kaimd drake,
  To gie the duck a dreel.
    'O bide, lady, bide,' &c.

She turned hersell into a hare,
  To rin upon yon hill,
And he became a gude grey-hound,
  And boldly he did fill.
    'O bide, lady, bide,' &c.

Then she became a gay grey mare,
  And stood in yonder slack,
And he became a gilt saddle,
  And sat upon her back.

'Was she wae, he held her sae,
And still he bade her bide,
The rusty smith her leman was,
For a' her muckle pride.'

Then she became a het girdle,
  And he became a cake,
And a' the ways she turnd hersell,
  The blacksmith was her make.
    'Was she wae,' &c.

She turnd hersell into a ship,
  To sail out over the flood.
He ca'ed a nail intill her tail,
  And syne the ship she stood.
    'Was she wae,' &c.

Then she became a silken plaid,
  And stretch'd upon a bed,
And he became a green covering,
  And gaind her maidenhead.
    'Was she wae,' &c.

Anon.

The Milk White Doe

'It was a mother and a maid
   That walked the woods among,
And still the maid went slow and sad,
   And still the mother sung.

"What ails you, daughter Margaret?
   Why go you pale and wan?
Is it for a cast of bitter love,
   Or for a false leman?"

"It is not for a false lover
   That I go sad to see,
But it is for a weary life
   Beneath the greenwood tree.

"For ever in the good daylight
   A maiden may I go,
But always on the ninth midnight
   I change to a milk white doe.

"They hunt me through the green forest
   With hounds and hunting men;
And ever it is my fair brother
   That is so fierce and keen."

. . .

"Good morrow, mother." "Good morrow, son;
   Where are your hounds so good?"
"Oh, they are hunting a white doe
   Within the glad greenwood.

"And three times they have hunted her,
   And thrice she's won away;
The fourth time that they follow her
   That white doe they shall slay."

. . .

Then out and spake the forester,
  as he came from the wood,
"Nor never saw I a maid's gold hair
  Among the wild deer's blood.

"And I have hunted the wild deer
  In east lands and in west;
And never saw I white doe yet
  That had a maiden's breast."

Then up and spake her fair brother,
  Between the wine and bread,
"Behold, I had but one sister,
  And I have seen her dead.

"But ye must bury my sweet sister
  With a stone at her foot and her head,
And ye must cover her fair body
  With the white roses and red.

"And I must out to the greenwood,
  The roof shall never shelter me;
And I shall lie for seven long years
  On the grass below the hawthorn tree."'

Anon.

Hares on the Mountains

A

Young women they'll run like hares on the mountains
Young women they'll run like hares on the mountains
If I was but a young man I'd soon go a-hunting
To my right fol diddle dero, to my right fol diddle dee.

Young women they sing like birds in the bushes
Young women they sing like birds in the bushes
If I was a young man I'd go and bang the bushes
To my right fol diddle dero, to my right fol diddle dee.

Young women they'll swim like ducks in the water
Young women they'll swim like ducks in the water
If I was a young man I'd go and swim all after
To my right fol diddle dero, to my right fol diddle dee.

B

If all those young men were as rushes a growing
Then all those pretty maidens will get scythes go a mowing
Fal lal etc.

If all those young men were as hares on the mountains
Then all those pretty maidens will get guns go a hunting

If all those young men were as ducks in the water
Then all those pretty maidens would soon follow after.

Anon.

The Song of Wandering Aengus

I went out to the hazel wood,
Because a fire was in my head,
And cut and peeled a hazel wand,
And hooked a berry to a thread;
And when white moths were on the wing,
And moth-like stars were flickering out,
I dropped the berry in a stream
And caught a little silver trout.

When I had laid it on the floor
I went to blow the fire a-flame,
But something rustled on the floor,
And some one called me by my name:
It had become a glimmering girl
With apple blossom in her hair
Who called me by my name and ran
And faded through the brightening air.

Though I am old with wandering
Through hollow lands and hilly lands,
I will find out where she has gone,
And kiss her lips and take her hands;
And walk among long dappled grass,
And pluck till time and times are done
The silver apples of the moon
The golden apples of the sun.

W. B. Yeats

The Loyal Lover

I'll make my love a garland,
It shall be dressed so fine.
I'll set it round with roses,
With lilies mixed with thyme,
And I'll present it to my love
When he comes back from sea
For I love my love, and I love my love
Because my love loves me.
  Ri-tol-di-rol, ri-tol-lol,
  Ri-tol-de-tol-dee.

I wish I were an arrow
And sped into the air,
I'd seek him like a sparrow
And if he were not there
Then quickly I'd become a fish
To search the raging sea,
For I love my love, and I love my love
Because my love loves me.
  Ri-tol-di-rol, ri-tol-lol,
  Ri-tol-de-tol-dee.

I wish I were a reaper,
I'd seek him in the corn.
I would I were a keeper,
I'd hunt him with my horn,
I'd blow a blast when found at last
Beneath the greenwood tree,
For I love my love, and I love my love
Because my love loves me.
  Ri-tol-di-tol, ri-tol-lol,
  Ri-tol-de-tol-dee.

Anon.

Clerk Colvill

Out then he drew his shining blade,
  Thinking to stick her where she stood,
But she was vanished to a fish,
  And swam far off, a fair mermaid.

O mother, mother, braid my hair,
  My lusty lady, make my bed.
O brother, take my sword and spear,
  For I have seen the false mermaid.

Anon.

[London Bridge]

London Bridge
Is broken down,
Dance over my Lady Lee,
London Bridge
Is broken down,
With a gay Lady.

How shall we build
It up again,
Dance over my Lady Lee.
How shall we build
It up again,
With a gay Lady.

Build it up with
Gravel, and Stone,
Dance over my Lady Lee.

Build it up with
Gravel, and Stone,
With a gay Lady.

Gravel, and Stone
Will wash away,
Dance over my Lady Lee.
Gravel, and Stone,
Will wash away,
With a gay Lady.

Build it up with
Iron, and Steel,
Dance over my Lady Lee.
Build it up with
Iron, and Steel,
With a gay Lady.

Iron, and Steel,
Will bend, and Bow,
Dance over my Lady Lee.
Iron, and steel,
Will bend, and Bow,
With a gay Lady.

Build it up with
Silver, and Gold,
Dance over my Lady Lee.
Build it up with
Silver, and Gold,
With a gay Lady.

Silver, and Gold,
Will be stoln away,
Dance over my Lady Lee.
Silver, and Gold,
Will be stoln away,
With a gay Lady.

Then we'll set
A Man to Watch,
Dance over my Lady Lee.
Then we'll set
A Man to Watch
With a gay Lady.

Mother Goose

Trickery

The Jolly Juggler

Draw me near, draw me near,
Draw me near, the jolly juggler.

Here beside dwelleth a rich baron's daughter:
She would have no man that for love had sought her –
  So nice she was.

She would have no man that was made of mold
But if he had a mouth of gold to kiss her when she would –
  So daungerous she was.

Thereof heard a jolly juggler that laid was on the green,
And at this lady's word, iwis he had great tene –
  An-angered he was.

He juggled to him a well good steed of an old horse bone,
A saddle and a bridle both, and set himself thereon –
  A juggler he was.

He pricked and pranced both, before that lady's gate:
She weened he had been an angel, was come for her sake –
  A pricker he was.

He pricked and pranced before that lady's bower:
She weened he had been an angel come from Heaven's tower –
  A prancer he was.

Four and twenty knightes led him into the hall,
And as many squires his horse to the stall,
  And gave him some meat.

They gave him oats, and also hay;
He was an old shrew and held his head away –
  He would not eat.

The day began to pass, the night began to come,
To bed was brought the fair gentlewoman,
  And the juggler also.

The night began to pass, the day began to spring;
All the birds of her bower they began to sing –
  And the cuckoo also.

'Where be ye, my merry maidens, that ye come not me to?
The jolly windows of my bower look that you undo,
  That I may see.

'For I have in mine arms a duke or else an earl.'
But when she looked him upon, he was a blear-eyed churl –
  'Alas!' she said.

She led him to a hill, and hanged should he be.
He juggled himself to a meal poke, the dust fell in her eye –
  Beguiled she was.

God and our Lady, and sweet Saint Johan,
Send every giglot of this town such another leman,
  Even as he was!

Anon.

Sing Ovy, Sing Ivy

My father gave me an acre of land,
  Sing ovy, sing ivy,
My father gave me an acre of land,
  A bunch of green holly and ivy.

I harrowed it with a bramble bush.

I sowed it with two peppercorns.

I rolled it with a rolling pin.

I reaped it with my little penknife.

I housed it into mouse's hole.

I threshed it out with two beanstalks.

I sent my rats to market with that.

My team o' rats came rattling back,
  Sing ovy, sing ivy,
With fifty bright guineas and an empty sack,
  A bunch of green holly and ivy.

Anon.

As I Set Off to Turkey

As I set off to Turkey, I travelled like an ox,
And in my breeches' pocket I carried my little box.
My box was four foot high, my box was four foot square,
All for to put my money in when guineas was so rare.

Chorus To my rite tol lol le riddle riddle lol
To my rite tol lol li day.

Then I bought me a little dog, his collar was undone,
I learnèd him to sing and dance, to wrestle and to run;
His legs were four feet high and his ears were four feet wide,
And round the world in half a day all on my dog I'd ride.

Then I bought me a flock of sheep, their wool it was so sleek,
And every month at the full of the moon they had six lambs apiece.
Then I bought me a little hen, on her I took much care,
I set her on a mussel-shell and she hatched me out a hare.

That hare it proved to be a milk-white steed about fifteen hands high,
And they as can tell a bigger jest, oh dear, oh dear, what a lie!

Anon.

As I was Going to Banbury

As I was going to Banbury
Ri fol latitee O
As I was going to Banbury
I saw a fine coddlin apple tree
With a ri fol latitee O.

And when the coddlins began to fall
I found five hundred men in all

And one of the men I saw was dead
So I sent for a hatchet to open his head

And in his head I found a spring
And seven young salmon a learning to sing

And one of the salmon as big as I
Now do you not think I am telling a lie?

And one of the salmon as big as an elf
If you want any more you must sing it yourself.

Anon.

[Under the Broom]

My father he died, but I can't tell you how,
He left me six horses to drive in my plough:
With my wing wang waddle oh,
Jack sing saddle oh,
Blowsey boys bubble oh,
Under the broom.

I sold my six horses and I bought me a cow,
I'd fain made a fortune, but did not know how:
With my wing wang waddle oh,
Jack sing saddle oh,
Blowsey boys bubble oh,
Under the broom.

I sold my cow, and I bought me a calf;
I'd fain made a fortune, but lost the best half:

With my wing wang waddle oh,
Jack sing saddle oh,
Blowsey boys bubble oh,
Under the broom.

I sold my calf, and bought me a cat;
A pretty thing she was, in my chimney corner sat:
With my wing wang waddle oh,
Jack sing saddle oh,
Blowsey boys bubble oh,
Under the broom.

I sold my cat, and bought me a mouse;
He carried fire in his tail, and burnt down my house:
With my wing wang waddle oh,
Jack sing saddle oh,
Blowsey boys bubble oh,
Under the broom.

Mother Goose

Blow the Wind Whistling

Up jumps the salmon
The largest o' em all
He jumps on our fore deck
Saying: Here's meat for all.
O blow the wind whistling
O blow the winds all
Our ship is still hearted boys
How steady she go!

Up jumps the shark
The largest of all

He jumped on our fore deck:
You should die all.

Then up jumps the sprat
The smallest of all
He jumps on our foredeck
Saying we shall be drowned all.

Anon.

A Nursery Song

When I was a wee thing,
  'Bout six or seven year auld,
I had no worth a petticoat,
  To keep me frae the cauld.

Then I went to Edinburgh,
  To bonny burrows toun,
And there I got a petticoat,
  A kirtle, and a goun.

As I came hame again,
  I thocht I wad bid a kirk,
And a' the fouls o' the air
  Wad help me to work.

The herring wi' her lang neb,
  She moupit me the stanes;
The doo, wi' her rough legs,
  She led me them hame.

The gled he was a wily thief,
  He rackled up the wa';
The pyot was a curst thief,
  She dang doun a'.

The hare cam hirpling ower the knowe,
  To ring the morning bell;
The hurcheon she came after,
  And said she wad do't hersel.

The herring was the high priest,
  The salmon was the clerk,
The howlet red the order –
  They held a bonny wark.

Anon.

[A Man of Words]

A man of words and not of deeds
Is like a garden full of weeds;
And when the weeds begin to grow,
It's like a garden full of snow;
And when the snow begins to fall,
It's like a bird upon the wall;
And when the bird away does fly,
It's like an eagle in the sky;
And when the sky begins to roar,
It's like a lion at the door;
And when the door begins to crack,
It's like a stick upon your back;
And when your back begins to smart,
It's like a penknife in your heart;
And when your heart begins to bleed,
You're dead, and dead, and dead, indeed.

Mother Goose

Notes

1 The Goddess and the God

The Goddess Worshipped

(p. 13), 'Queen and Huntress', Ben Jonson (1572–1637).

This song from *Cynthia's Revels*, while regarded generally as a tribute to Queen Elizabeth, is clearly a hymn of praise to the Great Goddess as Diana. Diana, the Queen of Heaven, was worshipped as a Moon Goddess, a Virgin, a Mother of all Living Creatures, and as a Huntress or Destroyer. As late as the fifth century the Gauls regarded her as the supreme deity. In the seventh century she was still worshipped steadfastly by the Franks. She was identified with Sophia, the Wisdom Goddess, by the gnostics, and as the Goddess of the Witches by the Inquisition.

She had many names according to the regions in which she was worshipped. In the Ardennes, for example, she was called Dea Arduenna. She differs only in small degree from the many other Goddesses worshipped all over the world, and who were named variously as Isis, Rhea, Minerva, Juno, Aphrodite, Demeter, Ceres, Beltis, Ishtar, Mulita and Nana, to give but a few. Her Greek name was, of course, Artemis.

Diana is portrayed frequently as a mother with a child, and her temples were frequently re-dedicated to the Christian Virgin Mary.

(p. 14), 'A Vow to Minerva', Robert Herrick (1591–1674).

Minerva was the Goddess as Wisdom. The owl was her sacred bird, and it appears in many rural superstitions. In Wales it was believed that when an owl hooted a maiden would lose her chastity. It was regarded as an unlucky bird, a bird of ill omen, perhaps because of its nocturnal habits. This distrust of night creatures may stem partially from the way in which the Christian Church was obliged to oppose those who worshipped the moon, the Goddess of the Night, and those who, following a moon calendar, counted their day from noon to noon, thus making midnight the centre of the 'day'. Minerva's night owl is still widely regarded as wise, especially in the British Isles.

(p. 14), 'Ode to Psyche', John Keats (1795–1821).
Keats's ode presents the poet as a worshipper of the Goddess as Psyche, who was regarded in the legend of Cupid and Psyche, as told by Apuleius, as being representative of the human soul. Psyche, however, is 'winged' and Keats sees her as being the Goddess herself, as Love, as Protectress of Nature, as Goddess of Song and Poetry, and as, indeed, the last and perhaps finest version of the Goddess in Greek myth and legend.

(p. 16), 'Dawn', anonymous Irish lyric, translated by James Carney.
This medieval poem presents the Goddess as Dawn. It was in Scandinavia, perhaps understandably, considering the long winter nights, that she was most widely worshipped. Her Scandinavian name was Eostre, which may be a form of Astarte. She gave her name to the Christian Festival of Easter, which is one of the few Christian Festivals that changes its date according to the moon. Eostre was, indeed, an aspect of the Moon Goddess. The Easter Bunny is derived from the sacred Moon Hare, and the Easter Egg derives from the notion, strongly believed in medieval Germany, that the Moon Hare would lay eggs for children on the eve of Easter.

(p. 17), 'Anima', John Knight (1906–1975).
John Knight was brought up in Cornwall, which he loved, and where he returned on retirement from the Civil Service. His first collection, *Straight Lines and Unicorns*, was published in 1960, a chapbook, *Other Causes of Love*, in 1969, and his posthumous collection *Edges of Fact* appeared in 1977.

John Clare (1793–1864) wrote in his Autobiography: 'I was a lover very early in life . . . my first attachment being a schoolboy affection was for Mary . . .' Mary was the daughter of a local farmer. At seventeen he fell in love with another Mary, Mary Joyce, whose father forbade a match, he being a farmer and Clare only a poor labourer's son. This Mary remained the subject of many of his poems throughout his life, and the very centre of his fantasies when he was committed to an asylum. Mary Joyce died in 1838 and he was writing to her as his 'first wife first love' until then, though she herself was married to someone else, as was he, and had children. Other Marys also became part of his life. In 1845 W. F. Knight became house steward at Northampton Asylum, and was responsible for collecting and publishing much of Clare's work. John Knight considered W. F. Knight an ancestor of his.

(p. 17), 'A Song to the Maskers', Robert Herrick (1591–1674).
Herrick's poem emphasizes the theme of the sacred dance which became, eventually, the dances of those who present masques and other entertainments at times of festival in the country. His reference to Isis makes it clear that he perceived this connection.

The Goddess and Muse

(p. 18), 'On Lucy, Countesse of Bedford', Ben Jonson (1572–1637).
Jonson's words, '. . . with even powers, / The rock, the spindle, and the sheeres controule / Of destinie . . .' allude to the Triple Goddess as the Three Fates. The Three Fates of Greek myth were called the Moerae. They were Clotho the Spinner, Lachesis the Measurer and Atropos the Cutter. They were the spinners of fate and controllers of destiny. The belief was that life was a thread spun by the Virgin, which was then measured and sustained by the Mother and cut by the Crone.

Magic charms were often based on the idea that one's life would be spared if the Moerae could be persuaded not to cut the thread. Knives were left out with offerings to the Fates in the hope that the thread cutter would not use her own.

(p. 19), 'A Hymn to the Muses', Robert Herrick (1591–1674).
In Greek mythology, the Muses, the Goddesses of Song and Inspiration, and of Literature and the Arts, were the daughters of Mnemosyne and Zeus. At one time the Muses were threefold and associated with the original Triple Goddess, but later they were always spoken of as being nine in number. They were: Clio (history), Euterpe (lyric poetry and flute), Thalia (comedy), Melpomene (tragedy), Terpsichore (dance), Calliope (heroic poetry), Erato (erotic poetry), Polyhymnia (sacred songs) and Urania (astronomy).

Among other offerings, worshippers left water, or milk, and honey for the Muses.

(p. 19), 'The Crystal Cabinet', William Blake (1757–1827).
In her *Blake and Tradition* (1968), Kathleen Raine points out that the crystal cabinet itself signifies matter, which according to Thomas Vaughan in his *Aula Lucis* (1652) is a 'Chrystall Castle' into which the human spirit is lured by 'liquid Venus', Blake's 'Maiden'. The spirit finds, however, that he is not in the embrace

of love, but in a prison, the human body. This poem therefore describes the descent of the human soul into the world of generation, and Kathleen Raine relates the poem to the Goddess by saying: 'This threefold Venus, whose heart is in her head and whose brain is in her body, is the enchantress, the witch, the feminine principle whose power over "gods and men" is the "cruel" . . . feminine power of "binding" the immortal within a mortal body.'

The Goddess and Nature

(p. 21), 'Chloridia, Rites to Chloris and Her Nymphs', Ben Jonson (1572–1637).

In this excerpt from the masque, *Chloridia, Rites to Chloris and her Nymphs* (1630), spring is seen as a rebirth of the Goddess. Chloris was a nymph whom Zephyrus (the West Wind) transformed into Flora, the Goddess of Flowers.

When the old matriarchal and matrilineal culture of the followers of the Mother Goddess was replaced, gradually, by a patriarchal and patrilineal culture, the rhythms of the seasons were reinterpreted. In the Old Religion, the Goddess ceases her reign in autumn and the winter months are the province of her consort, the male God. The Goddess returns to rule in the early spring, and in Celtic tradition, on St Brigid's Day (Saint Brigid being the Christianization of the Irish Great Goddess, Brigid). This is seen also in Greek mythology in the descent of Persephone to the Underworld and her return after the winter is over.

Patriarchal traditions, however, concentrate upon the God, who is seen as dying, or being killed, in autumn and being reborn in spring.

This is not wholly a vegetation myth. The story refers also to the deeply held belief in Reincarnation, in the return of the spirit to earth in another form. The Old Religion in the British Isles felt that people returned as people, but other traditions in Asia held that a person could return in a non-human form.

The theory of Reincarnation was tolerated by the Christian Church for many years, but eventually the doctrine of death leading to Purgatory or to an eternal Heaven or Hell became orthodox. As a consequence the Cathars, who believed in Reincarnation, were massacred, and the great thinker Giordano Bruno was executed in 1600 for heresy.

Once the doctrine of Reincarnation is accepted, death ceases to be a terror. Another life is to follow. (See Joseph Head and S. L. Cranston, *Reincarnation: The Phoenix Fire Mystery* (1977).)

(p. 22), 'The Succession of the Foure Sweet Months', Robert Herrick (1591–1674).

See the notes on 'Chloridia, Rites to Chloris and Her Nymphs' (p. 260) and on [Four-Leaf Clover] (p. 280) regarding the significance of four.

(p. 22), 'To Spring', William Blake (1757–1827).

(p. 23), [When Flora Fair], Richard Carlton (c. 1558–1638).

This song is from Carlton's *Madrigals*, 1601. Flora was an ancient Roman Goddess of Spring, the Goddess of Fertility and Flowers, and the queen of all plants. Annual May Day Festivals called Floralia, which celebrated nature and the female body, were held in her honour until the third century AD, at which time the Church put a stop to nude worship. As well as being called 'a Lady of Pleasure', and considered to be the patron of prostitutes, Flora was thought to be the secret patron of Rome and it was believed that Rome would die without help from the 'Flourishing One'.

(p. 24), 'Be Still as You are Beautiful', Patrick MacDonogh (1902–1960).

The rose and the white owl in this poem could be said to represent the Goddess. The rose, or Flower of Venus as it was known in ancient Rome, was the symbol for female genitalia, and a symbol of love. Here, the owl is the colour of purity, the symbol of the Virgin Goddess who was often represented cloaked in white.

(p. 24), 'To Mistress Margery Wentworth', John Skelton (1460–1529).

Mistress Margery's gown is embroidered with flowers in the same fashion as the Goddess figure in Botticelli's *Primavera*, and thus personifies Flora, the Goddess of Flowers and natural fertility.

(p. 25), 'To Mistress Margaret Hussey', John Skelton (1460–1529).

Isaphill, or Hypsipyle, was a Greek heroine who saved her father from death and helped him escape his enemies. She was noted as a mother and as a nurse. Euripides wrote a tragedy based on her life entitled *Hypsipyle*.

Coriander (Coriandrum sativum)

This herb was introduced into Britain by the Romans, and can be found growing wild in Essex and other parts of south-east England. It has a number of medical uses, and is included in the British Pharmacopoeia. It is a herb of protection for the household and also regarded as a herb of immortality. Bunches, tied together with ribbon, may be hung in the house to bring peace and protection.

In the line 'Good Cassander', Skelton was probably referring to Cassandra, the Trojan prophetess and twin sister of Helen of Troy, who warned King Agamemnon of his approaching death. Apollo gave Cassandra the art of prophecy, but because she defied him, he arranged that no one would believe her prophecies.

(p. 26), 'A Song of Yarrow', J. B. Selkirk (1832?–1904).
Most shrines to the Goddess were associated with springs, wells, lakes and the sea. It was believed that water (feminine) gave birth to spirit (masculine). It was therefore connected with the mother, creation, fertility and love. Without water, it was thought that even the psychic realm would suffer. Tantric scriptures mention the 'Mother of Creation' and a 'holy female river', and in the Middle Ages philosophers and magicians said that souls were born of the earth and the water. See the note on 'The Holy Well' (p. 288), regarding holy wells.

(p. 29), 'All That's Past', Walter de la Mare (1873–1956).
Not only does this poem refer directly to the pre-Christian Eden, it speaks of the power and cyclical forces of nature.

Amaranth (Amaranthus hypochondriacus)
This is also called Love-lies-bleeding, Red Cockscomb and Velvet Flower. It was sacred to Artemis, and used to decorate tombs and images of the gods because it is a symbol of immortality. It is an astringent and has a number of medical uses.

Love and the Goddess

(p. 30), 'You Meaner Beauties', Sir Henry Wotton (1568–1639). From the *Reliquiae Wottonianae*, 1651.

(p. 31), [My Beauty Named], Thomas Campion (1567–1620).
From his *Third Book of Aires* (c. 1617).

(p. 31), [The Chain], Francis Pilinton (fl. 1605–1624).
From his *First Set of Madrigals*, 1613.

Gold is commonly regarded as the metal of the sun, as silver is that of the moon. Gold, to the medieval mind, was the king of all metals, partly because of its sun-quality and partly because it was impervious to acids and therefore regarded as incorruptible. Thus gold was used for ceremonial ornaments, such as crowns, necklets proclaiming social position and, of course, wedding bands.

Pearls are, understandably, associated with the sea and therefore with the Moon Goddess who rules the tides. In various mythologies pearls are also associated with a Goddess figure, being formed of her tears.

The combination of gold and pearls on a garment therefore symbolizes the union of God and Goddess.

(p. 32), 'To Julia, The Flaminica Dialis, or Queen-Priest', Robert Herrick (1591–1674).

Inarculum is a twig of the pomegranate tree, which, Herrick says, the Queen Priest wore during sacrifices. Herrick has taken a liberty here, for the Flamen Dialis were male, being the special priests of ancient Rome who performed the daily sacrifices. The Flamen Dialis wore conical hats made of white leather, and if their hats fell off during sacrifices they were forced to resign. They were prohibited from wearing anything resembling a chain, and from touching dead bodies or anything unclean. They were, however, permitted to keep certain parts of the sacrificed animals. The Flamen Dialis were not taxed and they were exempt from the military.

Flowers, fire and wine were all involved in Goddess worship. Flowers, the symbol of fertility, contained the 'fruit of life', and Flora, the Goddess of Spring, was also Goddess of the Flowers. Incense was burned at altars as a sacrifice to the Goddess and it was also thought to carry prayers to the spirits. Fires played an important part in worship. Candlelight aided concentration and bonfires summoned power. Ashes from the sacred Hallowe'en and Midsummer fires were thought to have special powers of germination and were powerful charms. Ashes from these fires were mixed with seeds at sowing, and were also spread over crops to encourage further growth. Wine was thought to contain the essence of life, and sacrifices to the Goddess and offerings of wine were left at her altars. For more on sacrifice see the note on 'The Smell of the Sacrifice' (p. 266).

(p. 32), 'Like the Idalian Queen', William Drummond of Hawthornden (1585–1649).

Idalian refers to Idalium in Cyprus, a city sacred to Venus.

(p. 33), 'To Venus', John Fletcher (1579–1625).
From *The Mad Lover.*

This poem is an invocation to the Goddess. Invocations were often accompanied by offerings, sometimes of food and wine. The cave of the famous Mother Shipton in Yorkshire was positively festooned with gifts at one point in its history.

Forms of the God

(p. 34), 'Tom's Angel', Walter de la Mare (1873–1956).

(p. 35), 'Great God Pan', John Fletcher (1579–1625).
From *The Faithful Shepherdess*, 1609–10.

Pan, the Horned God, was one of the oldest Gods in Greece. He was said to have mated with the Great Goddess, and was God of the flocks and shepherds, and King of the Satyrs. Pan was accredited with the invention of the shepherd's flute; he led the nymphs' dances and amused himself with the chase; and because he often startled travellers, sudden fear or 'panic' is attributed to him.

With the advent of the Church, satyrs became 'demons' and Satan was given Pan's horns and cloven hooves. In his *Letters on Demonology and Witchcraft*, Sir Walter Scott says:

> It is not the least curious circumstance that from this silvan deity the modern nations of Europe have borrowed the degrading and unsuitable emblems of the goat's visage and form, the horns, hoofs, and tail, with which they have depicted the author of evil when it pleased him to show himself on earth. So that the alteration of a single word would render Pope's well-known line more truly adapted to the fact, should we venture to read –
> 'And Pan to *Satan* lends his heathen horn.'

The round dance is an old witch dance that imitates the movement of the stars and represents the wheel of life and the seasons. It is a dance of worship and is intended to raise power, and often has a hypnotic effect. The witches dance around their coven leader who directs the energy upwards in a 'cone of power', or they dance around a tree, a sacred stone or a bonfire. These dances united the witches with nature and summoned power for prayers, invocations and spells.

(p. 36), 'Hymn of Pan', P. B. Shelley (1792–1822).

The Greek Sun God, Apollo, was said to possess the Goddess's powers of healing, magic and prophecy. Among his other attributes, he was the God of Music and leader of the Muses. He has also been credited with the invention of the flute and lyre, and was known as the protector of flocks and cattle.

In the music contest between Apollo and Pan, the judge was Tmolus, the God of Mt Tmolus in Lydia.

Peneus is the main river in Thessaly that runs between Mt Olympus and Mt Ossa; Pelion (or Pelios) is a mountain range in Thessaly, and Maenalus a mountain range in Arcadia, where Pan was said to live.

The Sileni (Satyrs) and Fauns were woodland deities associated with, and resembling their King, Pan. The Sylvans were deities of the fields and woods, also identified with Pan. The Nymphs were mortal (albeit long-living) female divinities of great beauty who possessed the gift of prophecy, and the love of music and dance. They had different classes and were the representatives of nature. Among others, there were: the Nymphs of fresh water (Naiads), the Nymphs of the ocean (Oceanides), the Nymphs of mountains and grottoes (Oreads) and the Nymphs of trees (Dryads) who were said to die when the trees they inhabited died.

(p. 37), 'The Satyrs' Dance', Thomas Ravenscroft (1590–1633).

This song is from Ravenscroft's *Brief Discourse on the true use of Charact'ring the Degrees*, 1614. The Satyrs are performing a round dance as they sing. For the ring dance, see the note on 'Great God Pan' (p. 264).

(p. 37), 'Pan's Anniversary or The Shepherds' Holiday', Hymns 1 and 2, Ben Jonson (1572–1637).

This is an excerpt from the masque *Pan's Anniversary or The Shepherd's Holiday*, which was performed before King James's court in 1620.

For notes on Naiads and Dryads see the note on '*Hymn of Pan*' above).

(p. 39), 'Pan's Anniversary' or 'The Shepherds' Holiday', The Nymphs' Songs, Ben Jonson (1572–1637).

Extracted from the masque. 'Day's-eyes' are daisies, and 'Lips of cows' are wild cowslips.

(p. 39), 'A Hymn in Praise of Neptune', Thomas Campion (1567–1620).

From *Gesta Graiorium: Gray's Inn Masque*, 1594.

(p. 40), 'The Smell of the Sacrifice', Robert Herrick (1591–1674).
Males, human or animal, were thought to be expendable, and on the earliest altars, it was male blood that was shed. The victim's blood was intended to imitate female (life-giving) blood. Sacrifices were, however, looked upon as a god or king, and the rule was that 'whatever is killed becomes father'. Later, when human sacrifice was no longer acceptable, animals took their place. Of the animals, it was usually only the blood that was 'left for the gods' and the other parts were eaten.

11 Witches and Witchcraft

Flying and Bewitching

(p. 43), 'The Hagg', Robert Herrick (1591–1674).
It was believed that witches anointed their brooms with a flying ointment, hence 'greased staff'. Included in the recipes and concoctions for flying ointment were various hallucinogenic herbs which produced vivid dreams and erotic sensations. Contrary to some beliefs, bats' tongues, lizards' legs and baby fat were probably not used at all. Instead, they were probably listed in place of the true ingredients to keep the recipe secret. In fact, many herbs that do produce these effects are extremely poisonous if not used properly. See Doreen Valiente, *An ABC of Witchcraft Past and Present*, (1973).

(p. 44), 'The Witch o' Fife', James Hogg (1770–1835).
A bandalet, or bandelet, is a little band, fillet or string.

(p. 44), 'The Hag', Robert Herrick (1591–1674).
See the next note.

(p. 45), 'The Ride-By-Nights', Walter de la Mare (1873–1956).
Broomsticks were phallic symbols and it is said that witches represented copulation by straddling them. The notion that witches fly on broomsticks was derived, in part, from an old custom of leaping about in fields on a pole to incite the corn to grow taller.

Other flying implements included bits of straw, sheaves of corn, beans and, as in 'The Hag', pieces of bramble.

See the notes on [Green Brooms] (p. 299) and on 'Green Besoms' (p. 299).

(p. 46), 'Witch's Broomstick Spell', Isobel Gowdie (d. 1662).

This rhyme was recited by Isobel Gowdie at one of her many voluntary confessions during her trial for witchcraft in Scotland in 1662. Of the rhyme Gowdie said: 'When we would ride, we take windle-straws, or bean stalks, and put them betwixt our foot, and say [the rhyme] thrice. And immediately we fly away wherever we would.'

Some say that Gowdie was a young and deluded farmer's wife and others that she was a raving old woman, but it is agreed that of all the confessions hers were the most imaginative. In fact, hers was the longest and most detailed witch trial in Britain. Although there is no court record of her execution, it is believed that after her trial she was hanged first and then burned.

(p. 46), [Witch Song], Anonymous.

It is possible that this is a spell to cause pregnancy.

Sir Walter Scott says that this type of witch tune was popular at witch trials during King James's time, and in his *Letters on Demonology and Witchcraft* he gives a slightly different version.

(p. 46), 'Witch's Milking Charm', Anonymous.

It was believed that a cow would low in a peculiar manner if it was being milked invisibly by magic. One way to prevent this was to bind a twig of rowan-tree with a scarlet thread and place it across the threshold of the barn. See the notes on 'Against Witches' and [The Protection] (p. 273).

(p. 47), 'The Witches' Cauldron', William Shakespeare (1564–1616).

From *Macbeth.*

The cauldron appears in many varieties of the Old Religion in Europe. It was, of course, the three-legged iron cooking-pot that had many uses in the home, and was, indeed, apart from the roasting spit, almost the only means of cooking food. It was seen as a means of transformation, for it changed the inedible into the edible; it was a life-giver. Every important element in the rural economy took on religious significance, and in a particular fashion. Every deer or hare was an aspect of the Hare spirit or Deer spirit, of the Great Hare, the Great Deer. So it was with the cauldron; it was an aspect of the Great Cauldron of the Gods, or, sometimes, of the fairy folk.

In 1832 the *Gentleman's Magazine* reported on one such cauldron as follows:

> In the vestry of Frensham Church, Surrey, hangs a huge cauldron, hammered out of a single piece of copper . . . Tradition reports it to have been brought from Borough Hill, about a mile hence; if any one went to borrow any thing, he might have it for a year or longer, provided he kept his word as to the return. On this hill lies a great stone, about six feet long: the party went to this stone, knocked at it, declared what was desired, and when they would return it; and a voice answered appointing a time when they would find the article wanted. This kettle, with the trivet, it is said, was so borrowed but not returned at the time fixed; and though afterwards carried, it would not be received, and all subsequent applications have been fruitless. Another tradition ascribes the place whence it was borrowed to have been the neighbouring cave, called Mother Ludlow's Hole.

The cauldron also derives importance from its round shape, for it resembles the swollen belly of pregnancy; it is therefore yet another symbol of the Goddess.

(p. 48), 'A Charm Song', Thomas Middleton (1580–1627).
This is taken from Middleton's *The Witch.*

A Firedrake was a fire-breathing dragon, and Puckey (or Puck) and Robin are names for leaders of the fairies.

Libbard is an archaic word meaning sleep or sleeper. Libbard's bane, therefore, is a poisoner or destroyer of sleep.

Redheaded women, especially those with very white skin, were considered likely to be witches. This belief was utilized in Christopher Fry's play, *The Lady's Not for Burning.* It is also worth noting that henna, used to redden the hair, skin and nails was used in India, Egypt and Greece by worshippers of Hecate. It was the sacred colour of the Goddess and important in her sacrificial rites. In the Middle Ages it was associated with witchcraft and women were arrested for its use. In fact, this notion continued as late as the sixteenth and seventeenth centuries, and any woman who altered her appearance was considered to be practising witchcraft and was, therefore, subject to arrest. An Act of Parliament of 1770, as cited in *The Magic of Herbs* by Mrs C. F. Lyell, states:

> That all women of whatever age, rank, profession or degree, whether virgin maid or widow, that shall from and after such Act impose upon, seduce and

> betray into matrimony any of His Majesty's subjects by means of scent, paints, cosmetics, washes, artificial teeth, false hair, Spanish wool (red wool used for painting the face), iron stays, hoops, high-heeled shoes or bolstered hips, shall incur the penalty of the law now in force against witchcraft and like misdemeanours, and that the marriage upon conviction shall stand null and void.

There is even an account of an arrest made as late as the 1800s because some henna was found in an Essex woman's house.

(p. 49), 'The Masque of Queens', 9th, 10th and 11th Hags, Ben Jonson (1572–1637).

This is an excerpt from *The Masque of Queens* which was 'Celebrated from the House of Fame, by the Queen of Great Britain with her ladies. At Whitehall, February 2, 1609.'

Regarding these songs, Jonson says: 'Hemlock, henbane, serpent-tongue, nightshade, martagon [Jonson's 'moonwort'], doronicum ['libbard's bane'], wolf 's bane are the common beneficial ingredients, remembered by Paracelsus, Porta, Agrippa and others; which I make her to have gathered, as about a castle, church, or some such vast building, kept by dogs, among ruins and wild heaps.'

Jonson says that cat's brains were essential to witches' potions, and that the blacker the cat was, the more effective the potion. Black cats were, indeed, thought to possess special powers; the blood from their tails, for instance, was said to have medicinal properties. They had to be completely black; even one white hair disqualified them. Even though they figured in special rituals, they were never killed. See the note on [Black Cat] (p. 278).

Of toads, owls' eyes and bats' wings, Jonson states: 'These also, both by the confessions of witches and testimony of writers, are of principal use in their witchcraft.'

(p. 49), 'The Masque of Queens', Charms 4 and 5, Ben Jonson (1572–1637).

This is another excerpt from *The Masque of Queens*, 1609.

The Dame is the Hags' Chief, the Earth-Mother, and the blue drake is a dragon.

Burying sage, crossing sticks, and tossing ashes and flintstones into the air were rituals that were believed to be used by witches in order to create storms. It was also thought that they would seize egg shells and go out on them as boats, which also caused storms.

(p. 51), 'The Masque of Queens', Charms 7, 8 and 9, Ben Jonson (1572–1637).
Also an excerpt from *The Masque of Queens*, 1609.

> The whole throng of most wicked rabble sings the most abominable fescennine verses in honour of devils. One sings 'Har, har'; another, 'Devil, devil, dance hither, dance thither'; a third, 'Come frolic here, come frolic there'; still another, 'Sabbath, sabbath', etc. Nay, rather they rage and rave with shouts, hissing, shrieking and whistling, having received the powders or poisons which they scatter upon men and beasts.
>
> – Master Philip Ludwig Elich

Witches, For and Against

(p. 52), [The Night of Hallowe'en], Anonymous.
This is one of the many rhymes collected together under the title of 'Mother Goose', which are taken from several sources including Halliwell, Chambers, Sharp and Hazlitt.

Hallowe'en, originally the Celtic 'Samhain Eve' (Samhain meaning summer's end), is one of the four great witch sabbats. Samhain celebrated the end of summer and the coming of winter. The night of 31 October and the first week of November used to be observed with ritual bonfires on which the Celts symbolically burned the frustrations of the previous year.

Witches regarded Hallowe'en as a Festival of the Dead. Not only were the souls of the dead out and about this night, but so were goblins and spirits of every kind. Witches wore black capes or cloaks during their ceremonies in order to camouflage themselves in the dark, and they hung jack-o'-lanterns from poles to scare the curious away.

Beans were thought to contain spirits, and their flowers were associated with death. In Yorkshire it is said that 'Broad bean flowers contain the souls of the departed.' In Devonshire it is said, 'If in a row of beans, one should come up white instead of green, there will be a death in the family within a year.' To plant kidney beans on any day other than 3 May was tempting fate. The Japanese had a New Year's Eve custom that involved sprinkling beans around the house; this was said to appease the demons.

The Buckbean or Marsh Clover has been associated with the following rhyme:

Buckee, Buckee, biddy Bene,
Is the way now fair and clean?
Is the goose gone to nest
And the fox gone to rest?
Shall I come away?

This rhyme, given in Halliwell's *Popular Rhymes and Nursery Tales*, was said by children in Devon when they walked through a dark lane or passage. Buckee is a corruption of Puck, or Robin Goodfellow. 'Biddy' and 'Bene' are corruptions of the Anglo-Saxon words for pray or beseech, and for an entreaty respectively. Originally this rhyme was most probably said as twilight was thickening, before the supplicant went to a night-gathering. It is also probable that the questioner expected a sign in answer, a sound in the darkness, perhaps the hoot of an owl or the cry of a nightjar.

(p. 52), [Witches Gathering], Anonymous.
From a sixteenth-century burlesque poem, 'Montgomery's Flyting against Polwart'.

The Christian Church named 1 November All Hallows (or All Saints' Day) which meant that 31 October was renamed Hallowe'en, or as in the case of this poem, All-hallowe'en.

Bunwand, or bunewand, is an old Scottish name which meant anything that witches used to fly on.

(p. 52), [Ride a Cock-Horse], Mother Goose.
In *Faiths and Folklore of the British Isles*, William Hazlitt explains that in this witch rhyme, the 'fine lady' was Godiva, 'the Goddess', and that the cock-horse was her consort. There are many different versions of this rhyme: sometimes the fine lady is an old woman, and Banbury Cross is Coventry Cross, and the white horse a black horse.

The lady in one such version (c. 1790) has:

. . . a ring on her finger,
A bonnet of straw,
The strangest old woman,
That ever you saw.

Crossroads were sacred to Hecate, and also to the Roman Goddess Trivia. The horse is sacred to Demeter.

The children's game of 'riding a cock-horse' had its origin in Spain. The stick-horse was a cane with a horse head at the top that the Sufis brought to Spain in the early Middle Ages. The cane represented the fairy horse that they believed carried them to heaven and back. The result was that children used broomsticks to imitate the Sufis and their canes.

(p. 53), 'A Witch', William Barnes (1801–1886).
The notion of scratching or pricking someone to determine if they were a witch was one of many tests used during the witch trials in England and Scotland in the early 1600s. If the accused did not confess, they were stripped of their clothing and searched for 'the Devil's mark', or a teat. Third nipples, warts, moles, or anything remotely resembling a teat, were said to be used to suckle demons and were an incontrovertible sign of guilt. Men were not excluded from these searches and Christina Hole, in *Witchcraft in England*, says that some men were reported to have confessed to suckling imps.

The Devil's mark was more difficult to locate, and women in particular were subject to careful examination. The Devil's mark was sometimes a red or blue spot about the size of a flea bite, which, when pricked with a pin determined guilt if it did not bleed. There are reports of women being repeatedly pricked if the original attempt did not draw blood. Sometimes larger pins and special witch-pricking tools, such as three-inch awls, were introduced if those attempts failed.

Other witch tests included 'swimming' or 'ducking', which meant that the accused was bound hand and foot and thrown into fresh water. If the victims sank, they were innocent – if they floated, it meant that the water had rejected them and that they were witches. Less gruesome tests included reciting the Lord's Prayer faultlessly, and being weighed against the massive church Bible; the person was guilty of witchcraft if he or she weighed less than the Bible. These tests were forbidden in 1662, but the persecution of witches continued as late as the 1800s.

(p. 54), 'Another [Charme] to Bring in the Witch', Robert Herrick (1591–1674).

(p. 55), 'Another Charme for Stables', Robert Herrick (1591–1674).
Charms were often accompanied by the use of amulets or talismans. Stables were protected by horseshoes pinned with their arms upwards and this has been suggested as an image of the crescent moon of the Goddess. Hag-stones, which is

to say stones pierced through by a hole, were also used; these are still in use by some North American Indian Shamans.

(p. 55), 'Against Witches', Mother Goose.
A luggie is a wooden milk container, and a lammer is amber. Rowan-tree is mountain ash. Regarding the rowan-tree, Walter de la Mare says: 'So potent is the flower or berry or wood of the rowan or witchwood or quicken or whicken-tree or mountain ash against the wiles of the elf-folk, that dairymaids use it for cream-stirrers and cowherds for a switch.'

Also see the note on [Even Ash] (p. 280) regarding rowan-tree.

(p. 55), [The Protection], Mother Goose.
Another saying is:

Vervaine and dill
Hinder witches of their will.

Vervain and dill were used by the herbalists who were often termed witches. It is interesting to note that almost all the charms and symbols supposed to guard against witches are those which the witches themselves revered. Thus the horseshoes which symbolized the horned crescent of the Moon Goddess are both important to witches and used as a protection against them. The same applies to the rowan-tree. Saint Brigid's cross, which is pinned up on the threshold of the house to keep evil away, is, in fact, a sun-wheel, as also is the swastika that was used as a protective sign upon church bells. Witches are supposed to be unable to cross water, and yet the Old Religion's holy places were most frequently streams or places where streams cross underground.

(p. 56), 'Charmes', Robert Herrick (1591–1674).

Witches at Work

(p. 57), 'Alison Gross', Anonymous.
The grass-green horn, was so coloured because green was the colour of the fairies and it was thought that anyone wearing green could easily be stolen away by fairies. Although green is considered unlucky in Britain, it is regarded as lucky in other European countries, and is associated with woodland spirits. It is thought

that witches, demons and bad luck of various kinds can be driven away by hanging green branches over the doorway.

For the significance of silver and of pearls, see the note on [The Chain] (p. 262).

Silk was regarded as magical for two reasons. Firstly it was spun from threads created by a 'worm' to make a cocoon in which 'transformation' took place. Secondly, silk, when rubbed, creates a great deal of static electricity and can indeed give off sparks. Silk is still used by followers of the Old Religion and by occultists to wrap up their symbolic objects and their tarot cards to prevent them being affected by surrounding influences. Silk, being expensive, was also associated with the wealth and dignity of royalty.

(p. 59), 'The Witch of Wokey', Dr Harrington, of Bath (fl. 1730–50).

This ballad was written in 1748, and was published together with other poems in *Euthemia, or the Power of Harmony*, 1756.

Percy describes Wokey-hole as:

> . . . a noted cavern in Somersetshire, which has given birth to as many wild fanciful stories as Sybil's Cave, in Italy. Through a very narrow entrance, it opens into a very large vault the roof whereof, either on account of its height, or the thickness of the gloom, cannot be discovered by the light of torches. It goes winding a great way under ground, is crost by a stream of very cold water, and is all horrid with broken pieces of rock: many of these are evident petrifications; which, on account of their singular forms, have given rise to the fables alluded to in this poem.

Many of the menhirs and standing stones in Britain have been regarded as people who have been turned to stone, sometimes for dancing in a circle on the sabbath, sometimes for other reasons. Those wells which, because of their limestone content, turned objects placed into them into what appeared to be stone were always regarded as holy and magical, Mother Shipton's cavern being a notable example.

(p. 61), 'The Lunatic Lover', Anonymous.

Lamia is a spirit which appears to men in the form of a woman, and she may be related to the Serpent Goddess, for, when not in human form, she is frequently perceived as a serpent. She has been identified by some authorities as Lilith, Adam's first wife, and also as Lamashtu, the Babylonian Mother of Gods, who was envisioned as a serpent with a woman's head. The Lamia is predatory and destroys those men who fall in love with her.

III *The Craft of Magic*

Auguries and Foretellings

(p. 65), [A Prayer to the Moon Goddess], Mother Goose.
Charms like this worked best if made on the new moon. This one involved placing a prayer book, upon which was put a key, a ring, a flower, a sprig of willow, a small heart-cake (possibly similar to that of the dumb-cake described in the note on [To Dream of a Future Husband] (p. 277)), a crust of bread and four playing cards (the ten of clubs, the nine of hearts, the ace of spades and the ace of diamonds) under one's pillow.

Another charm like this is as follows:

> All hail to the moon! all hail to thee!
> I prithee, good moon, declare to me
> This night who my husband must be!

(p. 65), [Spell for Babies], Mother Goose.

(p. 65), 'To Know Whom One Shall Marry', Mother Goose.
In order to perform this divination properly, the girl hoping to see her future husband had to go to a different town and knit a left garter around the stocking for her right leg. While she was knitting, she had to recite this rhyme and knit a stitch at every comma. She then went to bed without supper and was sure to dream of her husband to be.

According to some, this was done on the night of 20 January, St Agnes Eve, a day purported to be of great importance to marriage-minded girls. (Ironically, however, it is said that Agnes was sanctified after being burned for refusing to marry.)

In Chambers's *Popular Rhymes of Scotland* (1870) there is another version of this rhyme, which he says was recited on Hallowe'en. The girl performed a similar ritual and said:

This knot, this knot, this knot I knit,
To see the thing I ne'er saw yet –
To see my love in his array,
And what he walks in every day;
And what his occupation be,
This night I in my sleep may see.
And if my love be clad in green,
His love for me is well seen;
And if my love is clad in gray,
His love for me is far away;
But if my love be clad in blue,
His love for me is very true.

Once this was done, she placed the garter under her pillow, believing that her intended would appear in her dreams and that the colour of his clothes would attest to the quality of the marriage.

(p. 66), [For Everlasting Beauty], Mother Goose.
The hawthorn was thought to be a sacred tree, not only a purveyor of beauty; its blossoms were thought to foretell the coming winter:

Mony hawes,
Mony snaws.

According to Chambers, in his *Popular Rhymes of Scotland*, in Germany it is said:

When the hawthorn has too early hawes,
We shall still have many snaws.

To cut the blossoms or damage the tree in any way was thought to bring bad luck, but an offering, such as a rag tied to its branches brought good fortune.

Hawthorn trees were planted at crossroads where earth spirits were believed to meet, and cairns formed around these trees because funerals coming across them would stop to add a stone.

(p. 66), [Divination with Yarrow], Mother Goose.
To make this divination work, take a sprig of yarrow which has been picked on the new moon and place it under your pillow, but don't speak to anyone after picking the yarrow, or else the spell will be broken.

In France, yarrow is known as 'carpenter's herb'. It was felt that yarrow could protect toolsheds from thieves and that it should at all times be kept hanging in the shed for it also staunches bleeding.

For more on yarrow, see the note on 'The Yarrow' (p. 290).

Rosemary and thyme can also bring about a vision of a lover. Sprinkle them with water and put a sprig in each shoe. Place a shoe on each side of the bed, and recite:

> St Valentine, that's to lovers kind,
> Come ease the trouble of my mind,
> And send the man that loves me true
> To take the sprigs out of my shoe.

For the significance of rosemary and thyme, see the note on [The Tasks] (p. 312).

(p. 66), [To Dream of a Future Husband], Mother Goose.

The custom of the 'dumb-cake' involved two girls who, together, on Midsummer Eve, 23 June, would bake a cake in silence. Once they had broken it in half, they would put a piece of the cake under their pillows in the belief that they would dream of their future husbands.

(p. 67), [Beseeching the Mirror], Mother Goose.

Mirrored surfaces were said to reflect the soul. If a pond was disturbed, or a mirror broken, it was thought that one's soul was put in peril. The superstition regarding seven years' bad luck after breaking a mirror can be attributed to this belief.

In Scotland mirrors were covered after a death in the house because it was thought that ghosts were able to steal the soul from reflections.

Before mirrors were in common use, divination would be accomplished by using a black stone in a bowl of water or cauldron. Dark wells were used for divination also, and many of the Holy Wells and Pools had this function. From this derives the belief in the Wishing Well. For Holy Wells see the note on 'The Holy Well' (p. 288).

(p. 67), [Sign of Rain), Mother Goose.

Weather prognostications were numerous in the oral wisdom of the countryside. Most of these were based upon natural observation. When gulls fly inland and settle on the fields one may expect a storm off the coast, for example. When scarlet pimpernels close their petals rain is likely to be on the way. This crow rhyme is making the same kind of point.

(p. 67), [To See Your Beau], Mother Goose.

(p. 68), [To Get a Wish], Mother Goose.
Blue is the colour of the Sky Goddess, and is also associated with dream and sleep. When the flame of a candle burns blue, it is said that a spirit is present.

(p. 68), [Good Omens], Mother Goose.

(p. 68), [Magpie Omens], from E. W. Wright's Rustic Speech and Folklore, 1913.
Magpies were regarded as magical birds, even as tricksters, partly because in flight they flash both black and white, and are therefore creatures of the two worlds of night and day, and partly because they are, like jackdaws, great thieves and will steal any small brightly coloured object they find lying about.

Crows are magical also, partly because they, like ravens, can be tamed and become companions to man, and partly because they are, observably, most intelligent and cunning birds. Members of the *corvinus* family – raven, crow, chough, jackdaw – have all been regarded as magical; raven, perhaps because it has an ability to mimic human speech, being the most magical of all.

(p. 69), [Crow Omens], Mother Goose.
In Maine it is said:

> One crow sorrow,
> Two crows joy,
> Three crows a letter,
> Four crows a boy.

(p. 69), [Black Cat], Mother Goose.
Cats were sacred in Egypt, and the Egyptian Goddess, Bast, was in the form of a black cat. Since cats are nocturnal, they were associated with the moon, the Goddess Diana, and later with witches.

Cats have been thought to be witches' familiars, and were credited with supernatural powers, partly because they can see in the dark, and also because of the static electricity of their fur. Witches were said to transform themselves into cats, but it was believed that they could only do this nine times in their lives; from this came the notion that cats have nine lives.

Black cats in particular were thought to share a special affinity with witches; one reason for this is simply that black cats are difficult to see at night.

In Britain it was thought to be lucky to have a black cat enter your house or cross your path, whereas it was unlucky in the United States, Belgium and Spain. For more on black cats and witches, see the note on 'The Masque of Queens', 9th, 10th and 11th Hags (p. 269).

(p. 69), [Charms for Luck], Mother Goose.

If you wish to have good luck, wear the stones on these days.

Through the ages, much importance has been placed on the magical and healing properties of gem stones. Coral has been credited with repelling witchcraft and the evil eye. Rubies have been associated with the blood, and a sudden colour change in this stone is said to reflect the health of the wearer, as is the case with opals. Pearls were thought to resemble tears, and opals and pearls are said to be unlucky when used in engagement rings, partly because they are so fragile.

Besides being worn as jewellery, gem stones are used as amulets and talismans, and sometimes hung in pouches around the neck in order to cure ailments or correct domestic circumstances. For instance, lapis lazuli, a blue stone flecked with gold, when carried in a pouch is said to relieve tension and conflict within the family, the colour blue being associated with rest and relaxation, and gold with the warmth of the sun.

Turquoise is purported to act as a sexual stimulant, and any change in its colour is a warning of approaching danger.

The diamond is the hardest of all gem stones, and perhaps the most mystical. It has the ability to break up light into all colours of the spectrum, and it was believed that these colours symbolize the trapped potential and future success and luck of the wearer. For men, diamonds represent courage, and for women, pride. Legend has it that Alexander the Great wore diamonds on his campaigns, and it is said that powdered diamonds were used to poison princes and popes.

(p. 70), [Winning a Pin], Mother Goose.

Pins were first made in France in the fourteenth century. Brooches were thought to cure sickness, and there are many superstitions about pins in general.

If you:

> See a pin and pick it up,
> All the day you'll have good luck;
> See a pin and let it lay,
> Bad luck you'll have all the day!

Superstition has it that it is good luck to pick up a pin only if it is pointing towards you, that one should never lend a pin for it brings bad luck, and that pins should never be worn in wedding dresses. A pin placed in the churchyard gate after a funeral helps ward off evil, and a pin stuck into a mountain ash is a cure for warts. It is possible that this cure for warts may have originated from the ancient and widespread superstition of 'Nailing Evil'. Nailing Evil, which works on the same principle as knotting does, was thought to trap the illness or evil and prevent it from getting back to the afflicted. Women in Algeria hammered nails into sacred trees in order to alleviate illness, and in Persia a nail was knocked into a tree trunk after an aching tooth had been pressed against it; the belief was that the nail took the toothache with it.

It was also a common belief that in their ceremonies, witches thrust thorns or pins into pictures or waxen effigies of their enemies in order to cause them pain or death. It is also said that at one time, young women indulged in this practice to bring back unfaithful lovers. The idea was that the lover would return to the girl thinking that she was the cause of his pain.

(p. 70), [Four-Leaf Clover], Mother Goose.
The number four was sacred to the Pythagoreans and to them it represented completeness. It encompasses the four elements: earth, air, fire and water, and is thought to be the luckiest of the even numbers; hence four leaf-clover. Apparently, almost any sprig of clover can be used to bring luck:

> Find a two, put it in your shoe;
> Find a three, let it be;
> Find a four, put it over the door;
> Find a five, let it thrive.

(p. 70), [Even Ash], Mother Goose.
'Even ash' is a branch of ash with an even amount of leaves on it. Other 'even ash' rhymes are as follows:

> The even-ash leaf in my hand,
> The first I meet shall be my man.

The even-ash leaf in my glove,
The first I meet shall be my love.
The even-ash leaf in my bosom,
The first I meet shall be my husband.

The even-ash I double in three,
The first I meet my true love shall be;
If he be married let him pass by,
But if he be single let him draw nigh.

The mountain ash (also called rowan-wood) was said to be connected with lightning, fire and clouds. Its wood was used to cure warts, pimples and ruptures, and was believed to possess the qualities of an aphrodisiac. Ash was used as a love charm, in part, because it is said that the dried flower, when held upside-down, looks like two people lying together in a curtained bed.

Ash wood was apparently used by witches to construct the figures they stuck pins into (see the note on [Winning a Pin] (p. 279) for wax figures), and it was especially good to have a coffin made of mountain ash.

(p. 71), [Bad Luck], Mother Goose.
The robin, commonly called Robin Redbreast in the British Isles, is regarded as sacred in Christian tradition because it is supposed that it gained its red breast by attempting to pull the thorns out of the crown of Jesus on the cross. It is also believed that, together with the wren, it will cover the bodies of unburied corpses with leaves and moss. The robin is very much in evidence in the winter months, when it appears even more vivid because of the lack of leaves and because of the snow. It was therefore associated with the God who is pre-eminent in the winter, one of whose names is Robin Goodfellow.

The wren is the only bird in the British Isles to be killed in an annual ritual. This is a mid-winter festival. In the Isle of Man it was performed at Christmas. At midnight on Christmas Eve the wren hunt would begin, and when the wren had been caught and killed it would be fastened to a pole and carried round in procession to every house, the celebrants chanting:

We hunted the wren for Robin the Bobbin,
We hunted the wren for Jack of the Can,
We hunted the wren for Robin the Bobbin,
We hunted the wren for everyone.

When all the houses had been visited, and money collected, the wren was placed on a bier and the procession moved to the churchyard where it was solemnly buried and dirges were sung over the grave. The celebration of Christmas itself then began.

In Ireland a similar ceremony took place on 26 December, St Stephen's Day, also called Wrenning Day, and Christian writers have suggested that the wren was stoned to death in memory of the martyrdom of Saint Stephen. This seems unlikely for the wren is a small bird and it would be difficult to stone it; also the Manx version clearly indicates an earlier pagan significance.

This pagan element is shown even more strongly in a Pembrokeshire custom of carrying a wren called 'The King' around in a glass box, decorated with a wheel hung with variously coloured ribbons, to every household. This took place on the Twelfth Day of Christmas. The hunting of the wren also took place in France on Christmas Eve.

The Welsh decorated wheel provides the clue to the wren's significance. The wheel represents the turning wheel of the year and the ribbons the rays of the sun. The wren is therefore the representative of the Sun God, who, at mid-winter, must be reborn in order to turn the wheel towards spring. Hence also the Yule Log and other fire festivals of mid-winter.

In the Manx version Robin the Bobbin was probably a weaver, for a bobbin is used in weaving, and Jack the Can would be a tapster, can being a name for a cup of metal or of wood. These two are therefore representative of the people as a whole.

Swallows are regarded as sacred because they are friends to man and nest in the eaves of houses and barns. They are associated with temples also; Shakespeare refers to 'the temple-haunting martlet'. To offend any bird with magical or sacred qualities is to bring evil upon oneself.

Spells

(p. 72), [Windmill Spell], Mother Goose.

(p. 72), [Spell of Power], Mother Goose.

(p. 73), [Spell against Warts at the New Moon], Mother Goose.
Cures for warts are almost countless. Here are just a few:

It has been said that certain people possessing supernatural powers can cure warts simply by being told how many warts the afflicted person has, and the warts disappear.

Snails are used in some wart cures. One involves rubbing a large black snail over the wart and then hanging it on a thorn; if this is done nine nights in a row, the wart will disappear.

A spell involving snails goes:

> Wart, wart on the snail's black back,
> Go away soon and never come back.

The snail was then hung over a bramble and pierced with as many thorns as there were warts to be cured.

Warts were said to vanish if one stole a piece of meat, rubbed the wart with it, and then buried the meat. The idea was that the warts would disappear as the meat decayed.

In Lancashire, a string was tied with as many knots as the afflicted had warts. Then the knots were touched to the warts, and the string buried. As the string rotted, the warts disappeared.

The Celts also believed, however, that warts are lucky in some instances:

> Wart on palm, luck to lad,
> Wart on instep, luck to lass.

(p. 73), [Ash Tree as a Cure for Warts], Mother Goose.
See the previous note. (For healing properties of ash, see the note on [Even Ash] (p. 280).)

(p. 73), [Bathe in Dew for Beauty), Mother Goose.
A very old rule for beauty is washing in the morning dew, especially on May Day.

(p. 74), [Spell for Marriage], Mother Goose.
The custom was for young girls to recite this charm while sowing hemp-seed. This was done on Hallowe'en, and was designed to bring about an early marriage. Another love charm that was recited on Hallowe'en is:

> Twine, twine, and intertwine,
> Let my love be wholly mine.
> If his heart be kind and true,
> Deeper grows his rose's hue.

The girl was to take two roses and name one after herself, and the other after her lover and then twine them together while saying the rhyme.

(p. 74), [Spell for a Good Harvest], Mother Goose.
This charm was sung to the fruit trees during Rogation Days.

(p. 74), [Snail Spell], Mother Goose.
Halliwell has two versions of this spell:

Snail, snail, shoot out your horns;
Father and mother are dead;
Brother and sister are in the back yard,
Begging for barley bread.

Sneel, snaul,
Robbers are coming to pull down your wall;
Sneel, snaul,
Put out your horn,
Robbers are coming to steal your corn,
Coming at four o'clock in the morn.

In Scotland it was thought that the next day's weather would be good if the snail shot out its horns. Snails were also believed to be capable of tracing out the initials of a future lover if they were placed in ashes.

(p. 75), [Five Spells to Banish Rain], Mother Goose.
Rhymes with regard to the rain appear all over the world and there are many versions. In 1687 John Aubrey said: 'Little children have a custome when it raines to sing, or charme away the Raine; thus they all joine in a chorus and sing thus, viz.

Raine, raine, goe away,
Come againe a Saterday.

I have a conceit that this childish custome is of Great Antiquity yt it is derived from ye Gentiles.'

(p. 75), [Spell for a Shower], Mother Goose.

(p. 76), [Self-Blessing Spell], Mother Goose.
It is believed to be lucky, in most European countries, to meet only one magpie,

raven or crow. For magpie and crow omens, see the notes on [Magpie Omens] and [Crow Omens] (p. 278).

(p. 76), [Horse's Spell], Mother Goose.

(p. 76), [Milking Spell], Mother Goose.

(p. 77), [Spell to Make Butter], Mother Goose.
This spell was said three times.

(p. 77), 'Charm of the Churn', Anonymous.
This and other spells and invocations included in this book were translated from Gaelic and are collected in Alexander Carmichael's (1832–1912) *Carmina Gadelica.*

This spell is as repetitive as are the movements of the person turning the handle of the churn, and it moves steadily from envisaging the beginning of the butter-making process to its conclusion. Like many verbal spells or charms it has a hypnotic quality intended to make the person speaking or chanting the spell achieve a trance-like state of mind in which the power of the magic can be most effectively employed.

(p. 80), 'Charm for Rose', collected by Alexander Carmichael.
'The rose' is a disease which affects cows.

(p. 81), 'Summoning Spell for a Fish', Jeni Couzyn (1942–).

(p. 82), 'Spell to Bring Lost Creatures Home', Kathleen Raine (1908–).

(p. 83), 'Fath-Fith', collected by Alexander Carmichael.
Fath-fith, the magic power of invisibility and transformation, was of particular use to travellers, warriors and hunters. It was voluntary or involuntary, and enabled or caused men to turn into horses, bulls or stags, and women into cats, hares or hinds.

Witches, members of the Old Religion, were credited with being able to change their shapes and also to change the shapes of others, transforming themselves into, most frequently, hares and deer, and turning their opponents into frogs or toads. There are many stories and poems involving these transformations.

> I shall go into a hare
> With sorrow and sighing and mickle care,
> And I shall go in the Devil's name
> Aye, till I come home again.

Recited by Isobel Gowdie at her trial for witchcraft in 1662 (see the note on 'Witch's Broomstick Spell' (p. 267)).

In a community partially or wholly dependent upon hunting for its source of food and clothing it has always been an axiom that the good hunter learns to think like his quarry, to almost 'become' the quarry. Indeed in North American Indian lore there are spells which involve the spell-maker in dressing up as the quarry; sometimes the hunter too will wear the skins of the creatures he is hunting. The witches, or shamans, were also practised in hypnotism. They would use it in teaching their pupils what it felt like to be a woodland creature, and 'transform' them just as stage hypnotists 'transform' cooperative members of their audience. Hypnotism was also used in healing. Someone afflicted with a lame leg might well be 'changed' into a running and leaping hare and made to exercise muscles without pain. Psychosomatic disorders would be cured by psychosomatic means.

Moreover, in dealing with his or her 'patients' the witch or shaman might well take on the shape of a creature of authority to give added force to his or her commands.

None of this is supernatural, but to the uninitiated it would appear so, and consequently witches who made use of hypnosis or self-hypnosis to 'change' themselves or others were regarded as having supernatural powers. It is interesting to note that in the rural religions of many countries there is always a 'trickster' figure who is able to change shape at will. Zeus had the ability to change shape; so does the raven of North-West Indian belief, and there are many others.

(p. 84), '*A Charme, or an Allay for Love*', *Robert Herrick (1591–1674)*.
Toads are covered in superstition and have long been associated with witchcraft. Like cats, toads were thought to be witches' familiars, even though it was also believed that witches turned their enemies into toads.

Generally, toads are regarded as good omens, because if a toad is near by so is a water source. A toad is said to bring good luck if it crosses the path of a couple on their wedding day. The heart of a toad, if carried by a thief, was said to prevent discovery. Another belief was that a toad stone (apparently found on the head), when worn in a ring, would indicate the presence of poison by changing colour or by 'sweating'. In sixteenth-century England, toads were associated with 'the evil one' and were burned in bonfires in order to ward off evil spirits.

(p. 84), 'The Bondman', Robert Herrick (1591–1674).

The ancients believed that a comet, then a portent of disaster, was a tendril of the Goddess's hair, and that the action of combing, and the binding and unbinding, of a woman's hair summoned the creative and destructive powers of nature. Later, the Christians thought that witches could cause storms, raise tempests and generally wreak havoc with the weather by letting their hair flow loosely. In seventeenth-century Scotland, this was still a well-known superstition, and Scottish women were prevented from combing their hair while their brothers were away at sea.

Fearing that women could command spirits by way of their unbound hair, St Paul determined that a woman's head must be covered in church; this is the reason women wear hats to church.

Christians also felt that a woman was rendered powerless if she had no hair, and it was for this reason that Christian nuns shaved their heads, and the Inquisitors shaved the heads of witches before torturing them. For more on hair, see the note on [Invocation to Fairies] (p. 307).

(p. 85), 'The Bracelet to Julia', Robert Herrick (1591–1697).

Lovers often exchanged locks of hair as proof of their devotion. The idea was that if betrayal occurred, the lock of hair could be used in a spell against the unfaithful lover. See the note on [Invocation to Fairies] (p. 307).

(p. 85), 'On Mistress S.W.', Thomas Flatman (1637–1688).

It is common to blame the messenger for the message he brings, as we know from the stories of bringers of ill-tidings being killed in ancient times. It is also common for small children to blame the furniture which has bruised them, and men have been known to curse the object upon which they have stubbed their toes. The healing, curing or cursing of the object which has done harm is, therefore, quite natural to mankind. Moreover in the case of a wound, the curing of the knife dissolves its malice and therefore prevents that malice from continuing to work and inflame the wound.

(p. 86), 'The Holy Well', John Fletcher (1579–1625).
From *The Faithful Shepherdess*, 1609–10.

Holy Wells played a large part in the Old Religion. Some were healing wells, because of the medicinal nature of their waters. Some were holy because they were surrounded by trees of a magical kind. Some were holy because they were dark and could be used for scrying. Water itself was also important for washing away ailments and evil and for renewal. The Christian rite of baptism derives from earlier customs. There are many stories of Gods and Goddesses rising from water, from the waves, as did Aphrodite.

(p. 87), 'A Conjuration to Electra', Robert Herrick (1591–1674).
The three forms of Hecate are: the virgin (or young woman), the mother (or mature woman) and the crone (or old wise woman, who is also the layer-out of the dead). Electra, the name meaning brilliant or shining, saved her brother's life after her mother, Clytemnestra, had murdered her father, Agamemnon. She then helped her brother, Orestes, to murder her mother. She is therefore the type of loyalty.

(p. 88), 'The Night-Piece, to Julia', Robert Herrick (1591–1674).

(p. 89), 'Love Charm', collected by Alexander Carmichael.

(p. 90), 'Love Spell', Kathleen Raine (1908–).

(p. 92), 'Summoning Spell for a Husband', Jeni Couzyn (1942–).

(p. 93), 'Spell to Protect Our Love', Jeni Couzyn (1942–).

(p. 94), 'Spell for Jealousy', Jeni Couzyn (1942—).

(p. 95), 'Spell to Release the Furious Old Woman', Jeni Couzyn (1942–).
There are many spells in which a sickness is taken from the sufferer and placed in something else. Sometimes the receiver is a creature, sometimes an inanimate object. The object is usually then destroyed or buried, and the creature either killed or driven away. The scapegoat that bears the sickness and evil of the tribe and is driven away to starve is the most familiar example of this custom.

(p. 96), 'Spell to Banish Fear', Jeni Couzyn (1942–).

(p. 96), 'Spell of Sleep', Kathleen Raine (1908–).

(p. 97), 'Charm of the Sprain', collected by Alexander Carmichael.
Here the spellmaker is not merely utilizing precedent; he or she is actually imitating the Goddess, with a sense that such imitation will cause her power to become available.

(p. 98), 'Charm for Chest Seizure', collected by Alexander Carmichael.
This spell begins with a self-hypnotic incantation which should produce a trance-like condition in which the power may be used. It is notable that the speaker does not ask for power to be given him or her; the power is there in the spellmaker once the trance has been achieved.

(p. 99), 'The Counting of the Stye', collected by Alexander Carmichael.
Once again the spell begins with an incantation. This is presented here in Christian terms. It is followed by a spell which makes use of numbers. The common numbering spell is a dwindling one, moving from ten to nine down to zero, and thus making the sickness dwindle as it proceeds. This spell uses the number technique differently, almost in an argumentative fashion.

(p. 100), 'Charm for the Evil Eye', collected by Alexander Carmichael.

Herb Magic

(p. 102), 'The Charm of the Figwort', collected by Alexander Carmichael.
'Scan' is Gaelic for herd, or swarm of bees. 'Foirinn' is Gaelic for land held in dispute and therefore watched. It can also mean help, remedy or strength.

In Uist it is said that the figwort was given as an offering to a spring on the island of Benbecula, between the islands of North and South Uist. A missionary named Torranan had blessed the spring for appearing to him when he was thirsty and named it 'Gamhnach' – or 'farrow cow' – which means 'a cow that does not carry a calf, but which gives milk of good quality and continuous but small in quantity'.

Carmichael says: 'On the mainland the figwort is known for its medicinal properties, and in the islands for its magical powers. On the mainland the leaf of the plant is applied to cuts and bruises, and the tuber to sores and tumours. In the islands the plant was placed on the cow fetter, under the milk boyne, and over the byre door to ensure milk in the cows.'

Figwort is a name for the Lesser Celandine (*ranunculus ficaria*). Culpeper tells us in his *Herbal*: 'It is certain by good experience that the decoction of the leaves and roots doth wonderfully help piles and haemorrhoids; also kernels by the ears and throat called the King's Evil, or any other hard wens or tumours.' Modern researchers have discovered that Culpeper was right and the herb has been recently included in the British Pharmacopoeia as a cure for piles.

(p. 103), 'The Tree-Entwining Ivy', collected by Alexander Carmichael.
Ivy is associated with the Roman God Bacchus, and it was not uncommon to see a piece of ivy hung near an inn. Ivy was said to protect houses from witchcraft, and if an ivy plant died on the wall of a house, the inhabitants would experience financial problems and lose the house. Ivy is used in a rare love divination practised solely by males: they are said to dream of love and marriage if they pick ten leaves of ivy on Hallowe'en, discard one of them and put the remaining nine leaves under their pillow. Ivy also cures whooping cough, skin diseases and cold symptoms.

(p. 103), 'The Yarrow', collected by Alexander Carmichael.
Yarrow has many country names, including Soldier's Woundwort, Knight's Milfoil, Bloodwort, Staunchweed, Devil's Nettle, Devil's Plaything and Old Man's Pepper. Tea made of yarrow is good for colds. It has been used to make snuff and to cure disorders as varied as toothache, baldness, ague and to heal wounds. Placed under one's pillow, the following should then be recited to receive a vision of a future wife or husband:

Thou pretty herb of Venus' tree,
Thy true name it is Yarrow;
Now who my bosom friend must be,
Pray tell thou me tomorrow.

This verse indicates clearly that at one time yarrow was thought to be sacred to the Goddess.

(p. 104), 'The Fairy Wort', collected by Alexander Carmichael.
The fairy wort is possibly yarrow (see the previous note).

(p. 104), 'The "Mothan"', collected by Alexander Carmichael.

Mothan, or Bog-violet, is put underneath pregnant women for a safe delivery; travellers use it to ensure safety; and it is sewn into women's bodices and under the left arm of men's vests. It is also used as a love-philtre.

The woman who is making up a love-philtre for a girl to use kneels on her left knee, picks nine roots of the mothan and knots them together into a ring. She then places it in the girl's mouth 'in the name of the King of the sun, and the moon, and of the stars, and in name of the Holy Three'. When the girl sees the man she wants, she puts the ring in her mouth and if he kisses her, he is 'henceforth her bondsman, bound to her everlastingly in cords infinitely finer than the gossamer net of the spider, and infinitely stronger than the adamant chain of the giant'.

Carmichael says that it is 'one of the most prized plants in the occult science of the people'.

There are over two hundred species of violet. The violet, in general, was used to comfort, calm and bring easy sleep. Violet garlands, according to Pliny, prevent headache and drunkenness. The violet is also a funeral flower, used to decorate graves, especially those of children. It is associated with the virtue of modesty. Its various species are used both in medicine and in cooking and perfumery.

(p. 105), 'St Columba's Plant', collected by Alexander Carmichael.

It is possible that St Columba's Plant is the same as, or related to St John's Plant; see the following note.

(p. 106), [The Nine Good Herbs], Anonymous.

These are the nine sacred herbs of Anglo-Saxon magic. Some are as follows:

Mugwort (Artemisia vulgaris) This is also named St John's Plant, Felon Herb and *Cingulum Sancti Johannis*, as John the Baptist supposedly wore a mugwort belt while in the wilderness. On St John's Eve a wreath of it was worn on the head as a protection from being possessed. It is supposed to preserve the traveller from exhaustion and protect him from sunstroke and wild animals. If gathered on St John's Eve it prevents misfortunes in the coming year. A pillow of mugwort brings visionary dreams. It is sacred to Diana.

Plantain (Plantago) There are no less than nine varieties of plantain, and all have medical uses. All are astringent, diuretic and refrigerant. The Anglo-

Saxons called the Common Plantain Waubroed and it was one of their nine sacred herbs. Culpeper's *Herbal* states that it is sacred to Venus, and good for curing wounds and abrasions.

Camomile or Chamomile (Anthemis) There are many chamomiles. In the Tudor period it was regarded as being sacred to the sun in Egypt and a remedy for all kinds of ague. It has many medical uses, and when planted in a garden protects neighbouring plants from both disease and insects.

Chervil (Myrrhis odorata) The chervil is also known as Sweet Cicely, Shepherd's Needle, British Myrrh, Anise and the Roman Plant. It is used as an antiseptic and aromatic, and is a carminative and expectorant. Its essence is supposedly aphrodisiac. It is a herb of immortality, enabling one to see beyond this life, and is particularly associated with the Goddess and with rituals involving the Cauldron of Cerridwen.

Fennel (Foeniculum vulgare) Fennel has many uses in both medicine and cooking. It is supposed to strengthen the eyesight. In the Middle Ages it was hung at the threshhold of the house to keep away evil spirits and witches. In Spain it was regularly cultivated as early as the tenth century. The Saxons used it in magical ceremonies.

Curses

(p. 109), [Curse on a Kitchen], Mother Goose.

(p. 109), [Curse on a Drunk], Mother Goose.

(p. 110), 'Another', Robert Herrick (1591–1674).

(p. 110), 'Charm against Wens', translated by G. *Storms in* Anglo-Saxon Magic.

(p. 111), 'The Curse', J. M. Synge (1871–1909).

This curse 'To a sister of an enemy of the author's who disapproved of "the Playboy"' was written in 1907, and on 25 March Synge wrote to Molly Algood: 'I have written a lovely curse on the "flighty one" but I'm half afraid to send it to you . . .' The person cursed, Molly's sister, Mrs Callender, did in fact fall ill shortly afterwards, which caused Synge some disquiet.

(p. 111), 'A Glass of Beer', James Stephens (1882–1950).

(p. 112), 'Thief', Robert Graves (1895–1985).

(p. 112), 'The Lament for O'Sullivan Beare', translated by Jeremiah Joseph Callanan (1795–1829).

(p. 114), 'A Curse on a Closed Gate', James H. Cousins (1873–1956).

(p. 115), [Curse of Nine], Anonymous.
Children say this when they want their friend's sweets.

A horse-lade is a horse's load. A curn is a grain, a corn, or a small quantity; an indefinite number.

This numbering spell proceeds from a small affliction to death itself. The chanting of such cumulative magic would probably be conducted in an increasingly loud voice or rising tone until the climax was reached.

(p. 116), [The Kelpy], Anonymous.
A kelpy is a bad-tempered and malicious spirit that takes the form of a horse.

This curse is said to have caused a prominent family, the Grahams of Morphie, to lose their fortune and their original male line. The belief is that the Lord of Morphie captured a Water-Kelpy, also known as a River-Horse, and made it carry stones to help him build his castle.

(p. 116), 'Highland Execration on the Commonwealth', Author unknown.
In *Popular Rhymes of Scotland* Chambers says that this curse was 'extracted from a manuscript usually styled *Constable's Cantus*, in the Advocates' Library.

The 'Rie' is the king. 'Gramaghee' seems to have been a Highland epithet for Cromwell, to whom it was not inappropriate, as the word signifies one who holds fast, as a vice or pair of forceps.'

Blessings

(p. 117), [A Charm to Protect One's Home], Mother Goose.
Robin Goodfellow was King of the Fairies. He was a woodland spirit from whom

Robin Hood was derived. Householders referred to fairies as 'Goodfellow' in order to keep on their good side.

(p. 117), [Sleep Blessing], Mother Goose.

(p. 118), 'The Blessing of the Parching', collected by Alexander Carmichael.
This blessing is used while drying ears of corn over a slow, smokeless fire.

(p. 118), 'The Beltane Blessing', collected by Alexander Carmichael.
While the trinity in this blessing may be regarded as Christian it could equally well be regarded as referring to the Triple Goddess. Ambiguities of this kind abound in the spells and charms of folk tradition.

Beltane, or Beltaine, is the Celtic name for the Festival held on the Eve of 1 May. See the notes on 'The May-Pole' and [Song for the First of May] (p. 302).

(p. 119), 'The Clipping Blessing', collected by Alexander Carmichael.
Bride, of course refers to Brigid, the Goddess. Michael was often substituted in Celtic charms for Lugh, the God of Light and the Sun.

(p. 120), [A Milking Prayer], collected by Alexander Carmichael.

(p. 120), 'Bless, O Chief of Generous Chiefs', collected by Alexander Carmichael.
Most often brownies are invisible, but when they are seen, they are either naked, or dressed in ragged brown clothes. Some have no noses, only nostrils, and some have no fingers or toes. They help out in the kitchen and are quick to anger and hurl dishes if they find that their chores have already been done by someone else. Brownies are particularly fond of brewing beer; they possess a sweet-tooth, and in Cornwall, they guard the beehives. They are easily insulted, but if not offended they will remain loyal to the household.

A banshee is a spirit that announces coming death. A ghoul is an evil spirit which preys upon human beings. Trolls are Scandinavian elves who live in caves, under bushes and trees, and under hills. They are said to know the secrets of the runes, are master smiths and, contrary to some stories, they are not ugly and malicious. Instead it is said that they are tall and thin and possess great wisdom.

(p. 121), 'Good Wish', collected by Alexander Carmichael.

(p. 122), 'Lob-Lie-by-The-Fire', Walter de la Mare (1873–1956).
Lob is a fairy house-dweller who lives by the hearth.

(p. 122), [The Crust], Robert Herrick (1591–1674).
There are many examples of pocket talismans in folklore. A raw potato in the pocket is supposed to keep away rheumatism for example, and cold iron in the pocket will ward off witches. One thinks of the herb moly which was used as a talisman by Ulysses, and cropped up again, inevitably, in James Joyce's book of that name.

(p. 123), 'The Wassaile', Robert Herrick (1591–1674).
A manchet is a small loaf of fine white bread.

Invocations and Incantations

(p. 125), 'The Love-Charm', John Fletcher (1579–1625).
From *The Humorous Lieutenant.*

Incantations are fundamentally songs and chants intended to alter the emotional and psychic condition of the people making them. Thus, before a magical ceremony of healing those involved might well perform an incantation referring to the healing powers of the Goddess.

Invocations differ from incantations in being a 'calling' up or down of spiritual powers. The spirit, or Goddess, invoked will be asked to provide power that the caller then can use.

(p. 125), 'Pray and Prosper', Robert Herrick (1591–1674).
This is a blessing of the fields. For incense, see the note on 'To Julia, the Flaminica Dialis', (p. 263).

(p. 126), 'To Larr', Robert Herrick (1591–1674).
The Lares, in Roman belief, were guardian spirits. The *Lares Familiares* took care of the household, and were worshipped at the hearth. They were also worshipped on important household occasions, such as weddings and births. They are associated with the Penates, the guardians of the *penus*, or store cupboard. At

family meals the Lares and Penates were given portions which were then thrown on the fire in the hearth. The name Larr is derived by Herrick from the word Lares, although the Romans never appear to have referred to a single member of the Lares in their writings.

Frankincense (Boswellia Thurifera)
Frankincense is most noted as an incense. Herodotus tells us that a thousand talents of frankincense were offered annually to the God Bel on his altar in Babylon. It has also been used in ceremonies devoted to Apollo, Demeter and Goddesses of the Moon. It is a herb of protection.

Garlic (Allium sativum)
There are many medical and culinary uses for garlic. It is a herb of protection, keeping away evil spirits. Sacred to Cybele, it was forbidden her votaries. In ancient Greece it was used in invocations to Hecate, in places where roads cross.

(p. 126), 'The Spell', Robert Herrick (1591–1674).
The Egyptians used salt in their embalming solutions, and the Roman pagans used it to bless their sacrifices. Salt was equated with iron and blood and it signified strength and kinship. Witches were said to hate it because of its strength and purity, and a pinch of salt over the left shoulder wards off demons.

The spittle of a fasting person was used for healing in the Middle Ages, and was regarded as magical. The custom of spitting on one's hands before a fight may have originated from the belief in the power of spittle.

(p. 127), [A Chant], Anonymous.
This appears to be simply an incantatory verse, carrying no meaning, but intended to arouse the speaker and the listener into an appropriate state of mind for working magic. It is possible that some of the words are corruptions of meaningful words, however. The fairies in Ireland are referred to as the Sidhe, pronounced shee (and thus spelt by J. M. Synge). Words ending in 'ar' were considered to be Moorish and therefore occult.

(p. 127), 'You Spotted Snakes with Double Tongue', William Shakespeare (1564–1616).
From A *Midsummer Night's Dream.*

(p. 128), 'Lucy Ashton's Song', Sir Walter Scott (1771–1832).
This song appears in Chapter III of *The Bride of Lammermoor*, from Scott's

Waverley novels. Lucy Ashton sings this song the morning after Lord Ravenswood's funeral.

(p. 128), 'The Invocation of the Graces', collected by Alexander Carmichael.

Emir was the wife of Cuchulainn, a Celtic hero. Darthula was the wife of Naois, and is the name of a type of affection. Many places in the Highlands are named after her. Maebh, the Queen of Connacht, wife of Ailill, was the cause of the 'cattle spoil of Cooley'. She is a type of bravery. Binne-bheul, or 'Mouth of melody', is a character in a Gaelic story, who caused animals to stand still when she sang.

(p. 130), 'God of the Moon, God of the Sun', collected by Alexander Carmichael.

This is an excellent illustration of the way in which the pre-Christian beliefs were modulated into Christian statements. The first line is clearly not Christian.

(p. 131), 'Queen of the Night', collected by Alexander Carmichael.

Clearly addressed to the Moon Goddess.

(p. 132), 'Benighted', Walter de la Mare (1873–1956).

(p. 132), 'Deirín Dé', translated by Thomas Kinsella (1928–).

Kinsella says: '. . . the nonsense refrain "deirín dé" probably had the original meaning of a last wisp of smoke, from the children's game where the players held burning sticks until one of them produced the last wisp of smoke'.

Lullabies are, of course, incantatory and hypnotic spells to bring sleep.

(p. 133), 'Greeting', Ella Young (1867–1956).

The four elements, earth, air, fire and water, are present in this poem.

(p. 133), [Invocation for Love], John Wilbye (1574–1638).

From his *Second Set of Madrigals*, 1609.

(p. 134), 'Invocation for Justice', collected by Alexander Carmichael.

Of this invocation, Carmichael says:

The litigant went at morning dawn to a place where three streams met. And as the rising sun gilded the mountain crests, the man placed his two palms edgeways together and filled them with water from the junction of the streams. Dipping his face into this improvised basin, he fervently repeated the prayer, after which he made his way to the court, feeling strong in the justice of his cause.

The bathing represents purification, the junction of three streams, the union of the Three Persons of Godhead, and the spreading of the morning sun, divine grace. The deer is symbolic of wariness, the horse of strength, the serpent of wisdom, and the king of dignity.

For shape changing see the note on 'Fath-Fith', (p. 285).

(p. 134), 'Incantation', Walter de la Mare (1873–1956).

(p. 135), 'Fragment', collected by Alexander Carmichael.
Although the word 'Triune' can be read as a Christian expression, it could equally easily be a reference to the triple Goddess.

IV *Country Folk and Feasts*

In the Green Wood

(p. 139), [Making the Fire], Mother Goose.
Trees were believed to be the homes of wood spirits, and there are many traditions and superstitions with regard to trees, including the following.

If children are passed through the branches of a maple tree, they will be assured of a long life. Often marriages were performed under oak trees, which were considered sacred. If a fir tree was struck by lightning, it was an omen of death for the land-owner. Hazel is used by water-diviners and if a twig is worn in the hair, and a wish made, the wish will come true. Nut-bearing trees such as walnut trees predict a hard winter if they produce a large crop. It was thought that the 'heart' of a willow tree would absorb the grief of a broken-hearted lover if he wore a sprig of willow.

(p. 140), 'In Sherwood', Robert Jones (fl. 1600–1611).
From *Musical Dream*, 1609.

For Robin Hood see the note on [A Charm to Protect One's Home] (p. 293).

(p. 141), [Green Brooms], Mother Goose.

Broom has been used medically from Anglo-Saxon times, and is included in the British Pharmacopoaeia. Its medieval name, *planta genista*, gave rise to the family name of Plantagenet as Geoffrey of Anjou wore a sprig of it in his helmet before a battle. It became an official emblem when Richard I included it on his Great Seal.

Margaret Murray claimed that the Plantagenets were devotees of the Old Religion, and certainly the green broom would be an appropriate emblem for a pagan family. The Christian Church did their best to vilify the symbol by saying that the Virgin Mary cursed the plant because, while fleeing from Herod, she trod upon broom pods which made a loud noise. Nevertheless in 1234 St Louis of France, on the day of his marriage, founded an order he called the Colle de Genet, and the order's collar combined the Fleur de Lys with the flower of the broom. The insignia continued to be greatly valued at least until the end of the fourteenth century, when Charles VI honoured his kinsmen with it.

The green broom is associated with magic, and the sweeping broom made from the plant is, of course, well known as an implement of witchcraft. If one wishes to prevent oneself from being followed by ghosts one should step over a broom or branch of broom. One marriage rite requires the bride and groom to jump back and forth over two branches of broom on the ground. In some gypsy marriages the bride is deflowered with a branch of broom, so that the hymenean blood will not contaminate her husband. The gypsies were, of course, makers and vendors of brooms, and the cry of the broom vendor may well have had some sexual implications. See the note on 'Green Besoms' (p. 300).

(p. 141), [A Soul-Cake], Mother Goose.

In England, children used to sing this song as they went from door to door on All Soul's Day.

(p. 142), 'Green Besoms', Mother Goose.

Brooms represented sexual union and fertility and figured in pagan marriage and birth rites. Pagan midwives, for instance, used to sweep the house of evil spirits after a birth, and an old wedding custom required that the bride and groom jump over a broom. Medieval European weddings were not recognized by the church, and marriages held in the old way were said to be 'by the broom'.

In Sussex, the Maypole used to have a broom on top of it, and in Yorkshire it was believed that if an unmarried woman stepped over a broom she'd end up becoming an unmarried mother. An unmarried mother was said to have 'jumped over the besom'. Besides being another name for broom, besom was a dialect term for 'a shameless and immoral female'.

It was considered unlucky to sweep the house in May, a superstition that may have originated from the pagan festivals held in May. A broomstick, if placed across the threshold, kept witches out of the house, and to burn a broom brought bad luck.

(p. 143), 'Hollin, Green Hollin', Anonymous.
Green wood was associated with liberty. For more on the colour green see the note on 'Alison Gross' (p. 273). 'Birk' means birch.

(p. 144), 'The Keeper', Anonymous.

(p. 145), 'Under the Greenwood Tree', Anonymous.
The word 'firk', in this instance, means a stroke or lash.

Love and Marriage

(p. 147), [Come, Lusty Ladies], Anonymous.
From *Christ Church* MS.I.5.49.

The gilliard, or galliard, was a popular sixteenth-century dance.

(p. 147), 'Song of the Cauld Lad of Hilton', Anonymous.
This rhyme has been attributed to an English brownie, the Cauld Lad of Hilton, who was said to help with the chores at Hilton Hall.

(p. 148), 'The Merry-ma-Tanzie', Anonymous.
In the seventeenth century the word 'jingo' was a part of the patter of a juggler or conjurer. The 'ring' is obviously a reference to dancing in a circle.

(p. 149), 'The Bride-Cake', Robert Herrick (1591–1674).

The Blacksmith

(p. 150), [Making Horseshoes], Mother Goose.
Here, the 'shoemaker' is a blacksmith.

Blacksmiths were regarded as shamans for they used all four elements in forging horseshoes, knives, sickles and rings, which were sacred articles. Theirs was the art of binding together, and in Gretna Green, on the border between England and Scotland, the village blacksmith performed legal marriages.

(p. 150), 'The Blacksmith's Song', Anonymous.

(p. 151), 'The Deathless Blacksmith', Sir William Watson (1858–1935).

(p. 152), 'Song of the Cyclops', Thomas Dekker (1572–1632).
From *London's Temple, or the Field of Happiness*, 1629.
Sparrowbills are shoemakers' nails.

Yule

(p. 154), 'Ceremonies for Christmasse', Robert Herrick (1591–1674).
Yule is the mid-winter festival. It occurs at the time of the winter solstice, when the sun is supposedly at the point of rebirth. Therefore this is a fire festival; the fires are intended to revive the sun by sympathetic magic.

(p. 155), [New Year], Mother Goose.

(p. 155), 'Saint Distaffs Day', Robert Herrick (1591–1674).

Twelfth Night

(p. 156), 'Twelfe Night, or King and Queene', Robert Herrick (1591–1674).
Twelfth Night was a time for feasting and revelry in the Middle Ages, and the custom probably derives from the Roman mid-winter feast of the Saturnalia.

Candlemas

(p. 158), 'Ceremony upon Candlemas Eve', Robert Herrick (1591–1674).
Candlemas, the Christian Festival, replaced the ancient feast of the Goddess Brigit, when the Goddess is welcomed into the home after her mid-winter

absence. On this day the Christians have a festival of light, at which time they relight all the church candles, which clearly continues the notion of the feast as being one in celebration of a rebirth or renewal.

Holly (Ilex aquifolium)

Holly was used by the Romans in celebration of their mid-winter Saturnalia; boughs of holly were sent to friends together with other gifts. The Druids also decorated their homes with holly during the winter months in order to provide a dwelling for woodland spirits. The Christians took over this custom as part of their Christmas celebrations, and the churches were decorated on Christmas Eve. Holly was called Christ's Thorn because it was said to have sprung up in Christ's footprints. In Turner's *Herbal* (1568) it is called the Holy Tree. The Christian Church did, however, recognize the pagan origin of these customs and Christians were forbidden to decorate their houses until the period of the Saturnalia was over.

For Christmas decorations see Rosemary in the note on [The Tasks] (p. 311).

In Christian tradition the greenery is supposed to be destroyed by burning on the twelfth day of Christmas. One connected belief is that if every piece of greenery is not removed before Candlemas there will be a death in the house. Candlemas is the feast of Brigid, the Great Goddess in Celtic tradition, and the day on which she returns to full powers after the winter in which her consort, the God, is regarded as being pre-eminent.

May

(p. 159), 'The May-Pole', Robert Herrick (1591–1674).

It was on May Eve when men and women danced around the Maypole. The accepted opinion of most authorities is that the Maypole itself was a phallic symbol and the ribbons that eminated from the centre symbolized the rays of the sun and the moon. Women danced around the Maypole moonwise (counter-clockwise), whereas men danced around it clockwise, or sunwise. The inter-twined ribbons that resulted signified the union of masculine (sun) and feminine (moon) powers.

(p. 159), [Song for the First of May], Mother Goose.

The month of May takes its name from the Greek goddess Maia, and the Romans regarded her as a Fire Goddess. She was the mother of Hermes, or Mercury, who was a phallic god. Thus Maia is the Goddess of sexual 'heat' or Desire. Her Festival was held on the first day of the month given her name. The Christians dedicated the month to Mary as the queen of flowers.

The month of May is presented as the time for love-making in almost numberless songs and stories.

(p. 160), 'The Milk-Maid's Life', Anonymous.
This is an excerpt from a song titled 'The Milk-Maid's Life'.

(p. 160), 'The Rural Dance about the Maypole', Anonymous.
From *Westminster Drollery, the Second Part*, 1672.

(p. 162), 'Corinna's Going a Maying', Robert Herrick (1591–1674).

(p. 164), 'It was a Lover and His Lass', William Shakespeare (1564–1616).
From As *You Like It.*

(p. 165), [The Month of May], Thomas Morley (1557–c. 1603).
From his *First Book of Ballets*, 1595.

(p. 166), [Sing Care Away], Thomas Morley (1557–c. 1603).
From *Madrigals to Four Voices*, 1600.

(p. 166), 'Padstow May Song: The Morning Song', Anonymous.
This song and the two following were sung during May Day celebrations in Padstow, Cornwall. The central figure in the Padstow rites was a wild horse, which signified male fertility.

(p. 168), 'Padstow May Song: The Day Song', Anonymous.
See the preceding note.

(p. 169), 'The Padstow Night Song (For May Day)', Anonymous.
See the note on 'Padstow May Song: The Morning Song'.

The white rose symbolizes the Virgin Goddess, and represents purity. The red rose symbolizes sexuality.

(p. 170), [Spring], Thomas Campion (1567–1620).
From his *Two Books of Airs*, c. 1613.

(p. 171), [Chloris Fresh as May], Thomas Weelkes (c. 1575–1623).
From *Ballets and Madrigals*, 1598.

(p. 171), 'The Masque of May', J. M. Synge (1871–1909).

Summer and Harvest

(p. 172), 'The Haymaker's Song', Anonymous.
Haymaking was long associated with love-making; indeed from the sixteenth to the nineteenth centuries the verb to mow meant to copulate. There are a number of bawdy songs that testify to the pleasures to be found among the hay ricks, or haycocks. Haymaking was a communal activity, as were other forms of harvesting in the Middle Ages, and it took place in Britain in June. At the close of July the yield of the whole harvest was celebrated at the feast of Lughnasad, the feast of Lugh the Celtic Sun God. This feast later became the Christian Lammas or loaf-mass, and the feast day, in the Roman Catholic church, of Saint Peter in Chains.

These feasts, termed sabbats by the witches, were times of celebration and re-dedication, and therefore also times for marriages or hand-fastings and betrothals. Moreover it was only on such communal occasions that people living far apart from each other would meet.

(p. 173), 'The Ripe and Bearded Barley', Anonymous.

(p. 175), [Harvest Time], Mother Goose.

(p. 175), 'Sir John Barleycorn', Anonymous.
The name John Barleycorn was used by Robert Burns in Tam o' Shanter, when praising malt liquor.

> Inspiring bold John Barleycorn
> What dangers thou canst make us scorn.

Barley according to some authorities is the oldest cultivated cereal, and the

Greeks worshipped a Barley Goddess at Eleusis. The Corn-Spirit, however, was also often regarded as male, as Zeus the partner of Demeter, the Corn-Goddess. According to *The Golden Bough* a representative of the Corn-Spirit, or Corn-God, was put to death at the harvest time to ensure that the corn would be 'reborn' in the spring. The death of Sir John Barleycorn is, therefore, a popular version of the death of the Corn God, which brings blessings and promises a secure future.

The word barleycorn is also a measurement of one third of an inch.

V *The World of Faery*

Song and Dance

(p. 179), 'The Fairies' Dance', Thomas Ravenscroft (1590–1633).

From his *Brief Discourse of the true use of Charact'ring the Degrees*, 1614.

Circles that form naturally in the grass were regarded as having magical properties and were termed 'fairy rings'. In Sussex these fairy rings are called 'hag tracks' and are believed, as the name implies, to be caused by witches dancing in the round. See the note on 'Great God Pan' (p. 264).

(p. 179), 'The Ruin', Walter de la Mare (1873–1956).

Fairies

Our general reliance upon methods of gathering and weighing evidence in a 'scientific' manner, and the widely held assumption that the only phenomena that can be adduced in evidence must be generally observable, has, over the centuries, led to a materialism that denies the existence of discarnate beings. Nevertheless, there is as much evidence for the existence of living creatures who are only occasionally visible to those with psychic ability as there is for ghosts who are now generally acknowledged to exist.

The discarnate beings of the folk lore of the British Isles are known by many names – fairies, pixies (or piskies), brownies, goblins, leprechauns, the little people and many more. In the folk lore of the Celtic parts of the British Isles they appear to have the gift of invisibility and of working magic; they are associated with places that have been centres of the Old Religion; they have powers of hypnotism and are able to change shapes. Emotionally they do not differ from the human race, and are capable of both generosity and vindictiveness; they are jealous of their chosen territories and boundaries; they celebrate seasonal feasts, especially the feast of Mayday or Beltaine.

Over the years these beings have become the subject of children's tales, just as much other lore has become thought of as nursery material. They have been explained, or explained away, in a number of ways, much as UFOs have been explained and denied.

In a religion which was not attached to the notion of a rigidly organized system of belief with a hierarchical attitude, the 'fairies' played an important part. (See Walter Yeeling Evans Wenz, *The Fairy-Faith in Celtic Countries* (1911, reissued 1966).)

Most fairies in Britain and Ireland were said to dress in green, which is associated with fairy mounds and vegetation, and makes a good camouflage. Some also wore red or blue caps with a feather in them.

In Scotland, fairies were thought to dress in brown and red, the dyes for their clothes coming from lichen. Others wore black and grey, and still others wore green kilts, coats and conical hats. Male fairies were thought to wear breeches and the females, linen and plaids. Some even wore stripes.

(p. 180), [The Fairy Ring], George Mason (fl. 1612–1649) and John Earsden (fl. 1618)

From Airs that were sung and played at Brougham Castle, Westmoreland in the King's Entertainment given by the Earl of Cumberland, 1618.

(p. 180), 'The Elves' Dance', Thomas Ravenscroft (1590–1633).

From his Brief Discourse of the true use of Charact'ring the Degrees, 1614.

(p. 181), [Song to the Spirit of the Wind], Sir Walter Scott (1771–1832).

This is an excerpt from *The Pirate*, Chapter XXVIII.

(p. 181), [Fairy Song], W. B. Yeats (1865–1939).

From *The Land of Heart's Desire.*

(p. 182), [Invocation to Fairies], Thomas Campion (1567–1620).

This invocation appears in Campion's *Third Book of Airs*, c. 1617.

Knots are used in many rituals and magical operations and there are many beliefs about them. When a woman is in labour, her hair must be let down and she should wear a seamless garment, so that there are no knots anywhere about her to keep the child tied within the womb. Similarly when a person is dying, there must be no knots of any kind about the place to restrain his or her free passage from this life into another. Sorcerers in Scandinavia bind up the winds by making knots in a cord, and when they wish to call up a wind they undo one or more knots according to how strong they wish the wind to be. Knots may be used in love magic to 'bind' a person's will within the cord and make him or her subject to one's will. Love-knots symbolize the binding together of two people, and knots of metal are made into 'eternity' rings to ensure fidelity. Sicknesses may be cured by 'tying' them into knotted cord and then burning the cord. A woman's hair, perhaps because it contains much static electricity, is regarded as containing a great deal of power, which is normally held in check by plaits or hair-combs; once these restrictions are removed the woman is given all her magical power. Coleridge clearly alluded to this when the maiden in his 'Kubla Khan' vision was described as having 'floating hair'. The same unknotted, long hair is characteristic of mermaids, who continually comb their hair, thus freeing it from any entanglement and ensuring the mermaids' power to enchant is at its most potent.

Faery Ways

(p. 183), [The Barge], Mother Goose.
It is possible that this rhyme is speaking of the way to Avalon, or Fairyland, since it was thought that it was reached by water.

(p. 183), 'The Shepherd's Calendar', John Clare (1793–1864).
From *The Shepherd's Calendar*.

(p. 185), [Little Lad], Mother Goose.
Among other things, fairies were said to eat honey, wine, bread, cow's milk and goat's milk. From these, they extracted the nourishment only and thus left the food behind. They were also believed to eat heather and poisonous mushrooms, and it was thought that if mortals entered Fairyland and consumed 'fairy food' they would be enchanted and would remain there forever.

(p. 185), [In Myrtle Arbours], Thomas Campion (1567–1620).
From Campion and Rosseter's *Book of Airs*, 1601.

Myrtle Flower (Iris Pseudacorus)
The myrtle flower, also called Yellow Flag, Yellow Iris, Jacob's Sword, Dragon Flower and Fleur de Luce, was used in purification ceremonies by the Romans, and therefore had a further name, *consecatrix.* It is the plant used for the heraldic emblem of the kings of France, and came to be known as Fleur de Lys. It has been regarded as an antidote to poison, and is used as a perfume.

Proserpine, or Persephone, was a Greek Goddess. She was the daughter of Zeus and Demeter. According to Homer, she was the wife of Hades, and the queen of Shades, ruler of the souls of the dead.

(p. 186), 'The Hosts of Faery', translated from Irish by Kuno Meyer (1858–1919).
This dates back to the twelfth century. 'Fidchell' is a game like chess, which fairies were fond of playing.

(p. 187), 'The Tale of the Wyf of Bathe', Geoffrey Chaucer (c. 1340–1400).
This is an excerpt from 'The Wife of Bath's Tale'.

(p. 188), Oberon's Feast', Robert Herrick (1591–1674).
An 'Emit' is an ant.

(p. 189), 'Queen Mab', P. B. Shelley (1792–1822).
Legend has it that this Celtic Goddess or Fairy Queen, whose name originally was 'Medhbh', meaning 'mead', fed all her consorts claret wine mixed with her menstrual blood. Claret, the traditional drink of kings, meant 'enlightenment' and was synonymous with blood, and Mab's claret was said to turn kings into gods.

(The Medieval Church believed that menstrual blood was the wine of witches and that they used it in their communions. Pliny felt that the touch of a menstruating woman could, among other things, cause wine to sour.)

(p. 190), 'The Fairies', Robert Herrick (1591–1674).
It was believed that fairies disliked unkempt houses and that they punished lazy housekeepers by pinching them. Fairies were also believed to sweep the house at midnight, grind meal in the mills and help with the dishes. In turn, and to keep on the good side of the fairies, the householder left a bowl of cream out for them

at night. If this was not done, it was said that the next day cheese would not curdle, butter would not come and ale wouldn't form a good head.

(p. 191), 'Now the Hungry Lion Roars', William Shakespeare (1564–1616).

From A *Midsummer Night's Dream.*

(p. 192), 'Over Hill, Over Dale', William Shakespeare (1564–1616)

From A *Midsummer Night's Dream.*

(p. 193), 'The Fairy Queen', author unknown. Percy informs us that this song is from an eight-volume book, The Mysteries of Love and Eloquence, *&c., London 1658.*

(p. 195), 'Song by Fairies', John Lyly (c. 1553–1606).

This song is from Lyly's play, *Endymion.*

(p. 195), 'Robin Good-Fellow'. Percy attributes this song to Ben Jonson (1572–1637), saying that it was likely intended for a masque.

For Robin Goodfellow, refer to the note on [A Charm to Protect One's Home], (p. 293).

Encounters

(p. 197), 'The Man Who Dreamed of Faeryland', W. B. Yeats (1865–1939).

This was written in 1893.

(p. 198), 'La Belle Dame Sans Merci', John Keats (1795–1821).

If a person were to fall asleep on a fairy mound, or fall asleep outside in twilight, it was said that they'd be stolen away by fairies.

In Scotland it was thought that if anyone should ever escape from Fairyland, they would be doomed to walk the moors in complete confusion, destined only to return to Fairyland.

Nursing mothers were also of great use to fairies because it was said that fairies couldn't nurse their own children, and if the mothers themselves weren't abducted, the fairies would exchange their children.

(p. 200), 'The Stolen Child', W. B. Yeats (1865–1939).
See the previous note.

(p. 202), 'The Wee Wee Man', Anonymous.
An effet is a newt. For the significance of green see the note on 'Alison Gross' (p. 273); note for gold, see the note on [The Chain] (p. 262). Fairy pipes are also called Celtic pipes, and Elfin pipes. They are very small pipes made of baked clay.

It is believed that crystal possesses magical properties. Rock crystal, wells, black stones and the like, were used in scrying to gain clairvoyance and for healing purposes.

(p. 203), 'The Elfin Knight', Anonymous.
'Eare' means to plough, 'bigg' to make and 'looff' is the palm of the hand.

In this ballad the elfin knight is requesting the maiden to make a seamless garment, that is to say, a garment without any knots. For another reference to a seamless garment see [The Tasks] (p. 311).

(p. 205), 'Lady Isabel and the Elf-Knight', Anonymous.
'Ban' means bound, and 'dag-durk' means dagger.

(p. 206), 'Thomas the Rhymer', Anonymous.
Thomas the Rhymer, or Thomas of Erceldoune, flourished in the fourteenth century. Erceldoune was the holy place of the Saxon Goddess Ercel. The river of blood has been interpreted as signifying the menstrual blood flow of the Goddess.

(p. 209), 'The Young Tamlane', Sir Walter Scott (1771–1832).
'Maik' means a match, 'eiry' means producing superstitious dread, 'erlish' or 'elritch' ghastly, 'esk' is a newt, 'coft' means bought and 'kane' means rent paid in kind.

(p. 218), [The Piper's Son], Mother Goose.
'Over the hills and far away' is a reference to the land of faerie or of eternal youth, which places Tom as a magical figure or shaman, who, like Orpheus, could use his music to charm and bewitch. He is also clearly related to the trickster god who occurs in many cultures – as Raven in North-west American Indian legend, as Loki in Scandinavia, as Anansi in West Africa, and so forth. His British counterpart is Robin Goodfellow.

(p. 219), 'The Elphin Nourice', Anonymous.

(p. 220), 'The Deserted Home', Anonymous, translated from the Irish by Kuno Meyer.

It is possible that this is from the eleventh century.

(p. 222), 'The Night Swans', Walter de la Mare (1873–1956).

The Fairies Farewell

(p. 224), 'The Fairies Farewell', Dr Richard Corbet (1582–1635).

VI Visions and Transformations

Love and Death

(p. 229), [The Tasks], Mother Goose.

Other versions of this begin with the line: 'As I was going to Scarborough fair . . .' As in 'The Elphin Knight' (see the note on p. 310), a request is being made for a seamless garment.

Parsley (Carum Petroselinum)

Parsley arrived in Britain from Sardinia in the sixteenth century. It is sacred to Persephone, and the Greeks used it in wreaths for the visitors of the Isthmian Games and for decorating tombs. It was believed that if parsley were thrown into a fish pond it would heal those fish that were sick. It is regarded as sacred to Aphrodite and should be gathered on a Friday when the moon is waxing. If given to a horse it will enable it to gallop faster and with greater safety.

Sage (Salivia)

Sage is now used primarily for cooking and as a condiment, but it also has many medical uses. Gerard's *Herbal* states: 'Sage is singularly good for the head and brain, it quickeneth the sinews, restoreth health to those that have the palsy, and taketh away shakey trembling of the members.' An anonymous charm of uncertain date runs:

> Sage make green the winter rain,
> Charm the demon from my brain.

It is sacred to the God, Consus, the God of Good Counsel.

Rosemary (Rosemarinus officinalis)
Rosemary is supposed to strengthen the memory, hence Ophelia's line in *Hamlet*: 'There's rosemary, that's for remembrance.' It is a symbol also of fidelity in love and was used as decoration at weddings and funerals, as well as in religious and magical rituals. It was used as a Christmas decoration along with bays, mistletoe, holly and ivy. It protects the household from witches and evil spirits, and if placed under the bed prevents bad dreams. In *Romeo and Juliet*, Friar Lawrence says:

> Dry up your tears, and stick your Rosemary
> On this fair corse.

Thyme (Thymus vulgaris)
Thyme has many culinary and medical uses. Like rosemary, it has been carried by the mourners at funerals and thrown upon the coffin. Thyme was one of the herbs that made up the bed of the Virgin Mary. According to Shakespeare and others it was a favourite of the fairies also, and girls used to wear springs of lavender, mint and thyme to bring them sweethearts. It is a herb of protection and used as an incense to keep away dangerous animals and other creatures.

(p. 230), 'The Youthful Quest', George Meredith (1828–1909).
Artemis/Diana is the Goddess of the Woods.

(p. 231), 'The Unquiet Grave', Anonymous.
There are many versions of this.

The theme of the return from the dead points to the belief that the dead are able to communicate with the living, especially at Hallowe'en (Samhain) when the veil between this world and the next is at its most permeable. The dead may visit us when there is a crisis which demands their attention, or when they are invoked. To what extent these returns are self-created hallucinations, vivid imaginings, and to what extent they are true apparitions must remain in doubt.

(p. 232), 'Fair Margaret and Sweet William', Anonymous.

This is an excerpt from the ballad 'Fair Margaret and Sweet William'.

See the previous note.

(p. 233), 'Song of the Murdered Child', Anonymous.

The belief in Reincarnation which was firmly held by followers of the Old Religion is often exemplified in song and verse and story by the changing of a dead person into another creature. This transformation occurs in a number of Greek myths, and is found in most cultures of the world. The spirit of a person, also, may 'enter into' a creature or an object, and there are many stories of people entering into trees, rocks and even household objects.

(p. 233), [Cock Robin], Mother Goose.

For Robin, see the note on [Bad Luck] (p. 281).

This has been regarded as a poem about the death of the god in autumn. He will be born again in the spring.

(p. 236), 'The Raven's Tomb', Walter de la Mare (1873–1956).

The yew tree was thought to guard the dead, and it was for this reason that yews were planted in churchyards. They have been known to live over nine hundred years, and yew wood was used in bows for hunting.

The Shape Changers

(p. 237), 'The Hare', Walter de la Mare (1873–1956).

See the note on 'Fath-Fith' (p. 285).

(p. 237), 'The Twa Magicians', Anonymous.

The smith is, of course, a shaman figure, and the lady a witch. Both therefore have the ability to change their shapes and this is one of many songs recording a shape-changing contest.

(p. 240), 'The Milk White Doe', translated from the French by Andrew Lang (1884–1912).

This was originally titled 'La Chasse'.

For animal transformations see the note on 'Fath-Fith' (p. 285).

(p. 242), 'Hares on the Mountains', Anonymous.

(p. 243), 'The Song of Wandering Aengus', W. B. Yeats (1856–1939).
Aengus is the Celtic God of Love.

(p. 244), 'The Loyal Lover', Anonymous.

(p. 245), 'Clerk Colvill', Anonymous.
This is an excerpt from 'Clerk Colvill'.

(p. 245), [London Bridge], Mother Goose.
All over the world there are stories about spirits interfering with construction sites. The opposing spirits were thought to dwell in nearby rivers, and there are reports of half-finished buildings being dismantled overnight, for which these spirits are credited.

In his notes to *Lay of the Last Minstrel*, Sir Walter Scott says:

> When the workmen were engaged in erecting the ancient church of Old Deer in Aberdeenshire, upon a small hill called Bissau, they were surprised to find that the work was impeded by supernatural obstacles. At length the Spirit of the River was heard to say:
>
> 'It is not here, it is not here,
> That ye shall build the church of Deer;
> But on Taptillery,
> Where many a corpse shall lie.'
>
> The site of the edifice was accordingly transferred to Taptillery, an eminence at some distance from the place where the building had been commenced.

There are many superstitions involving buildings and their construction, and at one time human sacrifice at these sites was common. When this became unacceptable, however, architects were said to lure an unsuspecting person to the site, measure their shadow and then 'bury' it.

Trickery

(p. 248), 'The Jolly Juggler', Anonymous.
From the fifteenth century.

The jolly juggler is another magician or shaman who is able to change his shape. The itinerant juggler in medieval times was often regarded as a magician because of the nature of his tricks. He also had the reputation, like the commercial traveller or pedlar and tinker of other folk stories, of being a ladies' man.

(p. 250), 'Sing Ovy, Sing Ivy', Anonymous.
The following fantastic and nonsensical verses are partly simply tall stories made for pure entertainment, and partly accounts of the magical feats possible to a shaman. The actual world has been challenged and conquered by the arts of the magician.

(p. 251), 'As I Set Off to Turkey', Anonymous.

(p. 251), 'As I was Going to Banbury', Anonymous.

(p. 252), [Under the Broom], Mother Goose.

(p. 253), 'Blow the Wind Whistling', Anonymous.

(p. 254), 'A Nursery Song', Anonymous.

(p. 255), [A Man of Words], Mother Goose.

Acknowledgements

For permission to include copyright items in this anthology, acknowledgement is made to the following copyright-holders:
Alexander Carmichael: to Scottish Academic Press for 'Charm for Chest Seizure', 'A Milking Prayer', 'Good Wish' and 'Queen of the Night' from *Carmina Gadelica*; Walter de la Mare: to the Literary Trustees of Walter de la Mare and the Society of Authors as their representative for 'Tom's Angel', 'The Ride-by-Nights', 'Lob-Lie-By-The-Fire', 'Benighted', 'Incantation', 'The Ruin', 'The Night-Swans' and 'The Hare'; Robert Graves: to A. P. Watt Limited on behalf of the Executors of the Estate of Robert Graves, and Oxford University Press, Inc., for 'Thief' from *Collected Poems 1975*, copyright © 1975 by Robert Graves; James Stephens: to the Society of Authors on behalf of the copyright owner, Mrs Iris Wise, and Macmillan Publishing Company, for 'A Glass of Beer' from *Collected Poems*, copyright 1918 by Macmillan Publishing Company, renewed 1946 by James Stephens; W. B. Yeats: to Macmillan Publishing Company for 'Faery Song', 'The Man Who Dreamed of Faeryland', 'The Stolen Child' and 'The Song of Wandering Aengus' from *The Poems of W. B. Yeats: A New Edition*, edited by Richard J. Finneran (New York: Macmillan, 1983); Ella Young: to Floris Books for 'Greeting' from *Celtic Wonder Tales*; Kathleen Raine: to the author for 'Spell of Sleep'; John Knight: to the author's estate and Margaret and Michael Seward Snow for 'Anima'; Thomas Kinsella: to the translator for the translation of 'Deirín Dé'.

Every effort has been made to trace copyright-holders. The editors and publishers would be pleased to hear from any copyright-holders not acknowledged.

Index of First Lines

Index

A selection of titles already published or in preparation

Weavers of Wisdom: Women Mystics of the Twentieth Century Anne Bancroft

Throughout history women have sought answers to eternal questions about existence and beyond – yet most gurus, philosophers and religious leaders have been men. Through exploring the teachings of fifteen women mystics – each with her own approach to what she calls 'the truth that goes beyond the ordinary' – Anne Bancroft gives a rare, cohesive and fascinating insight into the diversity of female approaches to mysticism.

Dynamics of the Unconscious: Seminars in Psychological Astrology Volume II Liz Greene and Howard Sasportas

The authors of *The Development of the Personality* team up again to show how the dynamics of depth psychology interact with your birth chart. They shed new light on the psychology and astrology of aggression and depression – the darker elements of the adult personality that we must confront if we are to grow to find the wisdom within.

The Myth of Eternal Return: Cosmos and History Mircea Eliade

'A luminous, profound, and extremely stimulating work . . . Eliade's thesis is that ancient man envisaged events not as constituting a linear, progressive history, but simply as so many creative repetitions of primordial archetypes . . . This is an essay which everyone interested in the history of religion and in the mentality of ancient man will have to read. It is difficult to speak too highly of it' – Theodore H. Gaster in *Review of Religion*

Karma and Destiny in the I Ching Guy Damian-Knight

This entirely original approach to the *I Ching*, achieved through mathematical rearrangement of the hexagrams, offers a new, more precise tool for self-understanding. Simple to use and yet profound, it gives the ancient Chinese classic a thoroughly contemporary relevance.

ARKANA – NEW-AGE BOOKS FOR MIND, BODY AND SPIRIT

A selection of titles already published or in preparation

Head Off Stress: Beyond the Bottom Line D. E. Harding

Learning to head off stress takes no time at all and is impossible to forget – all it requires is that we dare take a fresh look at ourselves. This infallible and revolutionary guide from the author of *On Having No Head* – whose work C. S. Lewis described as 'highest genius' – shows how.

Shiatzu: Japanese Finger Pressure for Energy, Sexual Vitality and Relief from Tension and Pain
Yukiko Irwin with James Wagenvoord

The product of 4000 years of Oriental medicine and philosophy, Shiatzu is a Japanese variant of the Chinese practice of acupuncture. Fingers, thumbs and palms are applied to the 657 pressure points that the Chinese penetrate with gold and silver needles, aiming to maintain health, increase vitality and promote well-being.

The Magus of Strovolos: The Extraordinary World of a Spiritual Healer Kyriacos C. Markides

This vivid account introduces us to the rich and intricate world of Daskalos, the Magus of Strovolos – a true healer who draws upon a seemingly limitless mixture of esoteric teachings, psychology, reincarnation, demonology, cosmology and mysticism, from both East and West.

'This is a really marvellous book . . . one of the most extraordinary accounts of a "magical" personality since Ouspensky's account of Gurdjieff' – Colin Wilson

Meetings With Remarkable Men G. I. Gurdjieff

All that we know of the early life of Gurdjieff – one of the great spiritual masters of this century – is contained within these colourful and profound tales of adventure. The men who influenced his formative years had no claim to fame in the conventional sense; what made them remarkable was the consuming desire they all shared to understand the deepest mysteries of life.

ARKANA – NEW-AGE BOOKS FOR MIND, BODY AND SPIRIT

A selection of titles already published or in preparation

The TM Technique Peter Russell

Through a process precisely opposite to that by which the body accumulates stress and tension, transcendental meditation works to produce a state of profound rest, with positive benefits for health, clarity of mind, creativity and personal stability. Peter Russell's book has become the key work for everyone requiring a complete mastery of TM.

The Development of the Personality: Seminars in Psychological Astrology Volume I Liz Greene and Howard Sasportas

Taking as a starting point their groundbreaking work on the cross-fertilization between astrology and psychology, Liz Greene and Howard Sasportas show how depth psychology works with the natal chart to illuminate the experiences and problems all of us encounter throughout the development of our individual identity, from childhood onwards.

Homage to the Sun: The Wisdom of the Magus of Strovolos
Kyriacos C. Markides

Homage to the Sun continues the adventure into the mysterious and extraordinary world of the spiritual teacher and healer Daskalos, the 'Magus of Strovolos'. The logical foundations of Daskalos' world of other dimensions are revealed to us – invisible masters, past-life memories and guardian angels, all explained by the Magus with great lucidity and scientific precision.

The Year I: Global Process Work Arnold Mindell

As we approach the end of the 20th century, we are on the verge of planetary extinction. Solving the planet's problems is literally a matter of life and death. Arnold Mindell shows how his famous and groundbreaking process-orientated psychology can be extended so that our own sense of global awareness can be developed and we – the whole community of earth's inhabitants – can comprehend the problems and work together towards solving them.

ARKANA – NEW-AGE BOOKS FOR MIND, BODY AND SPIRIT

A selection of titles already published or in preparation

Being Intimate: A Guide to Successful Relationships
John and Kris Amodeo

This invaluable guide aims to enrich one of the most important – yet often problematic – aspects of our lives: intimate relationships and friendships.

'A clear and practical guide to the realization and communication of authentic feelings, and thus an excellent pathway towards lasting intimacy and love' – George Leonard

The Brain Book Peter Russell

The essential handbook for brain users.

'A fascinating book – for everyone who is able to appreciate the human brain, which, as Russell says, is the most complex and most powerful information processor known to man. It is especially relevant for those who are called upon to read a great deal when time is limited, or who attend lectures or seminars and need to take notes' – *Nursing Times*

The Act of Creation Arthur Koestler

This second book in Koestler's classic trio of works on the human mind (which opened with *The Sleepwalkers* and concludes with *The Ghost in the Machine*) advances the theory that all creative activities – the conscious and unconscious processes underlying artistic originality, scientific discovery and comic inspiration – share a basic pattern, which Koestler expounds and explores with all his usual clarity and brilliance.

A Psychology With a Soul: Psychosynthesis in Evolutionary Context Jean Hardy

Psychosynthesis was developed between 1910 and the 1950s by Roberto Assagioli – an Italian psychiatrist who, like Jung, diverged from Freud in search of a more spiritually based understanding of human nature. Jean Hardy's account of this comprehensive approach to self-realization will be of great value to everyone concerned with personal integration and spiritual growth.

ARKANA – NEW-AGE BOOKS FOR MIND, BODY AND SPIRIT

A selection of titles already published or in preparation

Encyclopedia of the Unexplained
Edited by Richard Cavendish Consultant: J. B. Rhine

'Will probably be the definitive work of its kind for a long time to come' – *Prediction*

The ultimate guide to the unknown, the esoteric and the unproven: richly illustrated, with almost 450 clear and lively entries from Alchemy, the Black Box and Crowley to faculty X, Yoga and the Zodiac.

Buddhist Civilization in Tibet Tulku Thondup Rinpoche

Unique among works in English, *Buddhist Civilization in Tibet* provides an astonishing wealth of information on the various strands of Tibetan religion and literature in a single compact volume, focusing predominantly on the four major schools of Buddhism: Nyingma, Kagyud, Sakya and Gelug.

The Living Earth Manual of Feng-Shui Stephen Skinner

The ancient Chinese art of Feng-Shui – tracking the hidden energy flow which runs through the earth in order to derive maximum benefit from being in the right place at the right time – can be applied equally to the siting and layout of cities, houses, tombs and even flats and bedsits; and can be practised as successfully in the West as in the East with the aid of this accessible manual.

In Search of the Miraculous: Fragments of an Unknown Teaching P. D. Ouspensky

Ouspensky's renowned, vivid and characteristically honest account of his work with Gurdjieff from 1915–18.

'Undoubtedly a *tour de force*. To put entirely new and very complex cosmology and psychology into fewer than 400 pages, and to do this with a simplicity and vividness that makes the book accessible to any educated reader, is in itself something of an achievement' – *The Times Literary Supplement*

ARKANA – NEW-AGE BOOKS FOR MIND, BODY AND SPIRIT

A selection of titles already published or in preparation

The I Ching and You Diana ffarington Hook

A clear, accessible, step-by-step guide to the *I Ching* – the classic book of Chinese wisdom. Ideal for the reader seeking a quick guide to its fundamental principles, and the often highly subtle shades of meaning of its eight trigrams and sixty-four hexagrams.

A History of Yoga Vivian Worthington

The first of its kind, *A History of Yoga* chronicles the uplifting teachings of this ancient art in its many guises: at its most simple a beneficial exercise; at its purest an all-embracing quest for the union of body and mind.

Tao Te Ching The Richard Wilhelm Edition

Encompassing philosophical speculation and mystical reflection, the *Tao Te Ching* has been translated more often than any other book except the Bible, and more analysed than any other Chinese classic. Richard Wilhelm's acclaimed 1910 translation is here made available in English.

The Book of the Dead E. A. Wallis Budge

Intended to give the deceased immortality, the Ancient Egyptian *Book of the Dead* was a vital piece of 'luggage' on the soul's journey to the other world, providing for every need: victory over enemies, the procurement of friendship and – ultimately – entry into the kingdom of Osiris.

Yoga: Immortality and Freedom Mircea Eliade

Eliade's excellent volume explores the tradition of yoga with exceptional directness and detail.

'One of the most important and exhaustive single-volume studies of the major ascetic techniques of India and their history yet to appear in English' – *San Francisco Chronicle*